Beware the Exit

Version 1.2

By Alexander Francis

Beware the Exit

Copyright ©2014 by Alexander Francis

Arcus Verba Publishing
P.O Box 210
De Forest, Wisconsin
53532

www.arcusverba.com

Cover design by Alexander Francis

ISBN: **978-1-942420-05-7** print edition

ISBN: **978-1-942420-04-0** e-book

Other Novels by Alexander Francis

Are We A Band Yet?

Mick Grundy....Spy Hunt

Mick Grundy...The Russian Connection

Mick Grundy...Elapid

Geminknot

The Green Scarf

Revenge of Jesus

Memory Gap

The Copy Candidate

Visit afnovels.com

TABLE OF CONTENTS

You Can Never Return

*T*om stood up slowly, facing the balcony, his hands and arms spread out for balance while turning his back against the darkening sky and ocean. The curved wall that supported him was roughly waist height but narrow, topped with a rough natural stone. Far below him, waves impacted huge rocks at the base of the cliff with enough force to create waves of vibrations reaching his feet, further unsettling his balance. He tottered for a long moment, eventually reaching a precarious steady state, allowing him to carefully drop his arms by his side. A small breathless crowd started assembling near the big French doors with hushed murmurs and pointed fingers. Jeanette stood facing him from several safe feet away with her hands on her hips. She was wearing her dark purple evening dress with scattered sequins, the color contrasted with the tiny yellow bows and matching trim. Her bracelets jangled softly as she adjusted her hand to a defiant thumb-forward position.

"Sweetie, I would rather have my leg broken jumping off this cliff than have you feel that way," Tom said loudly. The onlookers behind Jeanette collectively gasped.

"Don't dare call me sweetie right now. Why don't you prove it by jumping off the cliff? I'll just stand here and watch. Go ahead, jump!"

"Would it help if I got down on my knees and begged forgiveness?" he asked above the puffs of wind ruffling his dinner jacket. Jeanette didn't answer and continued to watch him defiantly. Several more people pushed onto the balcony from the ballroom.

Tom's brain seized on the fact that there was nothing behind him but air, which continued to grab at his clothing. He had a sensation of falling backward for a moment, and his hands shot up and forward, accompanied by gasps and moans from the women spectators. He realized that standing on the rail was not softening his beautiful wife, and after three...or was it four?...cocktails, his reaction time was slowed to dangerous levels.

Tom just stood there and looked at her. What would she do if I got down from the wall he wondered? She was waiting for something, some act or words from him to prove his love and make amends. He glanced down at the stone pavers at her feet and decided to try to beg instead of continuing to chance the wall. His black tux was going to just have to take the punishment. Jumping off, he lowered himself to both knees and struggled toward her, his hands clasped as in prayer.

"Please forgive me, Jeanette. I promise to make it up to you," he said, hearing various giggles from the shadows. Several couples were watching, enjoying the humor of Tom groveling on his knees.

Jeanette backed out of his reach and said, "Not this time. It's not enough, and besides, I don't believe your story."

Tom stayed on his knees, ignoring the laughter in the corner. "I mean it, Jeanette. Children? Want to have a child? I'm ready. Want to visit your mother? I'll go also. New clothes? Anything? Oh, please, Jeanette." Tom was convinced he sounded sincere.

"No go, I'm afraid," she retorted. There was more laughter, this time from separate sources, some male.

Tom got up and dusted off his knees and the toes of his polished shoes. He held up a finger indicating that she should wait for a moment. Digging his phone from his jacket, he rapidly punched in a number.

"Hi, Eric. Tom here. Need a favor, old man. Yes, this is about last night. Would you talk to Jeanette and answer any questions she has about what we did, where we went, whom we saw or anything she wants to know? Thanks, hold on please." He offered the phone to Jeanette who hesitated but reluctantly accepted.

"All right, Eric. Better make it good," she said. Tom watched her as she listened and when she was done, or actually when Eric was done, she hung up without a word and handed Tom the phone. He waited, and they both looked at each other in silence.

"I'm not convinced. Where did you go?" she persisted.

"Out for drinks at the Seaside. It was harmless, but I forgot the time. When I got home, you were already gone."

"That shows me what I mean to you, doesn't it?" she asked.

"You mean everything to me. Everything. I never get you out of my mind, and I cherish every moment with you. I almost broke out in tears tonight just looking at you in my arms."

"Tom, I know you find me physically appealing, but I think I also rate higher as a companion than you can ever find going out with the guys. You didn't even call me, and I sat there for two hours waiting. I'm hurt and angry, and there is not much you can do to please me right now." She turned back to her view of the ocean with her swaying hair fringed in shades of red and purple.

"Please, Jeanette."

After a long moment, the last of the light evaporated from the darkened sky, and urgent water hitting the rocks below seemed to grow louder. She moved slowly toward him and nestled into his arms with her head back and her long hair brushing his hands. "You will have to keep not just one, but all the promises you made, and I have at least four witnesses."

"I will. And anything else I can do or give you, it's yours. Do I have to jump off the cliff and break my leg?"

"The night is young. Want to stand here and hold me or dance with me inside?"

"Both," he murmured.

She smiled, her face caught in harsh half-shadow, and pushing back from his waist, she said, "Dance. It's settled." As they danced, Tom put his arm around her and held his hand lightly at the small of her back. He loved feeling her muscles work under his hand as they danced, and it always brought back strong images of her back arching during intense sexual pleasure. She stole a quick glance up at him as they danced and winked one green almond-shaped eye. Dancing with Jeanette was like dancing with a faerie. She was light on her feet, perfectly tuned to his movements, and the air around her swirled with her scent. During a reverse turn, Tom led Jeanette into a deep dip, and as she arched back on his hand, he could see her ivory throat blending softly into her chest and breasts. She was magnificent, a holy creation, a vision of perfection. Tom was so much in love with her that he nearly choked with tears at the sight of this perfect creature briefly suspended in air. He pulled her up toward him, watching the green eyes fix on his and dilate as she drew near. She came briefly by his face but close enough that he felt her body heat and the ever so delicate touch of her lips and then she spun away from him with a flash of her red hair.

The singing sensation, Betty Atamore, was just starting to sing her rendition of an old Billy Holiday tune. The sax died away as the lights dimmed, and Betty stepped under the spots. The couples paired up and formed an arc around the stage. Tom circled Jeanette's waist with his arm and drew her hips into tight contact with his. The singer was a strikingly attractive and energetic black girl who managed to sound even better than Billy Holiday. The words came floating off the stage and echoed from the walls giving the song palpable impact.

> *If you can't love me then I want to be lonely*
> *There is no one to make me happy but you*
> *Kiss me goodbye and leave me forsaken*

Tom was caught with the moment and leaned down to Jeanette's ear and whispered, "I hate to fight. I love you too much." It was like she didn't hear him at all. He tried again, "I love you, Jeanette."

"Please! I'm trying to hear the song," she said without looking at him. He relaxed his arm and gradually let her go. She didn't appear to notice. He tried to remember the last time he heard her say, "I love you," but couldn't place it. It had been too long. He looked down at her and could see that her full attention was on the singer. She seemed to be having a good time and was smiling, but it wasn't at him. Where was she last night he wondered? She was on the couch when he got up so he wasn't sure what time she actually got in. And she was mad at him? He realized that she had gone somewhere out of spite and was using all her tricks to prevent him from asking about it.

> *No room in my heart for anyone but you*
> *Without you my world is nothing but blue*

Tom realized the lyrics fit. He couldn't begin to think about losing Jeanette. There was no one else and never had been. Was he losing her, or had he already lost her? Only one person knew.

When the song ended and the applause died, he gently took her arm and led her toward a table on the edge of the room. She looked at him with eyebrows raised but didn't resist.

"Please sit with me for a moment," he requested. "Want a drink or hors d'oeuvre?"

"No. Didn't you want to dance?"

"I need to talk to you and be serious for a moment," he said. Jeanette sighed loud enough to make her point.

"I thought we cleared all that up on the balcony."

"Do you love me, Jeanette?"

"Are you serious?" she exclaimed with wide eyes.

"Sure. I want to hear you say it. Call me immature or insecure if you like, but please tell me that you love me."

Jeanette brushed back a lock of hair and looked around as if wanting to escape. "Tom, you just tonight promised to have a child with me. I sleep with you, and I'm married to you. What do you think?"

"If that means that you love me, it wouldn't hurt you to tell me. I just told you I love you, and you ignored me. I need to hear it from you."

"This sounds a lot like high school. First, you stand me up last night, and now you want to hear me whisper sweet nothings to you. I don't come down that fast little boy. You will have to wait until I'm ready to hear that."

"Does this mean that you don't love me?" he asked.

"It means that your little redhead is still wondering the same thing. You can put your male buddies ahead of me when you feel like it. Why don't you ask Eric if he loves you?"

"Jeanette, I recognize punishment when I am getting it. Enough. I apologized, groveled at your feet, promised you the world and told you how much I love you. What more do you want?"

"Don't you see that those are all words, Tom? Actions are more important than words. Promise of change isn't change. I'll let you know when it's enough. Another thing...If you are softening me up to discover what I did last night, you can forget it."

"Don't you think I deserve to know where my wife goes in the middle of the night?"

"You lost that right some time ago. This isn't the first time you took me for granted."

"I don't recall any such thing."

"Well, that's the problem. You love my body but not me, and you don't even know when you put me second, I'm that low. Dress me up, take me to an expensive event and tell me how much you care, but tomorrow you'll read your paper at breakfast, and I won't hear a word from you all day, then you'll expect me to be bowled over by your nightly sexual appetite. I am not your toy. You don't know how women work and never will. Since you are too dense to figure it out all by yourself, I'll spell it out for you. Sex for a woman is part of a package, not the entire package. We are real people under the layers of appeal and easily your equal, if not better."

Tom sat and tried to collect and organize what she had said. The singer started with her rendition of another old tune, and her smooth voice swelled above the crowd and penetrated Tom's consciousness as when the persistent patter of rain on the roof finally gets your attention.

The woman I love is in love with some other man

If only she could kiss me

And hold me like I remember once she did

Her eyes, her body remain the same, but not her love

He suddenly felt lost. Unknowingly, he had disappointed the only person on earth who meant anything to him. Had she taken on a lover or at least become interested in another man? He didn't know what to do, and he looked again at Jeanette, who was looking away.

"I can see that I've failed you, Jeanette. I don't know if you will let me make it up to you, but if you will, I will try as hard as I can. You can never imagine what you mean to me, and whatever it takes to make you happy, I'll do. From now forward, you are first before anything, I promise."

"At least you listened to me. That's a change. I'm not trying to punish you, Tom. This is how I feel right now, and it's not just about last night. And I am not trying to find an excuse for feeling the way I do. It's just that...." She was suddenly awash in tears, real big ones that spilled onto the polished wood table. Putting her face in her hands, she leaned forward sobbing. He instinctively reached for her in earnest compassion, but as soon as his hand touched her shoulder she twisted away. "Kindly don't touch me right now," she said from behind her hands.

Helpless, Tom stood, part of him wanting to scoop her up in his arms and comfort her and the other part wanting to run away from the emotions. He recalled a lecture in college that concerned the limbic system of the brain and its effects on emotion. He could recall that the hypothalamus was the part that regulates human emotions. Once stimulated, it takes awhile for the neurotransmitters to dwindle. Clearly, Jeanette couldn't calm down quickly from this height of emotion. He had to be patient.

"Would it help if we went for a walk or back out on the terrace?" She shook her head, no. "Could I get you something to drink, cocktail perhaps?" He took his handkerchief from his jacket pocket and offered it to her. Again the headshake, no. Dancing resumed for the rest of the crowd as the band started another number. The room was easily 150 feet long and about 100 wide with large arched passageways to other rooms. The terrace to the sea was on the right from where they were and restrooms to the rear. There was a massive and ornate mahogany bar across the distant wall backed by large gold-trimmed mirrors which reflected the band on the circular elevated platform in the center of the room. A vaulted ceiling faded into the distance high above them in an arc culminating in a dome of leaded glass.

Jeanette sat up sniffing and wiped her eyes. "Sorry for that. It's been coming for awhile." Tom sat down beside her but was careful not to touch her until she wanted him to. He just sat uncomfortably, silently, wishing things were different.

"Honestly, Jeanette, I had no idea. I am so sorry. If you will let me, I'll take a couple of weeks off from work, and we can spend some real time together. We can even go somewhere like New York, even Paris."

She sniffed and looked up at him with her red-rimmed eyes. Normally, she was ablaze with abundant energy, defiance and appeal, but right now she looked older, sadder and deflated. In a word, pitiable. It was the first time Tom had ever seen his vivacious wife like this, and it hurt deeply. It was one of those moments in life that teach that our existence and our happiness are temporary. Tom reclined in thought. He was unable to change the facts as they now exist, and he searched his mind for when and how things went wrong. However unintentionally, he had hurt Jeanette, and now he understood that his previous actions could not be undone. They started out happy together, and he knew that they had shared many moments of love, both physical and mental. At some point, he must have forgotten the person she is while only remembering her beauty. He imagined a door or turn in the road, once taken, leads away into the far distance. The choices he had made were wrong, but now, perhaps, it was not too late to turn around. She was just at his shoulder, and they were still married. Surely he could find a way to restore her feeling for him.

"With your help, Jeanette, I can be a better husband. I want to start fresh, if you will let me, and make our marriage one of equals. You already know that I don't realize all the things I could have done differently, but I am willing to learn and change. For me, losing your love is like dying. Seeing you in tears rips at my soul."

"Well, that's too bad. Now you know how I have felt for a long time. I came to this party with you, because we both had social obligations, and it was scheduled for a long time, and I tried to have fun and pretend to be the girl you expected. It's a lie. I'm not that girl any longer, and I am through pretending. There will be no trip for us right now to party and get over it. You are on notice, Tom. You will change toward me or part ways, and I am not going to hold your hand doing it. It has to come from inside of you, otherwise, it will not be true."

"You'll see that I mean it, Jeanette. Things are different from this moment on. My full attention is fixed on making you happy, because I realize that without you, I have nothing of value."

"Oh, you would manage to survive without me. You have your profession as an architect, and you are very attractive, successful and well-known. You can get another me by snapping your fingers. The woman is always the loser, because she ages and her choices become more limited by the day. Nevertheless, I want to be happy and fulfilled, and I am starting to think that I chose the wrong path when we met. All I saw was the good-looking and enthusiastic boy in you. I never saw the self-centered egotist under the sharp clothes, until recently. Mostly, you care for you. My attractiveness keeps me in the picture. If I were to lose my looks, you would be gone, because you don't love me for what's inside."

"That's not how I feel at all. I do love you, every molecule inside and outside. I wouldn't change anything at all about you. No matter what may happen to you, I will be there for you until we die. What I need to do is to let you know it. I haven't been what I should have been in your eyes, so I plan to change that starting now."

"You are good at words, Tom, better than me. I'll never try to sweep you away with words or romance, but I am going to give you that chance to do what you say you will, as of right now. Now be a good boy and go find something for me to drink."

Tom shot to his feet and said, "Thank you, Jeanette, thank you. I won't mess this up." He started looking for a waiter with a tray, but they seem to have disappeared when the dancing started. The bar was a long way across the crowded room, and he could see a small group waiting for drinks. He pushed his chair back and knelt on one knee beside her and took her hand and kissed it. "Will you stay right here and wait for me?"

A bit of color came back to her face, and there was a hint of sparkle to her green eyes. "Depends on how long you plan to be gone. You'd best hurry back."

Tom nodded and headed with purpose around and through the dancers. The singer was winding down the old favorite, *Oh, how I would cry,* and he started listening without intending to.

> *If you said bye bye*
> *Oh, how I would cry*
> *When you ask to leave me*
> *Pain that you couldn't know*
> *Pain that I could never show*

He looked around more than once to be sure she was still at the table where he left her. She looked so alone there, almost as if a spotlight was above her and she was on a stage. The little wave when she saw him looking was touching. Things were looking up, and we are going to work this out, Tom thought. While he was in line at the bar, Jeanette and her table were out of his sight. He finally was serviced and headed back with two drinks firmly in his fists. It was like being a cowboy on his horse, picking his way through a herd of steers. The people were invisible to him except as a barrier, and he saw no one, except the image of his beautiful wife, floating in his mind's eye.

Finally, the path cleared and when he looked at the little table, she was gone. He walked slowly forward looking in all directions. Her bright red hair was always easy to identify. He even stood on tiptoes but couldn't spot her. Standing there with the drinks, he started feeling more and more foolish but patiently waited. At last, in the distance, near the balcony, he saw a familiar flash of red. The line of his vision was interrupted by the moving dancers, but he could see clearly a long red-haired woman talking with a handsome man in a dark tuxedo. He could see her animated hand motions, and her occasional caress on the man's chest. Was this man his replacement?

Tom felt anger and rage well up into his throat like a water glass being overfilled. There was no other explanation except that she had made a fool of him. She had let him pour his heart out to her and then left him standing alone while she dallied with someone within his sight. It was her retribution to him for whatever it was he had done. What was it she had said? Oh, yes, it was something like, "Well, that's too bad. Now you know how I have felt for a long time." The worse part was that he had meant every word and genuinely did love her far beyond his ability to express it, and he did intend to try to win her back, whatever it took. Well, this is how she wants it and perhaps he deserved it, he was no longer the best judge. He looked down at the two drinks, drank one down in a gulp and took the other one and carefully sat it down on their table. He scanned the room one more time. She was still there talking to the stranger, because there was no mistaking that hair. He could just see into one of the adjoining rooms under the arch, and though the lighting was dim, he thought he could see shadows of people inside. It's likely a private bar area, he thought, and headed that way. The archway was broad and high, decorated in the deco style of the rest of the room. As he approached, he still couldn't make out any detail other than scattered table lights and the perception of movement.

Just as Tom stepped across the threshold, an impulse made him turn and look back. He could see Jeanette emerging from the ladies' room to the rear of their table. It wasn't her across the room after all! When he saw her looking around for him, he started back toward her but couldn't seem to go past the threshold of the opening. He tried over and over, but the smallest part of him would not pass the threshold. He waved and shouted to her, but it was obvious that she could neither see nor hear him.

While he watched, she sat down and picked up the drink he left. Someone was tapping him on the shoulder, making Tom turn in anger.

"You can't get back, can you?" the man said. He was older than Tom and wore a cheap, ill-fitting suit, his tie hanging loose. There was an odor of alcohol and tobacco about him, and he needed a shave.

"What did you say?" Tom asked, still trying to keep Jeanette in view and attempting to push against whatever was holding him back.

"You might as well stop trying, fellow. You won't get through."

"What do you mean, I just came across? I don't understand what is happening. Why can't I go back?" Tom said in an increasingly irritated voice.

"It's really simple," the man said. "You can never return."

"I can never return?" Tom shouted and then backed up for a run at the opening.

"No, fellow, you can't ever go back. You chose to come in here. Things are different now. What you see in there is only your memory of what was. Things are different now, they've changed, you've changed. Welcome to your new world. I hope, for your sake, you made the right decision."

Chapter 2

Choices...But None Good

$\mathcal{T}$om slid to his knees, his arms extended against whatever was holding him back. He tried anger, rage, then tears, but nothing he did would let him back into the ballroom where Jeanette was still waiting at the table. Worse, the light in the ballroom seemed to be dimming, and the room behind him was getting brighter. Two men grabbed him by the shoulders and picked him up to his feet.

"We've been through the same thing, buddy. We understand, but there is no point fighting it. In a few minutes you won't be able to see in there any longer, and after an hour, the door will disappear. You have to face facts. You are in here to stay, just as we are," one of them said as they turned him around. Tom could see that he was in a nightclub with a stage on one end and a bar along one wall. Most of the tables and bar stools were occupied. Now and then, a scantily clad cocktail or cigarette waitress bustled past with a tray. The ambient noise was high, and occasionally someone broke into a hardy sustained laugh. Smoke, there was lots of cigarette smoke, hung as a definite layer just under head height.

Bewildered, Tom asked, "Where the hell am I?"

"The only answer I know is that you are here. Sounds stupid, but you are here, the same as you were there a few moments ago," the second man said.

"Did everyone here come from the ballroom?"

"No, likely we all came from different places. Your place was unique to you. It's the same story though, we all chose to be here. The problem is that we didn't know what we were choosing at the time. Now, it's too late. The past has disappeared for all of us."

"What do I do now?" Tom asked. He was trying not to tremble visibly, but he could feel that tight feeling of fear inside his chest. He looked down and realized that he was no longer wearing a tuxedo or black shoes.

"Do? You live your life. You are a person just like us. You go to bed, wake up, work. It's called living. Just like before, only different."

"You mean that Jeanette is in here someplace waiting for me?"

"I wouldn't get worked up on that one, buddy. If that was your girl...well, you'll get another one. Different. You'll see."

"My name is Chase, Tom Chase. I live on Ventura. I'm an architect. Can I just go home?" Tom was breaking down quickly and felt his legs trembling.

"How nice to meet you, Tom. I'm Frank Collins, and this is Vance Burke. To answer your question, you should look in your wallet. Your address will be there. Our bet is that you are not an architect. Now come with us to the bar and buy us and you a drink. We all need it."

They led a weakened Tom to the bar and helped him onto a stool. He looked in the mirror just in time to see the door to the ballroom wink out and disappear. He hung his head in absolute despair. What will happen to Jeanette? How will she get home? The thoughts raced through his mind, but there were no answers, only questions.

"What'll you have, brother?" a thick-armed bartender asked. He had a bald head with wrinkles of flesh instead of hair. Tom looked up into penetrating black eyes set deeply into a florid full face. "Well?" he said again. Tom looked lamely at his two new friends who sat on either side of him.

"He'll have a whiskey sour, on the rocks. Us, too." Frank said.

"Uh, I don't usually drink whiskey," Tom said quietly but not with conviction.

"Change? Remember, Tom, things are different now and so are you. You'll like it, don't worry," Frank said.

"What were you two in the other life?" Tom asked them.

"The thing is, Tom, in a couple of days you will forget most of that stuff. Oh, it's going to come back every night in your dreams, and for a long time you'll wake up thinking you are back. It fades away, it really does. You are going to live this life now, and you might grow to like it. To answer your question, I have no clear memory to say if I even had another life. The only reason I know about what just happened to you is that both Vance and I have seen several, just like you, just appear and tell almost the same story. Things work out, though. People adjust."

Vance laughed. "In my dreams, I'm always a publisher. People come to me with their crummy little stories that they work so hard on, and I always tell them 'NO'. Sorta makes me feel good to do it. Maybe I really was one. This always reminds me about those beliefs from the Far East. They believe when you die you come back as another person. It makes me believe that they might be on to something."

The drinks came, and Tom paid the tab. All three bolted their drinks and drained the glasses. "More," Tom ordered, and the glasses were quickly replaced. While he had his wallet out, he looked closely at its contents. He was still Tom Chase, but he had an Iowa license and no photo of Jeanette. The wallet was well-worn, but he had no memory of ever seeing it previously. He studied the address. It seemed that he had a flicker of memory about that address. He pulled out other cards. The registration for his car was for a Ford, not a Cadillac, and the car was several years old. Things definitely were not the same.

They drank the whiskeys down in unison. Tom was starting to feel a little better, but the fear kept coming back in waves, clutching at his insides with sharp talons. Every time he thought of Jeanette back in the ballroom, he felt like he was going to throw up, and he had to grab his stomach and hold on to the edge of the bar.

"You got it bad, Tom. Must be a girl back there, huh?" Vance asked.

"Yes, my wife, Jeanette. The person that I always said I couldn't live without. I came close to losing her tonight, but I thought that we were getting past it when..." He trailed off, unable to finish.

"Let me guess, Tom," Frank said. "Everything was going to be OK, then you did something stupid, didn't you?"

"Yes."

"I've heard that one before. Say, there is something you have to know, Tom, and this is as good a time as any to tell you." Frank stopped talking and just stared at him.

"Go ahead and tell me, Frank. Tonight couldn't get any worse."

"Beware the Exit, Tom. Beware the Exit."

"What does that mean? Look, don't give me any crap tonight. I can't handle what's on my plate now."

"Want to tell him, Vance?"

"Look, Tom, there are exit doors all around us. As an architect, you would know all about that. All of them lead out, right? Some to staircases, the outdoors, you know...just out. Then there are other exit doors. They lead to the real exit. Out. Finished. Gone. Do you get it?"

"No. Do you mean if you take the wrong exit you die? That's fairly preposterous. How are you supposed to tell the difference?" Tom asked.

"Death? We don't know. We just know that that person disappears forever. I once was standing next to someone who went through. He opened that door, and I could see only black on the other side, a kind of nothingness. I remember pulling back in fear as if I could fall or be pulled in. The man stepped over the threshold and just vanished."

Tom frowned in thought. "Isn't that just like what happened to me? I am still alive, just in some new place."

Frank put his hand on Tom's shoulder. "No, Tom, this is different. You remember that you could see into the opening, at least a little, before you stepped in? Another thing, those apertures fade away and disappear after you come across. The Exit Door we're talking about stays right there, waiting for the next guy."

"I think I am losing my mind," Tom declared. "What a ridiculous world. You can just walk into a room and everything in your life changes forever, or if you go through the wrong door, you vanish. This stuff is nuts!"

"Want another drink, boys?" the bartender said with a growl. "Otherwise, push off and make room for someone who is thirsty." One glance and Tom knew that this was no easygoing, talkative, therapy kind of bartender. This one would like to take you in the alley and beat on you for entertainment.

"One more for the road, barkeep. Tom's buying," Frank quickly added. The drinks appeared as quickly as Tom's wallet shed its treasure.

After they polished off the next round, Frank asked, "Well, Tom, my boy, do you know who you are yet?"

"I think I remember being a sales rep for the Talic Corp. I travel a lot, and my car is in the far parking lot on Front Street where I left it. But I still remember Jeanette who was sitting at our table waiting for me. I still love her."

"Feel better now?" Vance asked.

"No, I have a crummy job, no Jeanette and no future. And I'm stuck here developing an alcohol problem."

"Welcome back to the world, Tom. Glad we could help!" Vance laughed.

"One final question, guys. I still don't understand about the doors. How do you know when you are going to go through one and not return?"

"Frankly speaking...sorry, Frank...you only know afterwards. We think that when you go through one, you intended to change something in your life, and when you find out that things really have changed, you can't unchange them. The Exit Door is for those who are ready to quit for good. It's all about what you want to do, you see," said Vance.

"Can you go through enough doors to get back to where you started?" asked Tom.

Frank scratched at his chin stubble and looked upward at the ceiling. "I don't know, and there is no way to find out since they don't come back to tell us. You have to realize that every time you go through one, you take a big chance. There could be some very ugly things on the other side, and you won't know until you get there. A circuit? Sounds nice, but I don't know if I would chance it. I prefer to stay right here where I know what is going to happen next."

The three sat there in silence for a while and then Tom noticed his reflection in the mirrors behind the bar. He was older. There were lines in his face that he hadn't noticed before and a touch of grey at the sideburns. The eyes looked the same, but his lids were sagging a little. He looked down and saw a small paunch of fat hanging over his belt. Was the memory of my other life just a dream he wondered? No, he remembered every detail of Jeanette, every wink of her eyes and every utterance she made. She was as real as he was, there was no doubt. "Am I dreaming now?" he asked himself. No, the place was real and so was he. There were too many sensations around for him to be dreaming. Dreams are never this complete or complex, he told himself. He slid off the bar stool and got his wobbly legs back under him. He patted the two beside him on the back.

"Thanks for your help, both of you. I'm going home, now. Perhaps I'll wake up in the morning and have my wife in my arms and forget this whole thing happened."

"No, I'm afraid you won't. Remember that we usually hang out here at Thursday's, if you need to talk some more. Best of luck to you my new friend, you are going to need it," said Frank.

Vance laughed his now familiar laugh and added, "Women are a dime a dozen, Tom. If you get lonely, go find one to keep you company. She'll help you to forget, all right." He was still laughing in the distance as Tom headed for the main entrance, avoiding the exit doors.

Chapter 3

A New Life

Tom woke with a start and looked at his watch. "Jeanette, it's time to get up." He patted the other side of the bed finding it empty. She must be up making breakfast, he realized. He sat up and spun around to find his slippers. The room was different. Shabby. Then it hit him. There was no Jeanette. He realized that he had just been dreaming about having a conversation with her. What was it about? Oh, yes, he had promised her that they could start a family. She was really happy about it, and he could still taste her kisses... but it was a dream. They never had that conversation. The realization hit him like the ceiling falling, and he was seized again with pain in his stomach folding him forward. Jeanette didn't exist.

Tom waved hello to some of his coworkers as he made his way to his desk at Talic Corporation. Immediately, it hit home about the smell of the place. What was the smell? It was kind of a metallic, dusty odor, and he remembered thinking about the smell previously. When the elevator arrived it made the same "clunk" when the door opened that he had heard a thousand times. The place seemed familiar but at the same time, strange. He felt like he was running on impulse or habit much like a robot would. Finding his cubical messy, he distantly remembered leaving it that way. With a sigh, he sat down and turned on his computer screen.

"Mr. Chase? Mr. Chase?" came over the small speaker above his workstation.

"Yeah, I'm here," Tom answered.

"Boss wants you," the mechanical voice said and clicked off.

Tom searched his returning memory and then understood why he was being called in. The monthly report was due but where was it? He dug around on the desk, pushing paper stacks to the side. No luck. Opening the desk drawer, he found it was on top, right where he left it. Tom quickly studied the graph at the top of the page. Red lines indicated a drop in sales, and his page was full of them. Bummer.

"He's waiting, Mr. Chase. Are you coming?" the voice piped in.

"Coming right now," he answered and got up with the paper in his hand. He sighed and started the long walk to the elevator bank in the center of the room. On the way past Sally's desk, he slowed and looked for her. Catching a glimpse of her yellow hair as he got closer, he could see that she had her back to him and was on the phone. Tom tapped on the partition, getting her attention, then gave a short wave. She ignored him. The ride up was short, and when the door opened, he could see Mr. Talic at his desk in the far room. The secretary indicated that he was to go right in.

"Tom Chase, I want you to explain yourself. Sit down," Mr. Talic ordered.

Another one of those days, Tom thought and sat down. "I have the monthly report, sir. Like you requested," he added.

"Never mind the report. I've already seen it. Your sales are down, Tom. Down, down, down. Why is what I want to know. Why, why, why?" His jowls shook as he spoke, and the few hairs on the top of his head waved around in little arcs. Tom was reminded of a turkey just before someone chopped his head off.

"Well, sir," Tom started.

"Another thing, Tom. I've been studying your records. Exactly what did you do before you were hired here? It should be listed here and it isn't."

"I was once an architect. A good one too," Tom said remembering the only occupation he could recall.

"Don't make me laugh. Architect?" He stood up and walked to the large window looking down on most of the downtown buildings. "Come here," he demanded.

Obediently, Tom joined him at the large window but didn't see much of interest.

"See that large building right in front of us?" Mr. Talic demanded. Before Tom could say that he saw it, Mr. Talic asked, "What style of architecture is it, Tom? You should know."

Tom looked carefully at the building. The style seemed familiar, but he just couldn't place it or come out with a erudite phrase. "It escapes me, sir," he admitted.

"All right, I'll give you another chance. In this area, how deep does the foundation for such a structure have to be and how is it formed?"

Tom realized that he had no idea, but he remembered being an architect just as clearly as he remembered Jeanette. "Sorry, sir, I don't seem to know the answer."

"Just as I thought. You are either pretending or you are sick. Which is it, Tom?"

"I don't know, sir, but I am feeling disorientated or distracted. It's like I just stepped in here from someplace else. I'm not sure I'm supposed to be here."

Looking at your declining record of sales, I suspect you are right," Mr. Talic said. "Tell you what, Tom, I don't want to act rashly or harshly with you since you have been with us for a long time, so I want to have someone see you for an evaluation. Will you go?"

"You mean a psychiatrist, sir?"

"You bet it's what I mean. I have just the person in mind. You step into the hall, and Miss Rodgers will set up the appointment. In the meantime, you get to work and raise your sales numbers. Understand?"

He stood in front of Miss Rodgers' desk waiting on her to make the call. It was easy to see why, at approaching fifty, Miss Rodgers was still a Miss. She occasionally looked at him over her glasses with something of a cross between pity and contempt. Finally, she finished and shuffled some papers.

"Mr. Chase, this is for your appointment with Dr. Simpson." She picked out one paper and slid it across the desk. "Sign this. It allows the doctor to tell us what she finds."

Tom took the small stack of papers and just stood there looking a little lost. Noticing his hesitation, Miss Rodgers added, "That's all, Mr. Chase. Get back to work."

Tom came by Sally's desk on the way back to his. This time she was reading some papers and not otherwise occupied. He decided to use a stronger approach.

"Hi, Sally. Got a minute?" he asked, then came in without waiting for an invitation.

"Well, Tom?" she said without looking up from her papers. She was once attractive but now was starting to sag in various places. More men in her life she didn't really need, especially this one. She finally looked up at him, because he didn't answer, and saw that he was seated in the only other chair in the cubicle, smiling his artificial salesman smile at her. "I'm waiting, Tom," she said, holding his gaze.

"Well, Sally, I just came in to say hello. We haven't talked much lately, and I wanted to see if everything is all right with you. That's all."

"Everything is the same with me, Tom, and I can see that nothing is changed about you either. Look, I don't want to be rude, but unless you have something to say beyond hello, I have work to do and I'll bet you do too."

"Before I go, Sally, any chance of lunch sometime?"

"Not much," she said without looking at him.

Tom made it back to his cubicle and sat down heavily. He starting thinking about failing Mr. Talic's little architecture test. He didn't understand why he couldn't recall any information about building design, but he did remember his actual graduation from Stanford. He also clearly recalled Eric and his latest drawings. Inside the drawer was a pad and pen, and Tom used these to start drawing a simple house plan. After a few strokes it was apparent that he had never done it before and didn't have a clue how to start. He threw the pad on the desk and slumped in his chair. What about Jeanette? Surely she was real. He could even recall her perfume and remember her slender body stepping out of the shower. The thought of her made him want to cry, and he tried again to think this through. It was obvious that he had worked at this place for some time, perhaps years, and he could remember a lot about it. But only yesterday, he was an architect with a stunning wife. He even remembered the penetrating words from the jazz singer floating through the air in the ballroom last night and how pertinent they were to what was happening at that moment. Had that all been a dream or is he asleep and dreaming right now? He was confused. Talic was right, he needed to see a professional to sort it out.

The day dragged endlessly on, and his telephone calls to stimulate more sales achieved nothing. As the second hand on the clock in the hall passed the 12 and quitting time was finally reached, he rose from his chair and stretched. This is not going to work, he said to himself. I am unhappy here. There has got to be something else out there for me. He couldn't seem to remember any schooling other than his time at Stanford, which appears not to have happened. What was he capable of doing for a living? He couldn't recall any interests or hobbies. Then, there was the question about Sally. She and he were closer at one time, he knew, but to save his life he couldn't remember any details or understand why she no longer wanted anything to do with him. Last night, that fellow at the bar said something about being reborn. Maybe that was it. He had died and entered someone's body. He wasn't meant to be in this body. Then he remembered his reflection in the glass. The image was his, Tom's image, just a little older.

When he reached the door to his apartment, he fumbled while trying to get his key into the lock when he heard a door open behind him. As he turned, he saw old Mrs. Fletcher waving to him. He walked over to her and bent down to her level.

"Mr. Chase, can I ask you to be a bit quieter tonight than last night?" she said in her antique and slightly quavering voice.

"I'm sorry, Mrs. Fletcher, I don't remember last night very well. What did I do?"

"Since you don't remember, I'll tell you, and I'm not surprised at all that you don't remember. You came home a bit intoxicated, Mr. Chase, and then proceeded to sing at the top of your voice. You finally quit about midnight. Willard and I will call the police next time. Just letting you know." She abruptly closed the door in his face.

Midnight, he thought. About the time I got home from the bar. This is even more confusing. He knew that he didn't sing last night, because he was in California at the ball with Jeanette. What does a crazy person act like? Like me, he realized. He opened the door to his apartment and looked around. Everything there was worn, outdated and had little worth. A television was propped up in the corner but was old and too small for the room. The couch had torn arm upholstery and sagged between the cushions. A stale odor to the place betrayed the fact that no woman had ever lived there. An idea occurred to Tom that he could check his files and papers to find out more about himself. He opened the metal desk drawer and pulled out everything and spread it around the floor. After an hour he sat back up and realized that there were no records of his life prior to six years ago. He had just appeared, got a job and lived every day much as the current day had been lived. He went into the small kitchen and opened the fridge. Almost nothing edible was evident, and what was there hinted of mold. He opted for a small block of cheese and a cheap beer and settled into the couch.

What was his next step, he wondered. This life so far was not worth living. He could buckle down and try to be a good salesman or look for another job. Either was somehow unpleasant to contemplate. He swung around, stretched out, and finally was able to relax.

Their lips parted ever so slowly, and he felt her breath on his face. "When are you coming back to me?" she asked. "Don't you want me any longer?"

"Of course I do. I can't help being away from you. You know that you are all I think about." Reaching around, he grasped her buttocks with both hands and drew her even closer. He kissed her face in every spot while she giggled and returned his embrace with one of her own. Through his closed eyes, he concentrated on feeling her skin against his, while moaning with the pleasure of the moment. He opened his eyes just enough to see those heavenly green eyes right in front of his. Tom twisted to roll on top of her and felt a brief sensation of falling as he rolled off the couch onto the hard floor. The impact woke him up, and for a moment, he couldn't recollect where he was. As his eyes adjusted to the diminished light, he realized that he was still an incompetent salesman, and Jeanette was only a dream.

Tom got up stiffly from the floor and brushed himself off. He needed someone to talk to, preferably a woman. Since he couldn't remember any friends to seek out, he decided to go for a walk. Perhaps something would come up.

He walked like a defeated man, his hands in his pockets, a slump to his shoulders. Aimlessly, he headed toward the nearest street with stores, bars and human activity. He strolled slowly by the windows, looking in at others laughing and enjoying being alive and having purpose. The isolation he felt was a heavy weight he carried with him, and he began to be aware of the shuffling sound his shoes made against the pavement. Ahead, he saw something familiar about a neon sign above a bar. The harsh light from it was twisting from red to blue and back, endlessly. There was a fog in his head trying to form into a shape, but as he moved forward, he still couldn't put it together. What was it about this place that he seemed to remember? A young woman was standing against the corner of the building, her foot planted on the wall behind her creating an attractive angle of her bare leg. She watched him approach with some interest. He vaguely remembered being here before, but was the experience pleasant or frightful?

"Well, if it isn't my old friend. 'Tom'...didn't you say?" the woman asked. Tom looked at her and saw a pretty face hidden behind heavy makeup. She was provocatively dressed with her blouse opened to her waist partially showing full, heavy breasts with hard nipples tenting the thin fabric. Tom remembered clearly the last time he reached under that blouse. He often came here looking for sexual relief. There were other faces which came back to him and caused him to recall quick and rough sexual encounters with them. The alley behind her stretched into the darkness like the opening of a cave. Yes, that is where it usually happened, these brief meaningless contacts with female flesh, abruptly ending with quivering muscles, orgasm and an empty vacant feeling. For one illuminating instant, he was able to compare his sexual craving for Jeanette to alley sex with one of those women. The first was somehow magical, holy, ecstasy at the top of the scale of human experience. The latter was dark, awkward, humiliating and always left him feeling worse about himself.

"Come here and let's see what you have for me tonight," she said and took his unwilling hand and led him into the darkness. He took in the overpowering and cheap perfume, the clicks her high heels made against the concrete, echoing off the brick walls. They passed a doorway just as he reached around her waist to feel the movement of her pelvis while they walked. The door was lit from above with a dim and flickering "Exit" sign, and he hardly noticed it until it crept back into his consciousness after they passed.

"Hold it, that's an Exit!" he said and noticed he had started breathing hard.

"It's always been there, my little honey. Haven't you ever noticed before?" the woman said. She tugged on his sleeve, but he remained fixed looking at the door.

"You don't understand, the exit sign is on the wrong side, so is the lever. This exit opens inward." He had a sudden feeling of foreboding, and his first impulse was to run away, far away.

"Who cares about the door?" Betty asked sarcastically. "We have better things to do than care about how some ninny put it in backwards."

Tom resisted her pull toward the recesses of the dark alley and remained fixated on the door. He moved closer, leaving Betty where she stood. As he approached, he felt something pulling him toward the door, some force of his own willpower.

When the door was close enough to touch, he stood there in the dim light and studied it. A ring of red rust had formed on the outline of the door and the attachment of the push bar handle. Dull black paint had flaked off in spots leaving a depressed rusty surface. He summoned all his courage and touched it, feeling the cold which nearly stuck his hand to the surface.

"It's just a DOOR," she said. "Christ, I don't have time for this. I'm losing business being back here. Do you want it or not?"

Tom had to know what was on the other side, and after hesitation, he kicked the push bar hard with his foot and jumped back. The door creaked while swinging open and then stayed open, revealing a dense and absolute blackness on the other side. Even the door was no longer visible. There was no air movement and no sound from that portal into the unknown.

"What the hell are you doing, Tom, if that's your real name? Will you leave that door alone or not? Look, I'll go in and prove there isn't anything there of interest. Watch this," she said and took steps toward the blackness. Tom quickly grabbed her and pushed her away.

"Look at this, Betty," he said and picked up several large pieces of fractured concrete. He tossed them into the opening and waited, listening.

"What are you doing now, you nut case? What did that prove?"

"Did you hear anything?" Tom asked.

"No," she admitted "What does that mean?" She looked more fearful this time, realizing that Tom was on to something and backed farther away from the opening.

"This is an Exit Door. If you go in there, you disappear forever. I heard about one, but this is the only time I have actually seen it for myself."

"You mean that all the times I came past this door with a John, we could have gone in there by mistake and died?"

"I'm afraid that sums it up."

"Oh, God! How are we going to get it closed?"

Tom looked at the opening again and saw the image of the door forming and becoming visible. "The door is closed," he said.

"You can forget about action tonight. I'm out of here...forever. Wait until the girls hear about this."

"I wouldn't tell anyone. They might try it out, not believing you, and disappear. Keep this to yourself."

"I guess that I should thank you, Tom. Next time, it's free, if you are interested."

"Thanks, I guess. There won't be a next time, though. I'm going to change. Things have to be different for me, because I don't like who I am. I'm a better person than I have seen today."

"Are you saying that you are better than me?" There was anger and hurt in her words, and her face became taut.

"No. I'm not as good a person as you. After all, I have degraded you because of your need for money. I'm not proud of it. I hope to be better, but I'm not, yet. How much do you usually charge me?"

"You are usually good for a hundred, depending on what you want."

Tom searched his wallet and pulled out a crumpled bill and handed to her. "This is for talking to me. That's what I really needed. A companion, not sex." She accepted the money and stuffed it into her loose blouse.

"Thanks, lover. Anytime you need to talk or whatever, you know."

Tom pulled himself upright seeming to shake something off and walked down the alley toward the street. When he reached the sidewalk, he noticed that the neon sign for the bar was gone, just as a bullet struck the brick beside his head sending a shower of dust and lead peppering the side of his face.

Chapter 4

Bug

Stay there, Chase, he's got you spotted!" she shouted from across the street. Tom could see her draw her pistol and crouch down behind the door entry. After a few moments, she opened fire with a burst of several shots, lighting up the darkness with flashes and tongues of light. She stood up and holstered her weapon. "Looks like he's down, Chase."

Tom stepped into the deserted street and looked around. Smoke from her pistol still hung in the air, and in the distance, he could hear a dog barking and the distant sounds of a siren gradually getting louder. He looked down at himself and saw a dark suit and polished shoes. He felt the hard bulge of a large automatic pistol hanging under his left arm. The woman across from him was more casually dressed in jeans and a loose pullover top. She started toward him, her short blonde hair glinting over an appealing smile. Her name was hovering in front of him, but he couldn't quite see it.

"Good shooting," he said.

"Nothing to it. I had the angle. You all right?" she said as she wiped his face on the side of the splatter. "Looks like you'll be picking junk from your cheek for a few days. It'll make you even more handsome than you already are!" she laughed a short husky breathless chuckle. Tom got a better look at her when the patrol cars started arriving, lighting the area with their headlights and spots. She was very attractive but also moved in a dynamic, energetic way and could turn on the focus of her eyes in a manner that was unforgettable.

A husky patrolman got out of his car and hiked up his pants. The curve of his abdomen wasn't a good fit with the weight of his gear. "You two in one piece?" he asked, looking around.

"Two pieces, thank you, Sergeant. Yeah, we had a close call all right. Suspect is over there and not moving," she said as she pointed to the body lying against the fence. Two more patrol cars appeared from the other direction, and silhouettes moved in front of the headlights in pantomime.

"We have the scene secured, Lieutenant. You guys can take off if you like," Sergeant Jones suggested.

"We like," she said. Turning to Tom she asked, "Want to grab a beer or something before we go off?"

"For saving my life, you can order just about anything, including gold and diamonds," he said.

"Don't be silly. No more than you do for me all the time. Just my job."

Tom remembered her name as other details came back to him. "Allyson, you were wonderful to watch. I'm lucky to have you around. Who else could be so tough, reliable and beautiful at the same time?"

"Allyson? That's different. You usually call me June or June Bug or just Bug. I don't get to hear my first name very often…I kind of like it. Reminds me of my mother." She smiled at him and slapped him on the back in a masculine way. "I'm driving. Wanna ride?" and laughed again, that mesmerizing little laugh of hers.

Tom turned and looked back toward the alley he had just left. There was only solid brick there now, and he could see the chipped brick where the bullet had impacted the middle of the wall. "June, wasn't there an opening on that wall? I remember coming out of an alley when the bullet nearly got me."

"I was too busy to notice. There isn't one now. Sure your head is OK?"

Tom was sorry once again that he agreed to let her drive. She was ferocious in traffic and slammed the car back and forth as she wove her way downtown. From the bridge, the outline of the city spiked into the night sky in an unreal display of vertical stone, glass and aluminum. Headlights crawled along on the streets near the waterfront, even at this hour. She was too busy driving, or racing, to be factual, to engage in much conversation. He had time to study her face in the moving lights of various colors which danced in ever changing patterns across her smooth skin. She was intense. That was the best summation of Allyson June, better known as Bug to most of the other officers. Her father had been Chief at one time but now occupied himself with occasional fishing, but mostly drinking beer. June worked hard to get the respect she deserved, and eventually earned, by her persevering bravery. Being cute didn't help, because it was always hard for men to take her seriously. She didn't see herself as others saw her, because in her eyes, she had no feminine softness or charm. She had beauty that she could use if she wanted, but either never realized what she had or just didn't want to be looked on as desirable. Her husband was a nice sort but refined and...well yes, Tom thought, different. Tom had been jealous of Peter for some time and always refused to think about Allyson submitting to sex with her husband, because he just couldn't bear the image in his mind.

At last, the ordeal was over, and she slid up to the curb in front of their favorite bar, The Golden Buffalo. She left the car awkwardly positioned in a no-parking area, but as usual, she didn't care. They went inside and felt the usual breath of the place hit them, like opening an oven full of baking bread. There was smoke curling off of the antique stamped-steel ceiling back near the open grill where a large slab of dark meat slowly spun over the coals.

"Hey! It's the Tom Bug come to pay its respect. Make room gents!" a booming voice called from the far corner. Bug and Tom continued, past the backs of patrons lining the stools at the bar and around the chairs blocking the walkway mostly occupied by intoxicated fat men. Tom remembered that he could never tell exactly what type of flooring was under his feet. It had taken on a nearly uniform brown surface trending slightly lighter under tables. A sample would likely prove to be compressed grease, dirt and tobacco, and nothing else.

The booth was big enough for four on a side, and the fellows all slid over to make room. Tom stopped short and looked them over. "Not a chance, fat boy. Get up and move to the other side. Bug gets to sit on the outside so that none of you is tempted to grope her and blame it on alcohol." After some grumbling and return quips, the seating was sorted out to satisfy Tom, and they sat down together with Bug on the outside. A hurried waitress appeared, left, and reappeared quickly with their order.

"Just to let you know, guys. June saved my life tonight...again. She took the perp out with the most amazing gunfire. I thought for a moment she was using an M16."

"And, she looked good doing it, didn't she?" Ralph asked and raised his glass in a toast.

"Hold off the praise, boys. It's too early in the morning, and I think my makeup is slipping," Allyson said.

"She doesn't like too many compliments, but I am the luckiest detective anywhere, because I have a partner like June," Tom said and raised his glass of beer toward her. She responded with her glass raised, and they briefly touched them with a click. She wiped the foam from her lip with the back of her hand in a purposely masculine gesture. Tom saw how much she wanted to be part of the team, and she obviously thought that being attractive and feminine would make her less so. After three years of being together nearly every day and night, he was no longer just attracted to her, he was achingly in love with her. His respect for her kept him from ever expressing it in words or even in hints. He was the consummate gentleman with her, as far as she would allow it, and never put her at risk unless, like tonight, he couldn't help it. The other officers were all supportive and understood, even if Allyson didn't. On the other hand, she probably knew, but like Tom, wasn't going to show it, especially to him.

Having her shoulder next to his was as close as he ever got. He made no attempt using body language to convey his feelings and neither did she toward him. It was a hands-off love affair. There were moments when her eyes briefly caressed his face, her pupils changing size and lingering a split second too long, that told him what was in her mind. Working beside her was the best thing that had ever happened to him. She was with him far more than she was with her husband, only Peter had the real deal and Tom didn't. Tom had gotten used to feeling both suffering and pleasure from being near her and if they split, or worse, if she were taken out, he would be lost forever. The joy was in the moments like the present where he could look at her and hear her voice and daydream of hugging and kissing her.

Tom looked toward the bar, lost in thought. This life felt more real than the last, but he still recalled the ballroom and his enchanting Jeanette in his arms and that thought, the memory of her, nearly brought tears. The image of her filled his mind, wiping out any other consciousness. He saw her green eyes set in clear white skin and felt her breath on his lips. His stomach pain returned in the grasp of her memory, and he sputtered beer and clutched his abdomen.

"Tom, Tom," she said as she patted his face. He looked vacantly back, emerging from the past which swept over and around his face like parting strands of straw. "What's the matter, Tom?"

Allyson asked. She looked concerned, and her brow raised and furrowed, reflecting her feelings.

"Oh, I'm all right, Bug. I just lost if for a moment. Things in the past sometimes come back when I don't expect it. Don't worry about me," Tom said, but didn't mean it. How could he possibly love two women at the same time? Both seemed so real in his two different lives, all crammed into one head. From his previous experience, he knew that in his present life, Jeanette didn't exist and never had. She was a dream, but there was more to it than just thoughts. He had touched her and loved her in a way that went past anything other than reality. No, Jeanette wasn't a dream but a memory of a real person and a real life. He couldn't understand or grapple with it just now. Later, he would think about it later.

"Want to drop me off, Bug, to my miserable, lonely apartment, free of any female perfume or refinement, and a refrigerator full of stale food?"

"How could I refuse? Sleep in and I'll make the report. You can come in just before lunch, and we'll see what goes then."

He heard the sound of the unmarked patrol car driving away and waited for the familiar sound of the tires biting into the turn as she took the corner too fast. The echo faded as she sped away, and a glance at his watch showed nearly four. There were already hints of light above the city. His apartment was in an older brownstone that someday could be worth some money if the neighborhood improved. The key turned with a rattle, opening the door to a neat and well-appointed apartment. He recalled all the trips to antique dealers to acquire his furnishings, and it was worth it. No woman, but the place was home nevertheless. He went into the bathroom and looked in the mirror at himself. He was still Tom Chase all right, but this time he looked fit and healthy. Older, though, with touches of grey at the temporal area. A simple line of dark hair masqueraded as a mustache, but a well-groomed one. Not bad, he thought. He quickly stripped and flung himself into bed.

"I thought I would never see you again," she said seriously. The bright sunlight displayed her red hair at its best, forming small intense red sparkles and swooping shades of red sheen which morphed into a somber red near the back of her neck. Every time her head moved, the display changed. The light caught her bright red lips and reflected as impossibly bright spots from the mirror gloss that she liked to use. Her hair hid parts of her face in shadow, but the slight depression under her cheek bones came and went as she turned her head. God, she was beautiful. Was there ever a woman so lovely? She smiled at him and leaned forward. "Where have you been, stranger? Tell your Jeanette everything." The last was spoken with a credible French accent. Four years of college French and two years in Paris tends to perfect the French.

"I have been busy trying to live. It's not easy without you being there for me when I come home. There is a permanent fog around me, and I find myself not really believing where I am. Do you miss me?" Tom asked. She nodded "yes" and took a sip of her drink. Behind her, on the water, a yachtsman was raising a large sail with a continuous clicking noise.

She put down her drink and winked one of those precious almond-shaped green eyes and said, "Of course, dear. I am waiting for you to come back. When?"

"Do you still love me or is there anyone else, Jeanette?"

"I love you with all my heart. There will never be anyone else. Same for you?"

"In this life, there is only you, and I love you completely. But in my other lives, you are not there. Where are you?" Tom asked.

"I am always right here with you. I will never leave," she said, and he could see some reflection from moisture welling up in her eyes. "There is no other man for me other than you. Come back to me."

Tom woke up and found himself staring at the ceiling as his world came back together. The clock said 9:20 am. Time to get going.

He pushed hard against the automatic double door, impatient to find Allyson. The area was alive with the usual noise from chatter, phones and movement. He nodded to other officers who were at their desks and several by the coffee machine. He saw her blonde head down and hard at work behind her desk, which was right beside his.

"Morning, Bug. Anything happening?"

She looked up from typing and said, "Just finishing the report for last night. If you want to help, just go over and pick it up at the printer. Captain has a case for us that just came in. Looks like a terrorist hunt. Tell you more in a minute." She frequently used clipped speech, long on detail at times but never language. He wondered again if she would be so abrupt in bed. He would like her to linger over every word. Even repeat the words over and over so he could hear her voice, her beautiful little throaty voice. He picked up the papers and grabbed a cup of coffee.

"Here I am. Now tell me what's ahead and more about the terrorists."

She swung her legs up on the desk and leaned back. From the corner of his eye, Tom sensed that some of the men had stopped and were watching her. "There is a pickup and arrest order from HS for one Jamal ibn Abd al-Aziz al-Filasi who is suspected of illegal entry and has been seen in the company of known Islamic fighters in Yemen. They said to consider him armed and dangerous. If they know his target, they didn't tell us. A fax with his photo is on your desk."

Tom picked up the photo and studied it. A young man with

black eyes, a short, full beard and a head wrap. Most of them looked like the same man to him. "How are we supposed to identify him? Likely, he won't tell us who he is, you know."

"He has a tattoo of a palm tree on his right wrist. In green."

"Great. Where are we supposed to look for him?"

"That would be the problem."

"You know, if I were him and trying to hide, I would shave the beard, take the turban off and wear long sleeves. We could never find him until he succeeded in blowing himself or someone else to smithereens."

"They don't ever think of that. You're smarter than someone who will blow himself up but that doesn't help catch him. We are not allowed to profile people, not allowed into the Mosques, and we don't get a lot of help from the Muslim community. As I see it, our only option is to go down to where they congregate and show his photo around," she said.

"What will actually happen then is that someone will tell him we are looking, and he will be that much harder to find," Tom said.

"Got another approach, my fearless leader?"

"Two things. One is that I am not going to allow you go alone anywhere in that area without me, and the second is that we should get in position in a van or a car and just watch for him. Probably a waste of time, I know, but it's all a chance thing anyway."

"Suits me," she said. "Let's go!"

They parked in the Flatbush area on Foster and settled in for a long stay. People walked by the car as individuals, in streams or in groups, but none were suspicious. After two hours, the stakeout appeared to be a hopeless idea. Tom looked at his watch. Three more hours, max, then back to the station.

"Tom, can I ask you a personal question?"

"Depends how personal. Can I ask you personal questions?"

Ignoring his little quid pro quo, she said, "We've been together for a long time, but I've always wondered. Were you ever married? You don't have to tell me, but I would like to know."

"I'm going to give you a completely honest answer, Bug, but you won't understand it."

'Try me. I'm open."

"Not in this life."

"I don't understand."

"You'll think I'm crazy."

"I already know that. Tell me more."

Tom sighed. "Before I tell you my most intimate secret, I have another shock for you. Both are related in a strange way."

"I'm going to guess. You are in love with me."

"Yes, I am, Bug. You knew this for how long?"

"There is no exact date on such things, Tom, but I knew it was going to happen by our second day together."

"You never said anything."

"Did I have to?"

"Do you have any feeling for me, Bug?"

"Don't you know?"

"I hoped, but didn't know. Is it true? You do love me?"

"Of course, I love you, Tom. You should have known."

"Do you love Peter?"

"In a way. He treats me good and he is attractive and well educated, but we never had a real marriage, at least what you would likely call a marriage. Peter is gay, you know."

"I always wondered about that," Tom said.

"I am still faithful to him, because that was my marriage vow. He feels that his thing with men doesn't count, because in his view, he is faithful also."

"Gee, Bug, how long can something like that go on?"

"Probably until I say so. Now, you didn't finish telling me about your marriage."

"You promise not to think I'm crazy? You have to really mean it, Bug."

"I have been with you nearly every day and some nights for three years. I know that I would die instead of seeing you die, and there is no doubt that you would do the same. I know everything about you, Tom, excluding sex, that is. Whatever you say won't change my opinion about you."

"You asked for it. So far, I have lived three lives. In my first one, I was happily married to a girl named Jeanette. She visits me in my dreams at night, and the sensation is so real that I wake up disorientated. I got angry at her one evening, for no good reason, and I walked through an archway. Just an archway, that's all there was, just an ordinary archway. After I went through, I was in another room, and I couldn't get back to her. My life changed radically. Suddenly, I was a no-account salesman, one that frequented prostitutes. I was only in that other life for one day and one night, and I decided to change my crummy life and become a better person. When I walked out of an alley, I was nearly killed, and I saw you across the street firing a gun. That's how I got here. The weird part is that I know that I have always been here just like I was in my other lives. I remember our three years together and can tell you the exact number of times you smiled at me. Don't tell me it is all a dream, Bug. I know that the other two lives happened. I can tell you about every moment I spent with Jeanette and every word she ever spoke to me. It sounds crazy to me too, but there it is."

"You're crazy, Tom."

"I know. Do you still love me?"

"Yes."

"What are we going to do about it?"

"You'll have to give up Jeanette first."

"I never could control Jeanette. She is a redhead, you know.

She'll come back in my dreams when she wants to. I don't have anything to do with it."

"You can't have both of us, Tom."

"You are right, Bug. Any ideas?"

"Sure, you need a shrink. There is one other thing which could drive her out of your mind."

"I'm waiting, Bug."

"Me."

Tom thought about this and looked into her eyes for answers. He didn't think that she was kidding, but with her, you could never be sure. "I love you, Bug. It's a deal."

Two men with beards passed by the car, and one of them caught Tom's eye. They seemed to know that Tom spotted them and started walking faster.

"There he is, June. Draw your weapon and hang on." Tom started the car and lurched forward with burning tires. He turned hard, and the car jumped over the sidewalk cutting them off. He was first out of the car and leveled his pistol at them. June positioned her elbows on the roof of the car from the other side with her weapon pointing at their heads.

"Hands up or be shot," Tom shouted. Four hands went up, but the two men had a strange expression. Not fear, not hatred, something else, Tom saw. "One move, just the slightest move, and I'll shoot you both in the head. Do you understand?"

The men nodded that they understood but started smiling. An odd response to a threat such as Tom just made, and it unnerved him. There was something that they knew that he didn't know.

"Lieutenant June!" he shouted. "You will drive the car to the end of the block and call this in. Do it now and don't argue." Tom continued to watch the men closely as he heard the car start and drive away.

"You two seem to have it all figured out, but I want to tell you something. I don't mind dying. This life is only a dream after all. You can't really kill me, but I can kill you." The two men had a puzzled look and exchanged quick glances. Something about Tom had thrown them off. He was like them after all. They seemed to be searching for a plan. Tom could sense that something was going to happen, and he tensed and waited, alert for any motion from them.

The Jamal guy started smiling again. He had figured it out. In a motion too quick to describe, he started lowering one arm just as Tom's bullet struck him in the head throwing him backward. The other one jumped, probably startled by the gunshot, which caused Tom to shoot again. He fell backward also, and the two ended up nearly touching with their arms stretched out on the sidewalk. Tom stood erect and moved toward the men and pulled Jamal's wrap open with his shoe. His chest was covered by a vest containing large packets of explosives and wires. The other one was the same. Tom started running and nearly made it to June before the first explosion. He was thrown into her, and they both were knocked to the ground with him on top. The second explosion picked them and the car up and flung them across the street.

"Tom, we need to talk," she said. Her green eyes twinkled when she wanted to discuss something on her terms. She reached across the table and patted the back of his hand. He knew that whatever it was, she had the upper hand, figuratively and literally.

"Go ahead, Jeanette, let me know where I've failed you. It will be much simpler if I go ahead and apologize right now, so I will. Jeanette, dearest, you are the breath of my life, and I deeply apologize to you for doing anything which could possibly make you unhappy. Is that enough or would you like more?"

"Be serious, Tom. You have no idea what I want to talk about."

"Sure I do, Jeanette. It's about Allyson June. What else could it be?"

"For starters, I think your little nickname of Bug for her is atrocious. How perfectly disgusting to call a lovely young girl a name like 'Bug.' "

"Is that all that's really bothering you?"

"No. I worry that you can't love two women at one time. On this, I am only considering you, Tom, and what is best for you. I know that she said that she could replace me, but I wonder. Have you thought this through?"

"Jeanette, my lovely and breathtaking Jeanette. No woman can compare to you, and no man could be luckier than I have been having the privilege to be near you and wake up beside you. I love you with everything that I am but...even you will admit that in my life right now, you are only a dream and Bug is real. I have to go with real, Jeanette, no matter how much I love you."

"It isn't going to work in the long run, Tom. I am not going away. Let me show you something." She leaned across the table and slowly, very slowly, planted her lips on his and pressed into his face. She withdrew looking into his eyes, leaving him with her taste on his lips and his entire being yearning for more. "I am real, Tom, and I am here for you and you alone. No woman can replace me, because I am part of you and always will be."

"Jeanette, if I could only find you in this life. Is it possible?"

"You have me, Tom. I am right here beside you."

The first crack of his eyelids was painful. Sound and light poured into his senses like the first cold winds of winter, reaching into every corner and making him aware of where his pain was most intense. It was his right leg, he decided. The pain was grabbing him like a dog bite that wouldn't go away.

A warm hand held his and another hand with a delicate touch was on his forehead. "Tom. Can you hear me?" Bug said tenderly.

He turned his head toward the voice and opened his eyes wider. She was right beside the bed, and as he returned to the present, he could feel the warmth of her abdomen pressing against his elbow. She had wrinkles on her brow, but her eyes were wonderfully familiar, like the first sight of homeland when returning from a long sea voyage.

"Bug? Are you injured?"

"So you can talk. We were wondering how long that would take. Injured? Not much, Tom. You protected me with your body. You got the fracture and the head trauma, and I got a few scrapes and cuts. You also got all the headlines, the adulation, the respect and, yes, the love. You could run for president and win and still remain unconscious."

Tom tried to move but was seized with pain from several areas. He reconsidered and remained as he was. "To see you beside me is all that I could hope for, Bug. I don't mind being injured if I can wake up and find you here."

"Oh, then you are going to like the next part. We are both on official leave until you get well. I am going to be with you night and day until you kick me out."

"Then, I'll never get well, Bug. I'll never let you go."

"You didn't have to tell me that. Remember, I know you, Tom. I know what you think and what you'll do."

"What happens to Peter?"

"Peter is on an extended trip to Europe with his boyfriends. It's happened before so I know to expect him when I least expect him. He doesn't care what I do, really. Taking care of you is my number one priority and nothing, especially Peter, matters as much." Tom turned his hand over and clasped hers. He realized that this was the first time he had ever held her hand or ever touched her in any meaningful way. Her energy and love poured into him, and the pain in his head and leg ebbed away.

"Want to tell me what happened?" Tom asked.

"Simple. You shot the two bad guys, but timers exploded the bombs as they had planned. You were only two feet from me when the first went off, and we tumbled together with you on top. I didn't have much time to enjoy you being on top, because the second one detonated and seemed to be larger. I don't remember what happened exactly, but when I woke up you were still holding on to me, protecting me, and there were sirens and cops everywhere around us. I still can't get the smell of the Penta from my skin or my hair. I don't need to tell you how many lives you saved, the papers will do that, but I do want to tell you about saving mine. Twice, that day. The first was ordering me out of the area, and the second was putting your body in the path of the blast, sparing me both times at your expense."

"Forget it, Bug. First of all, you would have done the exact same thing, and second, I just protected something I loved. It was, after all, a very selfish move, and you don't need to thank me. I would let them blow me up over and over if I knew you would be there with me afterward."

She leaned across the bed and kissed him gently on the lips. Tom made a smacking sound and said, "Say, as far as I can tell, my lips are the only part of me that aren't injured. You don't really have to be careful, so if you don't mind, please do that again and be really reckless with it." He felt her tears dropping on his cheeks when she leaned over him the second time, but the kiss was a lot more vigorous than the first.

"Better, but you need a lot of practice to come up to my standards. As soon as I'm well, we'll work on it until we get it right."

A shadow fell over him, and he felt Allyson stiffen. "Well, isn't this a sight," a deep booming voice practically shouted. It was Sinclair Simpson, himself, come to pay a visit. "My daughter always said that you were a real man, and you proved to all of us that you are. You certainly did, young man. I was so proud of you that I cried into my coffee. You saved a lot of people with your quick action, and most of all for me, you saved my precious Allyson. I am indebted to you for the rest of my life, and I am proud to call you a fellow officer."

"Thanks, Sinclair, and thanks for coming by. It's nice to see you again. I wish I could stand up and return hugs with you, but that will have to wait for a while. But I promise to find you and share a beer with you when I'm able. By the way, I was just paying your daughter back for saving me more than once. That's what partners do."

Sinclair leaned forward and whispered rather loudly, "Sure wish you had her with you all the time instead of her going home to the man she married."

"Careful, father. I'm not going to hear anything negative about Peter from you," Bug said loudly.

"We're working on that, Sinclair, but it's good to have your blessing on it," Tom responded.

"Look, Tom, you have gotten so much publicity about what you did, you can run for public office in about any capacity. You are practically guaranteed to win. I still have friends downtown, you know, and I just happen to know that the Chief of Police job will soon be open. Just a suggestion, Tom, but I want you to start thinking about it, and we'll talk more later."

"You are the best, Sinclair. I always wished to know you better, but I thought Allyson would feel pressured if I did. Now, that's all behind us, and you have a new fishing buddy."

"Two fishing buddies," Bug said with a smile.

Sinclair said goodbye and kissed Allyson on the forehead, and they were alone again. Tom could see the tears still trying to come out of her eyes, and she continued to look at him without blinking or smiling.

"Your thoughts, Allyson?"

"I love you."

"Yes. I love you also. Is there more to say?"

"We should have had moments like this three years ago. I feel foolish for being loyal to someone who has no use for me except as an ornament. The kiss we just shared was the best for me in my lifetime. Now I know what was there all along."

"Allyson, there is something that we have to discuss. Now that we are going to be more than partners, you should know that I couldn't put you in a risky situation ever again. Seeing you hurt would be something I couldn't bear. If we are going to be a real couple, we can't be out on the street looking for perps any more. And I couldn't let you do it with another partner, because I wouldn't be there to watch over you. Either way, it won't work."

"I've got news for you, Tom. You never wanted to put me at risk even when we started. You have always protected me as much as you could. I knew it all along, and because I was in love with you, I let you do that for me. You have to remember, though, I am a detective through a lot of hard work of my own. You can't expect me to give up what I have wanted so badly all of my life."

"I do understand, dear Allyson. How about this? I make Chief, and I will give you any position in the force you want as long as the risks to you are low. Surely we can come up with something that satisfies us both."

Allyson started crying again and leaned over him and took both her hands to steady his face and kissed him long and hard. She laughed as she wiped his face dry of tears. "Wait a minute, some of those are your tears!"

"That was a kiss and a half. It made me cry," he said.

"Tom, I have to go back to the station for a while to meet with the interagency council. I am scheduled to be deposed about an hour from now. Will you be all right without me for that long?"

"No. Make them come over here."

"Silly. There is a plainclothes guard out there in the hall. I'll ask if he won't come in and keep you company while I'm gone."

"First, tell me why I need a guard. Do they think I'm about to escape?"

"I couldn't pass a day without hearing some of your humor. No, it's because of the publicity. Someone upstairs feels that friends of Jamel might want revenge."

"That may well indeed be the case, Bug, but one guard armed with a pistol would never stop that crowd."

"I know, Tom. I'll be back soon, and I have a gun also. You'll be safe until then, and when I return, you are again mine forever."

"In that case, I'll just sleep until you get back. That way the time will pass quicker."

"About Jeanette?"

"I wouldn't be surprised."

"Tell her hello from me. And tell her that she better make time with you while she can because soon you will only dream of me."

After Allyson left, Tom looked blankly at the ceiling thinking about the two women in his life, or more exactly, lives. Was there any solution? One for the day, one for his dreams, and both aware of each other. All there was left was a cat fight between the two. If he had a real relationship with Allyson, was it betraying Jeanette? And if he said he loved Jeanette in his dreams, did that betray Allyson? It wasn't like two different men at two different times loved these women. It was he that loved them both. Even though he knew that his present life was real and long, so were the others, and besides, the last time he saw Jeanette was only several days ago, not years and not lives, days. Jeanette kissed him a few minutes ago while he was asleep, and he could still taste her when he wakened. If both women were standing in front of him, he might know what to do but this way?

As he became agitated over his dilemma, his leg started pounding, and he pushed the nurse call button.

"Well, the famous Detective Chase is awake!" she said as she came in. "You are all over the news, you know. Do you need something, dear?"

"Well, my leg hurts a lot. Anything I can do?"

"No, but I can. See this button right here?" she said and pointed to another small device hanging by the bed. "Just press this button if the pain gets too bad, and the machine will dose you. Don't be afraid of it, because it won't let you use but so much. I'll do it this time for you," she said and pressed the little red button. Nearly instantly, he felt a warm flush, and the pain cased.

"Not bad. Much better, in fact. Thanks."

"Not at all, Tom. We all here want to help you as much as we can. You are our hero too."

"That's appreciated, but it's just my job. I have a trigger instead of a button, that's all."

"Modest. Cute too. Some of us would be even more attentive, but your lady friend wears a very big gun." She laughed and waved goodbye. Tom felt relaxed, and although he wanted to watch the clock for when Allyson was due back, he soon drifted off.

"I think I'm jealous, Tom. You and Bug make such a lovely pair. The kiss was nice too. And I just loved the threat from her. What a challenge!"

"She said to say hello in case you missed that part," Tom said.

"I heard. Some nerve," she said lazily and stretched her arms in front of her toward the ceiling. She let one of them fall across Tom's face so that he had her skin against his lips and nose. Her familiar fragrance filled his nostrils, and he had to resist the impulse to lick her arm as it slid over his partially open mouth. She rolled over on the bed to face him and pulled his face toward her. She brushed her red hair back and tucked a strand behind her ear. There was a funny look in her eyes, like she was plotting her next move. Her hand slid up and down on his bare chest and neck, and she leaned toward his face until they were nose to nose and her green eyes blinked into his.

"You remember me, don't you?" she asked.

"Need to ask me that?"

"Still love me?"

"Absolutely, without question, without qualification, without hesitation, I love you, Jeanette. If I could lay here with you forever, it wouldn't be long enough."

"You know I am waiting for you. Want to come back to me?"

"How, Jeanette? How do I come back? I went through the door, and I couldn't get back. Tell me how I do it."

"When you find the way, you will return to me. I don't want you to give up or get too distracted. There is still time yet, but I want you back as soon as you are ready. I thought I would give you a little incentive," she said, and stood up beside the bed and took a step backward. She had that look, that look of desire and passion mixed with fire, that he had seen on other rare occasions. Partially extending her arms like a dancer while keeping her eyes fixed on his, she let her robe fall away behind her leaving perfect skin in unashamed full view. She turned slowly so that he could see her from every angle, nearly like a ballerina without her costume. She was breathtaking. Her fair un-tanned skin was nearly transparent and magnified her nudity several fold. Tom took a deep breath, transfixed by the view of this apparition from heaven.

A burst of automatic gunfire came from just outside his door, and it woke him up with a jerk. A volley of returning fire came from close by, and he could hear the shattering of glass and wood as bullets struck the wall and windows in the hall. More and nastier bursts started coming from another location. A terrific explosion shook the room and the door partially opened. New automatic fire bursts lasting several seconds at a time grew louder and then suddenly stopped. The quiet was deafening, and smoke curled into the room from the hall, spreading silently against the ceiling. Pieces of glass were falling to a hard floor from some unseen place. Tom patted the bed for a weapon but only hurt his leg in the process, and he grimaced in agony flopping back down. He was helpless against whatever next came through that door.

Without warning, the door was forcibly kicked open and hit the wall with a crash. There was a moment of hesitation then a gun barrel appeared followed by a crouching man dressed in a black jumpsuit complete with helmet and face shield. He stood upright after looking around carefully, then raised his shield.

"You okay, sir?" he asked.

"Glad as hell to see you come through that door. Yes, they never made it this far. Can you tell me what happened?"

"As far as I know, three heavily armed fanatics tried to shoot their way in here. Summers was our guy in the hall and was taken out but not until he got one of them. The Chief had positioned two of us downstairs as a precaution and looks like he was right. Both the other perps are down and Swat is on the way over to canvas the area. I'm not sure it's over yet, sir."

"Do you know if Lieutenant June was involved?"

"Don't have that info, sir. Sorry."

"I need your handgun, officer. I can't be defenseless in here."

"Sure thing," he said and pulled out his black Beretta and handed it over.

Tom slipped the gun under his pillow and listened to the sirens and commotion erupting all around them. The black-outfitted officer remained just outside the door but in view, his assault rifle at the ready. Tom pushed his little red button a couple of times and settled back to wait things out.

After a few minutes, he heard someone running down the hall toward him, and he reached behind his head and grasped his new weapon. He relaxed when he saw his guard point his gun at the ceiling and step back. Allyson burst around the corner and nearly flung herself on him. "Can't I leave for a few minutes without you attracting some maniacs?" she said breathlessly.

"No, I told you that I would do anything to get you alone. Now you know it's true. I worried about you, Bug. Thankfully, you were gone at the time it all went down."

"Well, they better not return, because I am here to stay."

"Unfortunately, it looks like I am too," he said looking down at his swollen leg.

"We may need to move you to a safer place, Tom. With all the publicity, everybody knows where you are. It would be symbolic for them to be able to kill you, and they are sure to try again."

"I could just walk through an Exit Door. Simpler for everyone."

"What in the world are you talking about," she asked.

"That one, I don't want to discuss with you. You are too young and innocent."

"You are soon going to find out that I'm not very innocent." Her voice had that touch of huskiness that he found so appealing.

"Know what I'm looking forward to the most? Don't answer me. It's hearing that voice of yours in my ear over and over again no matter what you are saying."

"Right now, it's saying that I'm glad that they didn't make it this far." She got up and closed the door and pulled up a chair next to his bed. "We have a summer cabin in the lakes, and I don't think Dad's been there in years. It's quiet and safe, and no one knows about it. Think you might be willing to try it out?"

"Do I have to be there alone? It might be awkward and make

me a little crazier than I already am."

"You are a real piece of work. No, I have in mind being there also and finding out if I can make you tired of my voice," she said.

"Well, we need to bring plenty of food, because that is going to take a really long time."

She reached over and pushed his red button. "That will keep you for a few minutes. I want to go downstairs and meet with Swat and find out what's going on. You have a real tiger outside that door, and he won't let any bad thing in. I'll be right back." She got up and left just as the narcotic was hitting him, and the room faded away as if night was rapidly sneaking into his room.

Her perfumed hair was sweeping across his face, and the sweet feel and smell made him open his eyes. Jeanette's face was hovering just above his and he could see that he was in a soft tent of hair on both sides of his head. She was supporting herself on her arms and sitting softly on his lower abdomen. She smiled as the recognition of her came into his face.

"Hi! Am I bothering you?"

"Never. To see your face near mine is one of the great gifts of life. You smell wonderful."

"I just had a bath and am clean all over, just as you like me."

Tom reached around her with his arms and pulled her down on top of him. He kissed her forehead and then her nose. "I love you," he said.

"Yes, you always have, but I'm worried now about things. This new love of yours threatens me. I'm afraid of losing you to her. What can I do to hold onto you, Tom?"

"Simple. Tell me how to get back to you so that you can be real and not a dream."

"I am not a dream. Can't you smell me and feel my skin and my kisses?" She gave him a long and sensuous kiss on the lips.

"If I could stay here with you, I would. I keep waking up to my real life and then you aren't there. I can't see you or touch you when I'm awake, and I have to live a normal life without you. I'm sorry."

"Which is the dream, Tom, me or her?"

"Sometimes I'm not sure. Certainly not now. You feel as real as ever, and I want to consume you with my love." He kissed her and caressed her bare back with his hands. "There isn't anything that compares to being with you, Jeanette."

He felt something was different about this kiss. The touch was softer, and it pulled him up like he was on top of a helium-filled bed that soared vertically as fluffy clouds parting on either side. He had the sensation of being pushed down into bed while being lifted by his lips alone.

"Awake now?" Bug asked as she pulled away from his face slowly letting her touch linger on his skin. Tom opened his eyes wider realizing that he had changed women, and the world was once again real.

"You are back! Was it long?" he asked, still fuzzy.

"Only half an hour or so. You were still sleeping when I came in, but I couldn't resist your lips. They were just lying there unused. Hope you didn't mind."

"I think I missed most of it. Care to try again so I can concentrate?"

She leaned over and softly caressed his lower face with her lips moving in slow circles toward his lips until they met. He felt her tongue contact his and then she pulled away quickly as someone knocked at the door.

"More, more, Bug. Please more," Tom said.

"Later," she said and opened the door.

Two senior, serious and highly decorated police officers entered together as Allyson stood back to let them in.

"Detective Chase, Detective June, we came to pay our respects and to apologize for the attempted attack on you just now." It was the Chief and Assistant Chief of Police. One of which, Tom was intently interested in replacing with himself.

"Welcome to you both. It's an honor to have you both here," Tom said and tried unsuccessfully to sit more upright.

"No, son, you stay right where you are," the Chief said. "We have the hospital and grounds secured, and they are just starting to clean up the wreckage downstairs. Looks like they will have to evacuate this wing of the hospital because of the damage inflicted. You might have heard that the three terrorists who led the assault were killed. At least two others were spotted but managed to get away from us. The Feds are helping on this one, and they seem to feel that more is to come out of this. We think you have to leave this hospital as soon as you can be prepared or else we risk injury to the patients and staff here from another attack. There is a medevac helicopter being prepared to take you someplace of your choosing as soon as we get medical clearance."

"Thank you, sir, for the update. I'll leave, but I'm taking Detective June with me."

The officers laughed and looked back and forth between Tom and Allyson. "We all knew long ago it would come to this, kids. I'm surprised that it took this long for the fireworks to start. Our best wishes to you. By the way, I look really fine in my dress uniform. Keep that in mind if you ever have a wedding," the Chief said.

Tom noticed the facial expressions and eyes of Deputy Chief Riggs as they talked. He was somewhere else with his thoughts. At first Tom thought that he was still thinking about the terrorists or the hunt for the rest of them, but all at once he became clairvoyant about the man's intentions. Tom realized, in a flash, that Riggs was thinking of him as a competitor for the Chief's job. The more he studied Riggs, the more he was certain that Riggs was jealous of him, hated him, and would likely want to get rid of him. Riggs was a heavyset man with dark darting eyes, and the few times he smiled, it was one of those tight, level, compressed smiles that people put on when they are expected to smile. Riggs' eyes shifted from Tom to Allyson to the Chief in quick succession as thoughts raced through his head seeking or forming a plan.

"Where would you folks like us to take you?" Riggs asked. Allyson started to blurt out the location of the cabin, but Tom raised his hand and interrupted.

"We haven't discussed it yet, Deputy Chief, but we'll let you know as soon as possible," he said. Allyson shot him a questioning look but remained silent, because she had learned to trust his judgment without reservation.

"Right, then. We'll send the surgeon in here in a little while and get his permission, if possible, and get started on it. Since the FBI and Swat are out there in force, we can assume your safety for the moment," Riggs said. There was that look again. Riggs could not be trusted.

The officers, having had enough of the formalities, excused themselves and left for downstairs. "What are you thinking, Tom?" Allyson asked when the footsteps faded away.

"Riggs and I are in competition for the Chief's job. I don't trust him, and we surely aren't going to tell him where we are going. Do you know anyone in the area of your father's cabin?"

Allyson thought for a minute and said, "There is an older caretaker who manages several of the cabins. He lives nearby and gets them ready when the owners want to come back for a vacation. As I remember, his name is Charlie Chuck, a Native American who grew up in the area. I can ask Dad how to get hold of him."

"Nothing doing, Bug. Your father trusts these guys, and they could easily get it out of him after a couple of beers. They might not even need to talk to him, if they remember that he has an out-of-the-way place. I've got a better idea."

"I'm all ears, Tom. Or should I call you lover boy now?"

"Premature, lover girl. If you use a phone that they can't trace, you could call and see if you can talk to this Charlie. Try to get him to let you use another cabin, like across the lake while your place is 'fumigated' or something. Offer him some money to keep it quiet. If he agrees, we will get the chopper to put us down fifty miles from the cabin and rent a car to take us in. That way we can keep a watch on your father's place to see if anyone follows us out there. It'll buy us a bit of time to get away if we have to run for it."

"Gee, you are conspiratorial, aren't you? Where do you get that stuff?"

"I was in the Army. That's called a plan."

"Well, perhaps I could do it while it's safe around here. Let me see what I can work out. I'll be back as quick as I can. Bring you something?"

"You, and be quick about it."

Bug left and since he could hear two officers talking just outside the door, he felt safe enough to push his little red button again to control his throbbing leg and get some rest.

He felt the weight of her in his hand and arm as they spun around while looking into each other's eyes. She let go of him and twirled neatly before coming back to face him in an instance of perfect grace, enveloping his upper body, pulling into close contact with his chest, her green eyes turned up toward his. They stepped to one side with legs intertwined as a pulsating accordion poured out the tango tune *Canzone della strada.* Jeanette was wearing a red silk dress, split widely and deeply in the front, bare in the back. One side was open along the full length of her long, perfect leg. Unrestrained by a bra, her breasts moved softly back and forth with her movement and her breaths as they danced. The band of tiny white flowers holding her long hair was matched with a small corsage on her left strap.

"You haven't forgotten the tango, my love," she said, and he glimpsed her perfect teeth behind parted red lips.

"Nor have I forgotten you. How could I?"

"You can't forget me, ever. I am a part of you. You remember saying that when we make love, it's like we fuse into one body?"

"Yes, it's starting to seem long ago, but that is a sensation I never want to forget," Tom said and twirled her out and back.

"Kiss my neck and close your eyes for a moment, and the memory will come back," she suggested very softly. Tom did as she asked and felt her warm neck against his lips, closed his eyes and they twirled, slowly shifting their feet in between each other's. Her perfume was strong, and when she moved slightly away from him, the fragrance clung to his lips and nose.

"Yes, I remember. No moment in a man's life could ever match that one."

"We had many, as I recall," she said.

"All the moments we spent together were memorable, Jeanette."

"Do you still find me beautiful?"

"You likely are the most beautiful woman ever to have lived. You have no equals, Jeanette."

"More beautiful than your Bug, then?"

"Different. She is pretty, wholesome, healthy, and most of all, Jeanette, she is alive and with me."

"So you choose pretty over beautiful?"

"Do I have a choice? Tell me how I come back to you and I will."

"You would leave this Bug, Tom?" The French accent was heavy, and her long eyelashes hung over her pupils complimenting her sultry, pouty look.

"I am married to you. You have heard a million times how much I love you. Tell me how I can come back to you, Jeanette."

"Can't you feel my caress and the curve of my hip? I am real, Tom. Stay here with me." Her eyes were pleading with him.

"Is that all there is to it, Jeanette? You mean I can stay here?"

The door opened, admitting the surgeon and his acolytes who poured into the room. "Mr. Chase?" the surgeon prompted. Tom reluctantly opened his eyes.

"We are tasked with getting you out of the hospital. Tonight, I have been informed. Truthfully, you are not ready, and transportation will be a painful ordeal for you. Your leg has been repaired surgically, but there is too much swelling for a cast at this time. We can splint it, but it's a second class solution. Roberts, unwrap his head and let's have a look," he ordered, and his intern immediately started taking the layers of gauze from around Tom's head.

"Yes, the head wound is fine. We can leave off the dressing. Now about the leg." An inflatable splint appeared, and they managed to position it without severe discomfort. "Well, you need supervision, Mr. Chase. Where are they taking you?"

"I don't know yet, Doctor. But I think there will be no supervision for me."

"This is pretty barbaric. I can see why they want you to leave, because none of us would appreciate being blown to bits along with you. My ethics demand that I protest this move, and before they take you, I want to have one more try at some other solution." He patted Tom's shoulder affectionately, and the team noisily exited and left him alone with his throbbing leg.

Pushing the red button didn't seem to do anything so he rang for the nurse. After an agonizing delay, he heard the swish of her clothing and looked up to see her face. There was a trace of hostility or perhaps sadness on her face but not compassion. She waited for him to voice his problem.

"Did you get injured in the attack, Nurse?" he asked her.

"I was off duty. We lost two brave nurses who got in the line of fire, and the guard outside your door was killed. The hospital is ruined and things are kind of crazy with all the heavily armed police."

"Are you angry with me, Nurse? Hold me to blame, somehow?"

"Of course, you are not to blame. You saved a lot of lives the other day. We all still consider you a hero, but we would be happier and safer if the hero was someplace else. I'm sorry to put it that way, but so many lives are at stake in a hospital."

"I understand completely, Nurse, be assured that I'll be leaving shortly, but first, I want to thank you for the care I have received here. There is no way I can make up for all the chaos and the deaths. Someday, when I am well, I would like to come back and thank you properly."

"Anything I can do for you, Detective, before you are taken away?"

"The pain in my leg is bad since they applied the splint. Anything you can do will be helpful." She nodded understanding and quickly left. After a few moments she returned with a small kit of medication and fiddled with the pump.

"We'll send the pain pump with you. Here are some supplies needed to recharge the narcotic dose and instructions on how to do it are inside the kit. It's the best I can do."

"Thanks. I can manage it from here. You can leave me now and get back to your other patients, Nurse." He patted her arm and smiled at her. She leaned over and pushed the red button again, and he felt the rush of warmth pulsate through his veins. Relief.

He watched Jeanette's back as she took down her hair. She was facing the large mirror over her dressing table, and he could see that she was watching him. He was lying sprawled on their big bed with his head propped up so that he wouldn't miss anything she did. A waterfall of thick red hair was unleashed which cascaded down her back, waving softly from side to side as she brushed it out. Jeanette knew that Tom was transfixed and wouldn't and couldn't look away. She leaned forward, purposely thrusting her hip to one side as she pulled off one high-heeled shoe and then the other. To increase his anticipation, she stood upright and motionless before the moment she knew he had been waiting for. Then, one strap at a time, the dress slid past her hips to the floor.

"Tom, Tom, better wake up. We need to talk," Bug said. Tom peeped at her, not knowing if he should try to ignore her. Watching Jeanette take off her clothes was one of the things he most enjoyed, and he was reluctant to give it up. "Tom!" She patted his face and his eyes opened again.

"Yes, Bug. It's me," he croaked.

"I know it's you. Wake up," she demanded.

"Okay, I'm awake now. Did you have any luck?"

"All I needed to do was offer fifty bucks. I didn't actually talk to Charlie Chuck but to his wife. She makes all the decisions, anyway. It should be all set, and I already have the address. Luckily, it is directly across Silver Lake from my Dad's cabin. We should have an unobstructed view."

"Well, the surgeon has reluctantly agreed to let me go. Have you looked at a map of the area yet?"

"Better than that. I know someone close who will meet us anywhere we choose and drive us in."

"Remember, we are going to need a car, and it's better that your friend doesn't know where we are headed."

"Don't worry, we are going to have to let some details get worked out at the time. It'll be fun to have you all to myself," she added.

"One small problem, Bug. With this leg, I am about half a man. It's not going to be as fun as you think."

"You'll mend. By then, I'll have a long list of things we can do together."

With ferocious beating, the awkward machine forced its way into the air as the buildings beneath grew insignificant. An uncomfortable and threatening tilt forward provoked the lights below to slide toward the rear and out of sight. Allyson tightly and protectively held his hand with love, but also from fear induced by the mechanical beast they were encased in. Away from the city, there were few lights below to judge their speed or altitude, and the experience was one of noisily riding through a dark cave.

Tom was still on a stretcher and tightly bound to it with straps. His IV apparatus bumped and swayed along with shifts in the air and gravity, making a strong semblance to a pendulum of a giant clock. Allyson never left his side and frequently laid her head across his chest or gave him small kisses in the dark. Conversation was limited because of the ambient noise, so the language of love was spoken with touch rather than with words.

The helicopter abruptly started sinking into the darkness. The little town underneath them had few lights which could be seen, creating the impression that there was to their descent. Tom tensed in anticipation of an inevitable impact with earth, and his leg began throbbing. He held off pushing his red button because he knew that he might need his full faculties, but to his relief, there was a light, almost imperceptible settling of the machine onto its skids. After the long rotors slowly came to rest, one of the crew slid the big side door open, letting in the moisture of the night accompanied by sounds of crickets.

"We're here, folks. Didn't you say that you expected a ride, Detective?" the crewman asked.

"They'll be here shortly," Allyson said. "Let's get him out and then you can get back to the city." They all helped make Tom's exit as smooth as possible, but each small movement brought new agony from his leg. They expressed thanks to the crew, and Allyson began pushing the gurney slowly across the parking area into the protection of a small building as they watched the beast lift back into the night, its lights slowly receding into the distance.

Silence. Nearly absolute silence compared to the city. Then, as their ears adjusted to the new environment, the sounds of a summer night in the woods came softly to them. First, the crickets, then frogs and insects and, occasionally in the distance, various animal sounds floated in the damp air. They began to relax in the warm fragrant air, feeling more at home as the moments extended to minutes then nearly to an hour.

"You know, I believe this is the first time I have held your hand in mine in the dark," Tom said.

"Excites you?" she said and caressed his hair.

"It seems that it was always meant to be, Bug. Something I have wanted for a long time but never expected it to happen. I can't see you very well in the dark, but I have your face and shape memorized anyway. It's your wonderful voice that really excites me."

"You're going to get tired of it. My voice, I mean," she said, giving her unique little giggle.

"I have had three years of being with you, and I have seen you hurt, angry, sad....about any emotion possible, except love. You hid that very well. But, I've never, ever, gotten tired of you. You were why I came to work in the morning, but also why I always came home lonely. If there is such a thing as love at first sight, I know I experienced it in the first minute after I walked into the Chief's office and he introduced you. It wasn't that you were just a lovely, cute little blonde who was full of energy and enthusiasm. Something inside me clicked like a switch. It was on the other side of your eyes. I saw into your mind, and I loved what I saw there. Every minute we were together reinforced my love for you. I recall that I used to dream about you almost every night for a long time.

"Used to? You don't anymore?"

"Since I came out of that alley from my other life, Jeanette has been there each time I drift off. It seems that I know her better than I even know you. She begs me to return to her, and when I am asleep, she seems to be so real, almost like I could just stay there with her."

"That is clearly impossible. She is a dream, Tom. You hear me? A dream your brain cooked up because you were denied being with me. It was sexual and romantic frustration. I have known you for three years, and I knew about you before that. You were never married, and I know that to be true. I'm betting your dream girl is a beautiful and desirable woman who thrills you just to look at her. Am I right?"

"That's true. She is really perfection in a woman. Long red hair, green eyes and a beautiful shape. When you woke me up to leave, she was taking her clothes off for me."

"I am not that beautiful, just normal. Hope you aren't disappointed when you get a good look."

"Books and books have been written about love and sexual attraction. Both have been described for ages, and most often, they exist separately. When they are there together, it's always been beyond a clear description. That's what I have for you. Love and attraction at the same time. You can throw lust in there for good measure."

"I am going to drive her out of your thoughts, I promise. Just give me time, and I will be the only one in that head when you close your eyes."

"When I am here with you, Bug, there is nothing else I think about. When I fall asleep, she is there with me and just as real as you are now and I love her just as much. I think something has to happen, because I can't live this way. It's tearing me apart."

"Remember when you mentioned the exit door? Can you explain it to me now?"

"I would, if I understood it. I haven't seen one since I came out of the alley, but at the time, it created a lot of fear in me."

A car's motor labored in the distance and grew closer, and soon they could see the glow of its headlights approaching. Both of them instinctively slipped their hands around the handle of their pistols and waited in silence. The car traversed a section of gravel making an ominous and threatening sound. As it approached the sleeping town, its speed was reduced to a crawl, like a beetle picking his way through fallen leaves. The headlights stopped and caught them in its brazen beam, frozen like a photograph.

"Allyson? Is that you?" the voice called out.

"Jim? Yes, we are here," she called back. They could hear the car door closing, and the footfall of an approaching man. When he came into the glare of the headlight, it was obvious that he was an older man, somewhat bent and slow.

"Great to see you again, Allyson!" he said and clasped her hands with his. "I brought the station wagon. You said your friend is injured?" He finally spotted Tom on the gurney and came over with his hand extended. "Any friend of Allyson is a friend of mine. Jim Evan is my name, son."

"Glad to meet you, Mr. Evan. I am going to withhold my name at the moment, sir, for reasons which will become apparent later."

"No need for that, Tom Chase. I read the papers, you know, even out here. There was a time in my life that I was a cop. You can trust me."

"Jim was my father's long time partner when they were on the beat," Allyson explained.

"Sorry, Jim," Tom said.

"No sweat, kid. I'll do anything for a genuine hero like you. What's this all about folks?"

Allyson spoke first, "There was an assault on the hospital that Tom was in, and we were not too politely asked to leave. The terrorists will likely try to find us, even out here."

"Got it. Let's pile in the car and get out of here. You can drop me off and keep the wagon. I won't tell anyone about this. Anything you need before you go to roost?"

"Food, mostly. I can go out later and get anything else. We might be here for a few weeks or at least until Tom is mobile."

The large capacity of the older station wagon was appreciated, and the gurney slid in effortlessly. Before dropping Jim off, they made one stop for food and came back with several large bags. At Tom's request, Jim supplied them with an excellent pair of binoculars and an old double-barreled shotgun. At last, after a long drive, they saw their new temporary home in the headlights and behind it Silver Lake shimmering in the moonlight.

"I would love to carry you across the threshold, Bug. It turns out that you might have to carry me across instead," Tom quipped.

"Whatever gets the job done," she answered.

They settled in for the night quickly. Tom remained on the gurney which Allyson positioned beside the double bed. "Tomorrow, Tom, my love, we start a new life together. All we have to do is to get your leg healed." She gave him a long and tender kiss on his lips and held her head along side his as she whispered into his ear. "I love you, Tom. Try dreaming about me tonight, and I'll show you what you have to look forward to.

Chapter 5

Hunters Being Hunted

om had his feet on his desk and was looking out the window for some sort of inspiration. The latest drawings were scattered around on the desktop and spilling onto the floor. He had been at it for nearly three hours and his brain needed a break. There was a soft click, and his office door opened a crack, then gradually revealed bright red hair emerging, topping a smiling face. When she realized that he was looking her way, she pushed it the rest of the way open and stepped in.

"Hated to bother you, but I knew you needed a little break. Got time for lunch?" Jeanette asked. She was dressed in a simple cotton shift, but her figure filled it in the right places. Her gorgeous hair was back in a pony tail, and except for her striking good looks, she could have passed for a young student, albeit one who would attract a lot of attention.

"Come on in, Jeanette. You know I'm always glad to see you. I would have called you, but this project is nearing deadline, and we have just a few hours left to get it right." After he spoke, he saw her favorite picnic basket swinging from her arm. He glanced at his watch. Half past two and he remembered that he was hungry. "Picnic with you? Why not? It's a fine day for it, and after all, the park is just across the street." He got up and swung his dress jacket over his arm and smiled at her.

"Can I invite Eric also? I have enough for three," she asked.

"Sure, I'll tell him to come over when he gets finished with his meeting. I'll just be a second." Tom quietly opened Eric's door and waited until he got his attention and then used sign gestures to make him understand the plan. Eric nodded yes with his eyes and resumed listening to the men around him.

They chose a quiet spot, and Tom spread the ground cloth as Jeanette unpacked the basket. They sat across from each other just at the edge of the shade of a magnificent elm.

"Sorry that I haven't been much of a companion to you lately, but I'll make it up to you soon. What have you been up to this week, Jeanette?"

She rolled her eyes and squinted like a little girl as she shrugged, "Oh, not really anything. You know the usual. Went to the gym, shopped, got fitted for my next photo shoot."

"What kind of layout is it this time? I seem to remember that you told me but, forgive me, you have to remind me about it."

"It's for the spring edition of the FashionEtta collection. They pay well and the shoot will only be for one day this year." As she spoke, he yearned for the usual flirtation she was so good at, but she seemed slightly reserved at the moment.

"You are looking radiant, dear. Even my imagination could never create something so lovely as you are this afternoon."

"Thanks," she said without looking up. He noticed that there was no return compliment from her or even a flash from those green eyes that she often used as a small reward for good behavior.

"Everything all right, Jeanette?" he asked.

"Of course. With you?"

"Busy, that's all." Soft footsteps in the grass were headed toward them, and they both turned at the same time to see Eric trudging up the grassy slope. Tom flicked his focus back to Jeanette in time to see something in her face when she saw Eric. It was hard to describe and fleeting, but there was a change in her for just a moment. Tom noticed that she glanced toward him, possibly to see if he had noticed.

"Sorry, I finally got that bunch satisfied and out of there. Thanks for waiting for me," Eric said with his boyish grin. Tom was studying his face intently now, and he saw Eric glance at Jeanette for just a fraction of a bit longer than he had ever done before. Just a second longer, but in that second, Eric's eyes paused on her face slightly too long for Tom's comfort. Eric sat between them but slightly more toward her than him. They exchanged smiles and Jeanette graciously passed Eric some food. Tom's attention was at full alert. There wasn't any reason to suspect these two of something wrong, none at all. They all had known each other for several years and were good friends. Nevertheless, there was more interest and of a different kind than before. Eric's divorce had been final now for some months, and Tom wondered if he had gotten back in the dating game yet. He made a mental note to ask. These two people were closer to Tom than anyone else, even his blood kin. He had known both for a long time and thought he could nearly read their minds. There was a hint of radiation between them that he had never seen before. Not enough to blow up about, or even question, but enough to make him wonder.

"I forgot to ask, Eric. Have you found some new female friends now that you are single again?" Tom asked with a smile.

"I'm working on it," he answered with a shrug.

Lunch was bereft of conversation, and the three spent much of the time looking over at the city skyline in silent thought. Eric got up first saying, "Thanks for the lunch, Jeanette. I've got a meeting I have to prepare for so I'm off. See you soon."

Tom and Jeanette sat there in pregnant silence. Tom spoke first, "Want to discuss anything?"

"What's to discuss?"

"I know when I say what I'm thinking, you will just deny any knowledge of it. It's tiresome at times. Can't we just cut the bull and talk?"

"Anytime you want to talk, I'm prepared to listen," she said and started picking up the paper plates.

"Are you just trying to make me jealous, or is there something to be worried about?"

"You have your little Bug that you are about to bed, and you ask me that?"

"You know how much I care about you. Tell me how I can return to you full-time and I won't hesitate," Tom said.

"That is something only you can do. I have pleaded with you, enticed you, even reminded you about what you are missing and still you stay away. If you pinch me I will cry. How real is that? You are apart from me in your new life, but that means I am apart from you also."

"Jeanette, you know that I didn't intentionally leave you. I was excited to have a chance to put our marriage back where it should be, then I couldn't get back to you. I wanted to, and I tried until I nearly collapsed, but the doorway disappeared. This life I have now is all I know. Do you think that there is a chance you exist in this life also?"

"I exist right here and now. You are here, I am here. We are looking at each other, aren't we?" Jeanette said with exasperation accompanied by continental hand gestures. "I know that you left intentionally. You were mad at me because you wrongly thought I was talking to another man, and in your mind, you called our marriage over, didn't you?"

"I made a horrible mistake, and I am paying a steep price for it."

"You made a mistake, and we are both paying for it," she retorted.

Pain in his leg radiated up the entire right side of his body. He must have tried to turn in his sleep, and he woke up with a start and tried to comprehend where he was. Bug was asleep in a bed right beside his gurney, and he looked at her affectionately for a moment. His mind churned over his latest dream about Jeanette. She seemed so real and was pulling away from him, inch by inch, and who could blame her? He had been leading a life apart, separated by some force that he couldn't understand, and he could only wonder if he ever appeared in her dreams like she did in his. Clenching his fist and his jaw, he thought of Eric and Jeanette together. His first impulse was a desire to kill Eric. Could he do it? The man he is right now could, without a doubt. Unfortunately, he no longer had a say in what Eric or Jeanette did. Nevertheless, thoughts about a dalliance between them still made him sick to his stomach. He laid back down and looked at the rustic ceiling and thought about the present. Now what? There hadn't been time to sort it out and think it through. His most immediate problem was to get better so that he could become mobile again. Their safety from the terrorists...was this hiding place enough? Probably not, given enough time and assistance from Riggs, they would be found. He knew that the more people who knew where they were, the more chance of being discovered. So far, only three people knew anything, and only two knew the exact location of the cabin. Being a detective, he knew that for the terrorists to find them, they would need to do some legwork and ask questions. There was still time yet.

"Are you feeling better?" Bug asked from bed. He looked down and saw her face peeping from a cleft in the covers, with just a little tuft of blonde hair showing.

"So far, knock on wood, I haven't needed the pain pump. Perhaps we can take the IV out today," he said.

Allyson got up and carefully checked his leg. "Looks less swollen," she remarked. She patted him on his head on her way past, like she would do with an affectionate dog. "Hungry?" she asked from the kitchen.

"Always."

Quickly and efficiently, she prepared a big spread of ham, eggs and toast. A pot of coffee simmered, leaving the wonderful aroma of morning drifting around the room. Tom watched her work, and the feminine and graceful in her seemed balanced by a strength of purpose. A woman is an amazing package, he thought. So easy to underestimate from a man's point of view. Jeanette is the same in some ways, he recalled, but is far more toward the alluring, provocative and sexual side of the female spectrum. He couldn't summon the image of Jeanette firing a large handgun, but he could easily picture her manipulating someone to do it for her. By the same token, he couldn't picture Bug in a revealing red gown dancing the tango with him. He sighed. He loved them both. In a dangerous situation, Bug would be there like a rock, but in the bedroom, Jeanette could not possibly have an equal. There really was no choice. Bug was the perfect woman for him in this present life, and she loved him as much as he loved her. She was no flighty thing consumed with her appearance and skilled at using the charms of a woman. Bug was dependable, strong, and moral. She had stayed true to her wedding vows in an empty marriage devoid of the physical closeness people need to get through life. When Bug committed to something, she would see it through, no matter what it took. Most of all, Bug was real.

His eyes had plenty of time to visualize her shape under her clothing as she moved. Watching her made him realize how much he wanted her whole being, body and soul. He wanted to consume her, to savor her, and to be with her physically and mentally forever. Previously, he had always forced himself to repress any desire for her. He made every effort not to cross the line, because she was his partner and his equal. Obviously, she had known what his subconscious was thinking all along, felt the same way, but never gave any indication. They had established some method of mental communication in their relationship. Perhaps that explained why they made such a good team for police work and the same thing would work as well for them as life partners.

There was a loud rapping at the cabin door, and Tom watched as Allyson picked up her handgun and looked out the window. "Yes?" She called out as she made sure there was a cartridge chambered.

"Charlie Chuck here, Miss," a strangely accented voice said through the door. Allyson tucked the gun behind her back and opened the door. "Came for my money, Miss. That's fifty, according to my boss," he chuckled at the humor and craned his neck looking into the single room.

"You might as well introduce us, Allyson. He's already seen me," Tom said. Allyson stepped out of his way, and a large man in a plaid shirt darkened the door as he came in. Tom had a good look at him and saw a very fit man, though older, dressed in loose clothing which hid what was obviously a lot of muscle. He wore his braided hair in shades of grey and black, and it hung over his shoulder onto his chest. A large brimmed felt hat partially obscured his face which was wrinkled and tanned from years of exposure. Tom watched as Charlie scanned the room, efficiently taking in every detail.

"What's wrong with you?" he asked Tom when they met eyes.

"I was injured in an explosion. My leg bone was fractured." Charlie nodded as if he understood the whole picture.

He turned to Allyson and said in his direct manner, "Why you want to stay here? What's matter with your cabin?" He gestured across the lake toward her father's place. Allyson looked at Tom to gauge his response on how much they should tell Charlie.

"Tell him, Allyson," Tom said.

Allyson came around Charlie so that they could be face to face. "We came up here to hide, Charlie. There is a pack of terrorists hunting Tom, because he was forced to kill two of them before they could set off some bombs. We need you to keep this to yourself. Understand?"

"Missy, I was in the Army, in 'Nam. Machine gunner. I understand. That your car outside?"

"No, it belongs to a friend," she said.

"How you think they find you way up here?" Charlie asked.

"There may be someone on the police force who would like Tom gone. He could tell the terrorists if he can figure this out. They could come looking," she explained.

"Hum..." he said as he thought it out. "Car outside no good. Most people gone for the season. They will look for car if they come."

Tom interjected, "Charlie, what do you think we should do?"

"Small red barn up the road half mile. Hide car there. No lights at night in here, you get me?"

"That helps. Thanks, we'll do it," Tom said and offered his hand.

Charlie ignored it. "Your name Chase?" he asked. Tom nodded yes. "I read papers, watch TV. You famous."

"Unfortunately, that makes it harder for us to disappear until I heal."

"Charlie give you good suggestion about your leg. Indian way is get up and move, and leg heal much faster," he said.

"As soon as I can, I promise to do just that." Charlie nodded as if he wanted it done right away and was disappointed that Tom wasn't up to it.

Allyson offered Charlie his money, folded up in a small wad. "Here is what we owe you, Charlie. Thanks for your help and advice."

"No money. Glad to help, and I'll keep watch for your bad guys. Charlie won't let you down."

After Charlie left they talked over what he had suggested. "Charlie was right about the station wagon. It's a giveaway. I would notice it and so would you. About the lights at night, he's probably right about that also. Too bad about my leg, because I sure could figure out how to use all that dark," Tom said.

"You don't need dark to do that. The light is evermore satisfying, isn't it?" Bug smiled, then continued, "I think we are going to need more food and some clothes, batteries and a lot more other things if we are going to stay for a while. How about behaving yourself for a bit, and I'll go shopping and afterward hide the car in the barn."

"As long as you tell me how I can possibly misbehave. Say, are you going to use a credit card?"

"Yes, otherwise I don't have enough cash to buy anything. What's wrong?"

"If Riggs is looking closely, he will spot the purchases and locate us. Better drive away from here to buy anything. Far away."

"Why don't I just drive into the city and shoot Riggs?" she asked.

"That's a lot better. Go ahead, you have my permission."

"Look, lover, this is going to take me a couple of hours, maybe more. Sure you'll be all right?"

"Not without a long wet kiss first, I won't. Now that I think about it, my leg is telling me that it won't mind anything I ask of it." Bug grasped his head in her hands and gave him what he wanted, then very slowly and reluctantly pulled away.

"That ought to last for a couple of hours. As to the rest of your plans...later."

Tom heard the car drive away, and the silence commenced and lay over him, smothering him as if it were liquid. He knew he had to get up, but he was afraid to try it. If he fell he would have to lay on the floor for a long time before Allyson returned. He felt as helpless as a vegetable in the supermarket. He sat up and studied his leg after removing most of the dressing. There was an incision extending from his right knee upward for nearly ten inches. A neat row of clips held the skin tightly together. His right leg was much larger than his left, but there was little redness over the surgical area. He put the bandage back in place, wrapping it tightly. He needed a crutch and realized that no one had thought of getting him one. The shotgun was handy. He picked it up and tested the length. It might work, and at least it would help. Pushing his red button two last times, he disconnected his IV and pulled out the needle. Now he was on his own. If he could make it to the bathroom then back to the bed by himself, it would give him a lot of confidence. He gradually eased off the gurney, steadying himself on the bed and his new 12-gauge crutch. Standing upright for the first time since his injury occurred, he just hovered there for a moment, swaying slightly, getting up nerve for the next move. The first step was on his good left leg. The second step taught him that his right leg would not support weight, and he nearly fell as his pain reflexes caused the leg to buckle rather than accept his body weight. Slowly and clumsily, he made it to the bathroom and back to the bed, lying down gratefully and sweating from the effort. At least he knew that he was no longer trapped on the gurney, so there was some chance of defending himself if danger came his way. He closed his eyes, intending to let the narcotic effect diminish so his head would clear.

Looking down, he could see his shoes extending over the edge of the stone. Without looking behind him, he somehow knew that nothing but the night was there. He started swaying with his arms out trying to keep his balance. Somewhere far below, the surf thundered into the rocks, vibrating the entire cliff with the energy of the sea. He looked up to see Jeanette standing just out of reach, her hands in front of her mouth as if in dread or fear. Looking to one side he could see the curved stone wall arching away from him. He was standing on a short wall high above the ocean, and it was nighttime. A clear recognition came to him of where he was…the ballroom balcony above the ocean. He remembered threatening to get up there to appease Jeanette's anger.

The awareness of where he was increased his instability, and he stiffened, terrified that he was going to fall backward. Fear welled up inside of him and he found that he couldn't move around any longer to maintain his balance. Incongruously, he could hear the jazz band playing from the ballroom and sounds of laughter mixed with tinkling glasses. The smooth voice of the singer swept past the open door and stabbed into his ears like pointed fingers.

We love together in my dreams…and
I' ll never change the way I feel…so
Should we part forever…please remember…dear
I'll always be there with you…if only in our dreams

Something was shaking him, and he became aware of pain in his right leg. "Chase, you gotta wake up. I've something to tell you," the mysterious voice called out to him from somewhere distant. "Come out of it, man. Wake up now," the voice said. A calloused hand began patting his face roughly. He opened his eyes expecting a woman, but he saw the ancient face of Charlie Chuck leaning over him.

"Charlie. Something wrong?" he asked with effort, his head still somewhere back in time.

"Can you hear me now, Chase?"

"Yes, I'm awake. Is Allyson...has something happened her?" Now he was fully conscious, and his mind raced with all the unwanted things Charlie's presence could indicate.

"Don't know about the Miss. I said I would watch for the bad people hunting for you. They in town right now. I spotted four, and they have an evil about them."

"What are they doing?"

"Just casing the place, walking around looking at people. I heard them talking to each other and didn't understand a word of it. I thought you should be warned."

"What time is it?" After he spoke, he realized that Charlie probably didn't keep time the way he did so he looked at his own watch. Allyson had been gone for three hours. She should get back anytime. "Charlie, help me over to the chair by the window, I want to have a look at Allyson's cabin across the lake." Without words, Charlie simply leaned over and picked him up and transported him across the room to the chair.

Using the binoculars, he studied the other cabin which appeared to be much like the one they were in. There was nothing that seemed out of the ordinary, and there was no movement in or around it. Perhaps there was another explanation for the group of foreigners Charlie saw, and perhaps not.

"How did you get here from town, Charlie?"

"Hitched a ride and walked the rest of the way. Wife's got the truck."

"You didn't tell anyone that we were here did you?"

"No. I said you could trust Charlie and you can."

There was a distant sound that grew familiar. A car was approaching rapidly. Charlie went to the door and stood there squinting into the distance. "It's the Miss," he said without emotion.

"Thank God," Tom said through his teeth.

Tom could hear the car door slam and the wonderful sound of Bug's voice when she spotted Charlie in the doorway.

"Hi, Charlie. Want to help me carry some packages?" she said from a distance. They returned bearing loads which were deposited on the floor. "Well, look at you up and about! I had nothing to worry about did I?" She came over and kissed Tom on the forehead, but he didn't respond in the usual way. "Want to tell me what's happening someone?" she asked.

"Charlie just came over to tell me that he spotted our terrorists. The are in town. At least four of them."

"That was fast. They had to have help to locate us this quickly. Looks like you were right about Riggs. Now what?"

"There is no way that they can discover where we are right now unless they search every cabin around the lake. From their point of view, we could be far away from here by now, and frankly, that is what we should have done."

"So, we just wait it out and hope?"

"If my leg wasn't broken, I would want to hit them before they find out we are here, but I can barely move, and I don't think I can take a car trip yet. We don't have many options except to hunker down."

"Charlie, why don't you take our car, go find a phone, and call the FBI and tell them what you saw. They'll probably send a team right out when they find out about those men in town.

"They would believe you better than me, Miss."

Chapter 6

Trapped and Helpless

As night seeped between the trees, the nocturnal forest sounds emerged from the woods as if trading places with the day. A glow of purple and orange turned the window openings into magical lanterns in the darkened room, the view of a perfect world that was slipping away, moment by moment. Tom put away the last bite of supper and relaxed, reclining on a pillow. Bug washed her hands and came to his bed nestling in the crook of his arm. Both had a feeling of safety and contentment that neither had ever experienced previously. Their little, dark nest away from the cares and stress of the world wrapped around them like a protective glove. Tom buried his nose in her hair and took a deep breath.

At last, as the auburn light was fading, Tom broke their self-imposed silence. "I don't want to go back to the city. Let's just stay here forever. I can get a job chopping wood, and you can stay and raise our six children."

"There sure is a lot of ugliness back there. Right this moment, I don't miss our lives in the city at all. Don't think a life in the woods is easy, though. There is a little thing called hard work and near poverty to be considered. Besides, six children is not enough. Make it ten and I'll agree."

"Bug, I have in my arm everything I could want in life. There is no poverty possible because having you beside me makes me a rich man. One to be envied."

"You haven't really experienced me yet. It's all in your imagination at the moment so how can you be sure I'll measure up to your standards? Remember Jeanette, the most perfect woman any man could hope to be with? Didn't you say that you were married to her? I assume that you know her intimately, and in detail. Since she is so perfect, there must have been times with her that are burned into your memory so deeply that you could never forget them. I wonder how I can replace her, how I will compare. There are not many women around who have had to compete with a dream."

Tom didn't answer at first because much of what she said was true. Jeanette was an intense experience. All of her, and that includes her fiery personality, is a true force of nature. Tom knew that he had to forget Jeanette because it would never be fair to love both women. Thanks to heaven that he didn't have to choose between them standing right there together. Jeanette was only with him in his dreams, and she seemed to be slipping away, even though he didn't want to lose her. What did he want, really? Could he just stay with her in his dream? And why did he keep waking up to find her gone again? If he could stay with Jeanette, he knew he would lose Bug, a loss just as great to bear. It seemed to him that there was no choice. Jeanette was a dream, and Bug was real. Jeanette would have to go.

"Bug, no dream can compete with a girl like you. You never have to fear Jeanette, because I think that you were right when you said that soon I will only dream about you. You should also know that I don't see a single fault, and I wouldn't improve anything about you or wish for anything different."

He felt the warmth from her face and her tears on his cheek as she started kissing his face. She started with his lips, then moved to his cheeks and forehead. She found his closed eyes, one at a time, and softly touched his nose. When she came back to his mouth, she pressed hard, and they exchanged breaths and tongues in what seemed to last for a short happy lifetime. The light in the room finally disappeared completely, leaving them alone in near absolute darkness, circling the earth slowly in their little craft far above the earth's surface and far away from harm.

"I could use a crackling fire and some soft jazz music right now," Tom said as he pressed her cheek into his.

"Better not. Wonder how Charlie made out with the Feds? We might not hear until morning," Bug said.

"Relax. Even we couldn't find us here quickly. We are safe for now. Tomorrow is another day." They lay together, side by side, feeling the heat from and the satisfaction of having the person you love so close. There was nothing to talk over and nothing to plan. Life was now, and they were enjoying it together.

Tom heard the tapping of high heels, and they both looked up as the couple came into the paneled room. Tom didn't choose to stand, but his attorney did, saying, "Come in and take a chair please," and extended his arm toward two matched arm chairs against the far wall. They sat separated from Tom and his attorney by several feet across a thick red carpet. A gulf of several miles. There was an uncomfortable silence. Tom stared at Jeanette, and she stared back. There were no words to convey what was obvious. Jeanette no longer loved him, and her new chosen partner was beside her. Eric had the same boyish grin that he always did and looked rather out of place in his plaid jacket.

Tom was angry and hurt, but he was trying not to let it show. Divorce from Jeanette was not his idea, because he still loved her passionately. Looking at her and knowing that she would never be his again created pain so deep that he knew he would be scarred inside for life. There was never a single harsh word that he had ever spoken to her, and every time he touched her, it was with tenderness and affection. She had everything money could buy and nothing was expected of her. Tom understood how attractive he was to women, and besides, he and Jeanette had a good sex life together. Why she wanted a divorce, he just couldn't fathom.

And to take up with the lightweight Eric? He had already been through two wives and countless live-in girlfriends. He is a romantic loser who spends most of his weekends drinking beer and watching football. Tango? Forget that or any other dance. It wasn't his looks either. Where Tom saw himself as fit and trim, Eric is an overweight softy, and to make matters much worse, Eric is Tom's employee. Did either one of them believe that Tom would just go on as usual and be the nice guy he always has been?

"This is the parties last chance at reconciliation, as ordered by the court. This is not part of a divorce decree but a mandated step in the divorce process," Mr. McGrery stated to the room to clarify why they were all present. He continued, "I, personally, am disappointed at you, Mrs. Chase, that you have the effrontery to be accompanied by your paramour to a divorce proceeding. It's clear that you don't want reconciliation with your husband, isn't that correct?"

Jeanette just smiled, keeping her eyes glued to Tom's face. Her answer was crystal clear. "No."

"Very well, then, we will record your answer for your signature at the conclusion of this meeting. Mr. Chase, how do you feel about reconciliation with your wife?"

"I still love her. I love the air she exhales, and the floor she walks on. I love every fragment of her skin, her discarded food and most of all her entire being. I don't want a divorce from Jeanette, because she and I belong together forever."

"For the record, Mr. Chase, your answer is 'Yes, you do want reconciliation?'"

"Reconciliation. Yes, that is what I want."

"Do you have any comment on that, Mrs. Chase. For the record, at least."

"Ask him about his girlfriend. Ask him if he has a woman that he loves other than me. Ask him if he took up with his new woman before I had any thought of divorce. And ask him if I haven't begged, pleaded, bribed, coaxed and flattered him relentlessly to get him to come back to me."

"Your response, Mr. Chase?"

"Yes, she has done all that. It's true. As for the girlfriend, ask her if she has ever seen this woman or know where she lives or how to contact her or anything at all that she knows about this alleged girlfriend."

"Mrs. Chase?"

"No, I have never seen her or do I know anything other than what my husband has told me. I do know that he loves this woman passionately, but I don't know if they have had a physical relationship. Yet."

"Comment, Mr. Chase?"

"She hasn't seen this woman, because she comes to me in a dream. A dream! Can I be cheating on my wife with a dream? Can I have a conjugal relationship with a dream? The answer is no. I hoped that Jeanette would be more understanding than she is. I need time to work this out. Jeanette has gone too far, because I don't deserve this kind of treatment."

"What you want, Tom Chase, is to have two women at the same time. It's like a harem. You have one for the day and one for the night. Perfect, isn't it? But I won't stand for it. I won't compete with a dream woman. I want a divorce," Jeanette nearly screamed at him. She was red in the face, and her pupils dilated. The anger she was showing was no pretense, and it came from the bottom of the well at him.

Mr. McGrery cleared his throat and stood up. "Since we don't have a conclusion and there remain strong differences of opinion between the parties, I recommend that we meet again and revisit this issue in hopes of amicability and concurrence between the parties. Mr. Chase...you are to seek the services of a psychologist and have the report sent to my office. Ms. Chase...you are not to bring this gentleman into a meeting like this again. To both parties...are there any questions?"

No questions were voiced, and the parties dismissed. The three left together, and once in the hall, and after the door closed, Tom motioned to Eric to stay for a moment. At first he seemed to want to run away, but after exchanging glances with Jeanette, he turned toward Tom. He knew, or thought he knew, what was coming.

"Yeah, Tom. Let me guess. I am fired...is that about it?"

"Of course you are. You don't have to be told that. You think I could look at you every day and know that you have been pawing my beautiful ex-wife and not get angry? No, Eric, there is more. I am going to gut you like a fish. The next time you see my face will be the last day of your life. I am going to make it slow and painful for you. Does that clear things up a bit?"

Eric suddenly lost his color, and his lip started trembling. "You got it wrong, Tom. I haven't touched her. We all know that she is too much woman for me. I couldn't hold on to her if I tried. I came with her out of friendship for both of you. I want to see you two get back together, and the way it was explained to me, this was supposed to make you jealous enough to dump the other woman. That's the whole story, I promise!"

"Well, the jealous part worked. I'll give you that. You remember what I said if you are ever tempted by her, and I'll warn you, she can make herself very tempting." He looked at Jeanette who was several yards away waiting for Eric. She was smiling broadly, and Tom wasn't actually sure what that meant.

He felt Bug get out of bed suddenly, and he came up from his dream like an explorer ascending from the depths of a cold green cave, upward toward the light and the real world. "Tom! Can you see the light from there?" He looked vacantly toward Bug's voice and finally made out that she was standing beside the window facing Silver Lake. There was an orange but flickering glow reflecting off the panes. He struggled to understand what was the matter.

"Our cottage is on fire," she said in a rather flat voice and continued to watch the blaze from the window. This statement brought all of Tom's brain cells to life, and his mind turned over with possibilities. He saw Bug looking through the binoculars with her hair catching some color from her burning property across the lake.

"Do you see anyone over there?" he asked impatiently.

"Nothing moving. Whole thing's going up. It's lighting up the entire lake." Tom caught a vision in his mind of someone looking back.

"Bug, get back from the window. They may be looking for us to notice the fire."

Realizing that he was right, she stepped to one side of the window and put away the glasses. "Why burn it down if no one was there?" she wondered aloud.

"A token of their esteem, perhaps, or in frustration. Or..." he trailed off.

"Or what?"

"Or it was a distraction. It could mean that they know where we are and are coming for us."

"Oh, God! I think you're right. Do you want to try to get away from here while we can?"

"For all we know, they are already out there. We should lie low and wait it out. Keep your voice down and try not to make any noise that they could hear." Just as he finished speaking, they could hear the sound of a car's tires on gravel making its way slowly toward them. Allyson got up and carefully peered out of a side window.

"No headlights." She drew her pistol and crouched as she was trained to do. They both listened carefully and heard the car stop just outside the cabin with its motor running. Tom tried to get up, forgetting his leg wound, but quickly was reminded of his incapacity to get to his feet. He felt utterly helpless as he watched his partner move behind the door in case it opened. After a long moment, the car gradually, and indolently crunched away from the cabin. Neither one dared to breath, and Allyson held her position. The car continued for a short time then the motor and gravel sounds stopped.

"Do you think they stopped or can we just not hear them?" Allyson asked quietly.

"Worse case is they have stopped and are returning on foot," Tom said with a whisper.

"I'm going outside and try an ambush. There's no other choice," Allyson said.

Before Tom could object he checked himself. She was right, of course. Hit them before they hit us. The hunted always have the advantage, if they use it. She quietly and slowly opened the door and slid ghostlike into the black night. Tom could hear the crickets, and in the distance, a bullfrog's plaintive call, but Allyson made no noise that he could detect. Tom looked around in the darkness for the shotgun but couldn't force the shadows to create its shape so he felt around the bed where he thought he had left it. Nothing. His handgun was in its holster hanging on another chair about eight feet away. He considered the distance and knew if he fell, there would be noise and he might even cry out in pain. Too far. From outside, there was no telling sounds or indication of where

Allyson had gone. Tom was alone and helpless, waiting with short impatient breaths.

A deep thunderous explosion followed quickly by another fractured the night. It was close because Tom could see the flash partially light up the room. That was no handgun, he knew. Tom instinctively compelled himself to act and nearly flung his body toward his handgun crashing to the floor in agony, just short of the chair. As he was getting ready to crawl the rest of the way, the cabin door flung open and a shape hovered indistinctly in the opening. Tom was momentarily hypnotized by the shadow and hesitated just long enough to see and hear two sharp cracks illuminate, for an instant, a face in the door before the form crumpled as if dropping into a sudden opening in the earth. Tom made it to his weapon by summoning his last bit of reserve and spun around on the floor leveling the gun toward the door.

"Coming in, Tom, hold your fire," Allyson said from outside. Her smaller form blocked the starlight followed by a much larger shape. "Tom, where are you?" she asked.

"Here on the floor. Who is that behind you?'

"Charlie here. You all right?"

"I wouldn't be lying here on the floor in pain if I was all right. I'm alive, thanks to you both."

"Charlie got the first one with the shotgun. I got the second when he bolted for the door. Looks like our boys, at least two of them."

"You two better get out of here, quicktime," Charlie said.

"He's right, Allyson. The others will be back. Obviously, they know we are here. Charlie, do you think that they could have forced your wife to tell them where we are?"

"It's the only way. I must get home as soon as I get you to your car."

"Well, if you left it in that barn, it's going to be interesting for me to get there," Tom said.

Tom could feel something tap him on the chest, and he reached out and grasped it and held on. Charlie pulled him nearly to his feet, and he felt Allyson grab him under his arms.

"Made this for you while I was waiting on your bad men," Charlie said and released the stick. Tom felt it and realized that it was a primitive crutch made from a sapling which had two branching limbs cut at the top making it a nearly perfect fit.

"This will work. Thanks, Charlie. You said we could depend on you, and you sure proved it. Allyson, grab whatever we have to have, and let's get out of here." Tom leaned over and picked up the handgun and shoulder strap and put it on. "Was that the shotgun from here?"

"Yes, it looked useful. Any more shells?"

"Look over in that box against the wall. Take them all," Tom said.

Charlie did just that, and after he filled his pockets, he stood in the doorway and looked silently out into the darkness. "Follow this road. You can't miss the barn on the left. Keys are in it. I will go ahead of you into the woods. If they are waiting, I will find them before they find you," and then he disappeared silently into the dark.

"Let's head out. I have everything, including a submachine gun I took from the one by the door," Allyson said.

Tom struggled to get a rhythm, trying to be careful where he placed the crutch in the dark. They walked as silently as Tom's condition allowed, with Allyson slightly behind him so that she could have a better view and could act quickly. By the time the barn loomed like a darkened monster lying in wait, Tom was running on reserve. His arm and leg on the right side were throbbing, and he was getting sloppy and in danger of falling. He gratefully pried himself into the front seat and rolled down the window to enable him to fire the submachine gun, if needed. They never saw Charlie or even heard him.

Allyson took one last look around before getting in. "Ready?" she asked. Then without waiting for his response, she started the motor and immediately started moving the big wagon. They decided to travel without headlights as long as possible and drove slowly to make less noise. When they reached the paved road, she turned on the lights and accelerated into the unknown. They had made it. Now where?

Chapter 7

Irreversible Decision

hey drove along listening to a tune from the car radio keeping time to the clicks of pavement under the tires. A big yellow moon finally showed his face nearly in front of them and rose like an inflatable craft, slowly leaving the trees and horizon attached to earth. It felt good to head into the unknown, because if they didn't know where they were going, then no one else could either.

"I wonder if Charlie contacted the Feds?" Tom asked.

"Frankly, I doubt it. He didn't seem to want to do it, for whatever reason. When we stop, I'll call them myself."

"We have a problem, you know."

"Such as?" she asked and puckered her lips in thought.

"We have to use a credit card to get gas or a room. If Riggs is looking, he's going to see it within minutes."

"You're right, but if we only use it for gas, they can't get to us before we leave the station. It means that we'll be sleeping in the car until we get some help."

"I don't like running. I want to stop and fight," Tom said.

"Sure you do. I do also, but until your leg heals, you are at a big disadvantage."

"I am dragging you into danger. You don't have to do this, you know. They are not after you, just me."

"Stop talking like that. Would you dump me if I needed you?"

Tom didn't answer, because he knew there was no way to get

her to leave him. He watched her as they drove west into a lightening horizon. Dawn was only minutes away, and the sky was impossibly clear. It promised to be a fine day, and the road and the future stretched endlessly ahead. Allyson's face was content, and her small dimples were outlined in shadows by the reflected light from the road. Tom could never get tired of her face and traced the contour of her nose and lips down to her chin with the sharp focus of his eyes. When the first rays of the new sun blazed into the car, the beams caught her blonde hair and set it bursting with orange and pink flames. With every imperfection in the road, her hair moved like thousands of tiny springs, up and down as if absorbing and accumulating energy in that wonderful and beautiful creation of a higher being.

She noticed that he was looking at her and smiled while keeping her eyes on the road. "What are you thinking?"

"Mostly about taking your clothes off, but some about food. Is the car ready for fuel yet, I hope?"

"Soon. Fifty more miles. Can you handle it?

"Can I watch you and think about you with no clothes while I wait?"

"If it will make you happy, go ahead, or you could take a little rest."

That made him realize how incredibly tired he was. He stretched his leg out as far as he could and leaned back into the corner of the seat and door. The rhythm of the road and the warming light from the rising sun made it easy to close his eyes and relax.

The moist sand oozed between his toes and pressed against the arches of his feet as they walked. The sand wasn't too hot after all, and a gentle breeze was coming off of the ocean, bringing with it the sound of gulls and occasional breaking waves. The day was shaping up to be a perfect one. Jeanette wore a big floppy straw hat and oversized sunglasses. She held the top of the hat awkwardly, keeping it in place. The multicolored towel she had around her neck proved helpful earlier, when they sat on a small sand dune and watched the surf fishermen catch nothing. Tom squinted into the bright sun and shielded his eyes with his hand.

"Another mile at least. I didn't know that we came this far," he said.

Jeanette was choosing her steps carefully to avoid sharp sea shells and didn't respond. In the distance, the red and blue buildings of the resort shimmered in the sun, as if their construction was from liquid instead of ceramic and stone. Tom watched the flags standing away from their supports in the distance. "Wind's picking up, too. We'll make it back just in time for a good lunch, I think." They walked in silence, shoulder to shoulder, thinking and occasionally watching a small sailboat beat against the waves in a reach toward the resort landing.

"Want to go sailing tomorrow?" he asked. Jeanette gave a small smile and shrugged. Yes, she would do it, but he could tell she wasn't enthusiastic about it.

"Something else, touring the local artifacts or shopping?" he asked.

"None of that matters to me right now," she said without looking his way.

"What then?"

"I want to be by you and look at you all day and hold your hand. Just to hear your voice will be enough. That's all I want, being with you. I don't want to be distracted by the tourist sights."

"I'm very complimented. That's the first time I ever heard that from you. It sounds more like one of my lines."

"Yes, but I'm sincere." That stung, but he let it go; whatever was necessary to make her happy and to regain what they had lost lately, he would gladly do. He wanted to return to the happiness of when they were first married, the intensity of it. They couldn't get enough of each other then. It was like always being starved, but you didn't know it and then led into a banquet room full of exotic food. That's it exactly. They feasted on each other, and their appetite was never satisfied. Now there is something between them, some metamorphosis of attitude. Tom knew that he loved her as much as ever, but somehow he was unable to show it to her, to convince her. The previous remark from Jeanette exposed how her thinking had changed for the worse. He noticed that she said nothing about making love tomorrow or even tonight. She wanted to look at him just so she could always remember him like that. Healthy, fit and happy. He remembered his high school annual. How the friends he had known were captured there just like they were, never changing or growing older and fatter. Looking at the pages, he always felt that he was their same age again and looked just like them. It occurred to him that this was the same thing. Jeanette wanted to capture him because she was going to live with his memory, not him, in the future. She loved him still, but as he was, not for what he had become or will be.

"Can you explain that to me, please? I mean about tomorrow?"

"You know in your heart the answer, Tom. We are separating, and you and I are going on different paths from now on. I want to remember something good when I think of you, and this place and time is as good as any. You chose this outcome when you went through that door. Some things can't be undone, and now we are drifting apart. I know that you and I have tried to keep together, but fate is fate. We are going to have to find our own way in the world from now on, like it or not. Tomorrow is the last day we will ever see each other, and all we will have are our memories. They were mostly good, and I am happy about keeping mine. No matter what the future brings, I have my fond memories of you and me together, walking through the sands of life, watching it push through our toes."

Tom felt his heart surge with pain and torment. This is not what he wanted. He always thought that they would be together, hand in hand, to face their aging world slowly parting from them and cling to the comfort and strength of each other until the end. He didn't want any other way, no other person could replace her. What a fool he had been to throw his life away so easily.

"Jeanette, I can't face life without you. It would have no meaning."

"You will. And you will discover another life out there which is different, but which will work for you. I will do the same. We won't ever forget each other, and I'm sure in some quiet moment, we will bring those happy, private times back and recall what our happiness felt like. Think of it as a gift. If we hadn't had our time together, what would there be to remember?" Tom reached for her and silently took her hand in his. How many times had he held her slender, beautiful hand? To think that he will never feel her warmth and her touch again. It was too much. He wanted instead to die.

The car changed speed, and he came awake suddenly. Allyson was turning off of the Interstate and heading toward a gasoline station.

"Where are we?" he said, wiping the sleep from his face.

"Here. I'm not sure it makes any difference. We are getting gas, some food and I'm calling the Feds. Can you make it to the men's room without me?"

"No, I can't do anything without you. You are my life's crutch, and you are a lot better looking than my forest one."

"I can see that you are awake. Go on now. I know you can do this all by yourself." She opened the door, searching for a credit card as he painfully and slowly emerged from the car. At least the weather was good, he thought as he beheld the distance to the men's room. A challenge, but at least not as bad as last night when they both felt that gunfire could suddenly erupt from hiding places all around them. When he slowly and painfully returned, he saw Allyson waiting, leaning against the fender.

"News," she said when he got close. Tom raised his eyebrows and waited for any bombshell. "I talked to the FBI headquarters in D.C. They knew all about us and what happened after you shot those two terrorists, and they are most anxious to help us. A couple of agents have just been dispatched to meet us. Guesstimate is about one hour travel time. Until then, they don't want us to move from here."

"Sounds good, so far. Any bad news?"

"They were close-mouthed, if they knew anything else, suggesting that we talk to the agents who will be fully informed by then."

"Next order of business is food. Any luck with that?"

"There is a small truck stop restaurant in there. I cased it out, and it looks clean. Want to try?"

They sat down at a booth so that Tom's leg could be extended on the outside of the table. They both warned the waitress that she would be shot if she accidentally bumped it. She responded with rolled eyes and a downturned mouth. The food wasn't bad, and Tom had worked up a big appetite. They sat across from each other and mostly made small talk.

"We have to get Riggs. I want to crush the life out of him if it's the last thing I do," Tom said.

"Not before we are sure he is the leak, you won't. When they get here, we'll discuss our suspicions, I assure you. If it was Riggs, the FBI will help us prove it."

Tom made it through his third cup of coffee and his second slice of apple pie when two large fellows suddenly appeared beside their table. Dark blue suits, loads of muscle and two gold FBI badges. It was the Feds, all right, and one glance told Tom and

Allyson that their new colleagues rarely smiled and certainly weren't today.

"Special Agents McMurphy and Wittlow," the larger one said. "You folks Chase and June?" he asked assertively.

"That's us," Allyson said. "Want to sit and talk here while Tom finishes his food?"

She moved over and the three sat across from Tom. He noticed that these two men were rather large, much larger than he was.

"Do you have an update on our terrorists, Special Agents?" Tom ventured.

"We have been authorized to provide you with a full briefing, Detectives. You certainly deserve it. The situation in New York is unchanged. No new activity and no additional arrests. Your recent location is different. We assume that you took out the three perps and wounded the fourth, but we can't seem to pull the facts in a straight line to figure out how you did that. Want to help us here?" one of them asked.

"I shot one," Allyson admitted. "You will find two of my slugs in him. We know that a local shot one other using a borrowed shotgun of ours. The other shootings, we have no knowledge of."

"Well, that local is one tough customer. Who is he?"

"His name is Charlie Chuck, and he saved our lives. So don't you dare treat him badly. He is a vet from the Viet Nam era, and he knows his stuff. Better check on his wife because the terrorists probably got to her to find us. That could be the reason he tried to kill the other two." As she spoke, one agent was busily typing into his portable and staring at the small screen.

"You Feds need to get in on this next bit. We are sure that someone in the police department tipped the terrorists off about where we were. That someone had access to up-to-the-minute information to feed them. That means at least several contacts were involved. We both have a very strong suspicion about a certain individual. If you listen to us, it will shorten the time needed to catch him."

Special Agent Wittlow looked incredulous at Tom. "This is unusual to level a charge like that toward a fellow officer. What motive could he have to do something like this?"

"Competition, Special Agent. The Deputy Chief, Riggs by name, and I are both seeking the job of Chief of Police. In my opinion, he did this to eliminate me."

"Wow, a deputy chief working with foreign terrorists! If this is true, it will tear the police department apart. Yes, we are interested. At that high level of corruption, a police force needs outside help. We'll start checking it out."

Special Agent McMurphy looked up from his computer. "A Vivian Chuck was treated for a broken arm this morning and then released from the local hospital. She is going to be fine. That's the motive for sure. I checked on this man, Charlie Chuck. He was heavily decorated by the Army, and his file said that he was a machine gunner on a Huey and saw extensive combat. If I were a terrorist, this is the man I would not want to meet. The wounded one is in FBI custody now and is talking. He was glad to get arrested to get away from Charlie Chuck who pursued him through the woods for two hours taking pot shots at him with the shotgun and slowly filling him with pellets." They all laughed at the image.

"What do you two have in mind doing, just now, that we can help you with?" Wittlow asked.

Allyson was ready with a response, "We need to find a safe place to park until Tom's leg improves. If we are right about Riggs, we can't use our credit cards without the risk of another attack." The two agents thought it over, then Wittlow said, "There is an FBI safe house not far from here. It's located on a private resort, and I'm sure you would like it. If that suits you, we can make arrangements and take you there."

"That's what we wanted you to say," Tom readily agreed.

The resort safe house turned out to be a very nice home situated on a lake large enough for water sports, next to a complex of small restaurants and upscale shops. Their hosts had a charge account set up for purchases and also provided a small sporty car.

"Awfully swank, fellows. I had no idea that the Federal Government had this kind of connections," Tom remarked.

"The previous occupant was a Russian General who defected. He lived here for about six months. Since then it has been empty, Don't worry about how much it costs because the City of New York will be paying for it. They just don't know it yet," McMurphy said.

After the agents left, Tom collapsed on the king-size bed and propped his leg up on two pillows while Allyson took a long overdue shower. The sun reflected from the lake, playing on the ceiling, making little bright bands of light that seemed to have a direction. From a distance drifted the exuberant shouts of young boys at play, combining with the hiss of the shower on the other side of the wall, lulling him into relaxing.

There were tears running down her face as she stood in the doorway, lit by the yellow light from the room, with darkness behind. Her hands were at her sides holding two rather large pieces of luggage, and her big green almond eyes were fixed on his. "This is an occasion I thought I would never have to see," she said. "I have packed away all my memories of us and you in a safe place, but this is likely the moment I will remember the most."

"I will, for sure," Tom said. "If I could live that life over and over, I would gladly do it. Being with you was always intense. You were either very happy or very sad but always very exciting and very beautiful. This is the absolute rock bottom moment of my life."

"For both of us then. You understand, really, don't you? I have to have a life now that you are gone. While I'm still young enough to start over, I want to find someone that I can give my love to and possibly have children with. You know that it isn't fair to just have you as a dream and not for real. It would mean a lot to me if you can understand."

"I understand, Jeanette. There are no hard feelings because I know you are doing the right thing. My love for you is so strong that, most of all, I want you to be happy in life. Standing here, I feel so real, and I can still remember the taste of you and how it feels to have your arms and legs wrapped around me when we embraced. It's not like I'm dead. I still have my yearning arms and my feeling of love for you just like I always did."

"This isn't any easier for me than it is for you, Tom. I love you just as intensely as you ever loved me. Walking away from you is ending something wonderful, a bright light that we floated around on not knowing that someday if would extinguish itself. Shows you what a careless moment or a wrong decision can do, doesn't it? Our lives changed by a moment that we can't ever undo. A path taken that leads farther and farther away."

"Can I have one last kiss, Jeanette?"

"No, Tom, I couldn't bear it, and it would only prolong our pain. This is goodbye, my love, and I expect that we will never meet again, not even in our dreams. We have to go on with our new lives and try to forget the past."

"I hope you can forget, but I never will, even after I die. You are the greatest treasure any man ever had. Surely I deserve some punishment for doubting you, but not this." They both stood helplessly in place looking into each other's face, trying to prolong this last look. Jeanette's shoulders started turning before she allowed her head to follow, but at last she turned around and slowly disappeared into the darkness leaving Tom looking vacantly at the void.

"Tom, are you in pain?" the soft voice asked. He felt her hand on his cheek and turned toward her voice.

"No," he said, then when he moved his leg, he changed his mind. "Well, I need to change that to yes."

"I thought you were crying. Was it because of your leg or something else?" Bug asked.

"Why would I cry if I can wake up to your voice?" he said. When he caressed her, it dawned on him that her shoulder was bare. His eyes opened wider, and she leaned over and kissed him gently.

"I thought you should get a look at what you are buying. Never pay for a package until you know what it contains."

Chapter 8

✦

Parting Is Never Sweet

That was Special Agent McMurphy. He wants us to come to lunch with him over at Jessica's Restaurant in a half hour," Allyson said as she put the receiver down.

"Fine by me. He's buying," Tom said. He stood, testing the leg and deciding if he still needed a crutch. No, today he would try without it. He always felt that Charlie would never have needed a crutch, and when he picked up the now familiar fragment of tree, he always paused to remember the man who made it. They grabbed their coats and headed down the groomed path along the water toward the cluster of red tiled buildings which could be seen through the trees. They went arm in arm, completely inseparable in their happiness. After three weeks of continuous nights and days together, the emotional bond grew larger than either could have imagined. Both wanted this interlude in life to last as long as it could but knew that any moment, it would burst like a soap bubble and return them to the cares of the world.

Special Agent McMurphy stood as they approached and held a chair for Allyson. The three had become good friends over the past weeks, and there was a bond of trust.

"What's the news, my friend?" Tom asked after they had all been seated.

McMurphy cleared his throat, never a good sign. "As you know, the two captured terrorists have both admitted that they got information from someone outside their circle. At first they were vague about it, but after transferring them to Guantanamo, they were more forthcoming. It was someone on the police force, just as you said, but neither of them apparently ever saw him. The only one who would have known whom we seek was killed by your friend in the mountains. We have put surveillance on Deputy Chief Riggs and have searched his apartment, his office, and taken a long look at all his records. If he is dirty, we can't find it. I think you both were right, but at this point, unless he makes a mistake, we can't prove anything."

"And the really bad news?" Allyson asked.

"The court order for surveillance is ending soon. That also means that we are kicking you out of this dump. Back to life and its risks for you. Sorry." He stopped abruptly and massaged his chin.

"There's even more, isn't there?" Tom asked.

"Yes, Chief Riggs has asked that you both report to his office in two days."

"Does he know that he has been a suspect?" Allyson asked.

"We don't think so, but you can never be certain. He is a powerful figure in a large police force. They have a lot of friends."

"So, we just take our chances?" Tom asked.

"Not exactly. We want you to wear a listening device when you meet with him, and we are enlisting a private security service to watch your apartment. Tom...I assume that both of you will live there?"

"Yes," they said.

"That's the best I can do. As far as we can tell, there are no more terrorists lurking out there ready to blow themselves up to get you. You'll just have to be alert, but you already know that."

"When do you want us out?" Allyson said.

"Tomorrow. We'll send a car to take you back."

Back in their room, tiny bright lights splashed off the lake making the room dance in the evening's mellow light as they sat on the bed holding hands and looking out the large window.

"This has been great, Bug. I'm sorry to see it end. You know, we could just head West and forget New York. Really start fresh."

"No. I was born and raised there. I'm not letting Riggs or anyone else chase me out. Besides, my dad is getting old, and I have to be there for him."

"I don't like being chased out either. It's what Riggs wants, and I want to bust him for what he's done. But, I don't want any harm to come to you, Bug. They are all after me, not you. It'll be my fault if something happens to you. With you beside me, I could be happy anywhere."

"Quit talking. You know you are going back. We are not going to use our last hours in this happy place to argue. I have other ideas."

At precisely nine, Tom knocked on the door under the brass plaque which said Forrest Riggs, Deputy Chief.

"Enter," a voice commanded from behind the polished mahogany door. Tom and Allyson entered together and stood wordlessly in front of the big desk. Riggs looked at them with thinly veiled contempt.

"Well, all rested and ready to provide service to the community in return for your paychecks?"

"Odd you should put it that way. Do you think that we haven't been working on behalf of the people?" Tom asked.

"Actually, I think you have been wined and dined by the FBI at the expense of the City of New York. Isn't that about it?"

No, I'm afraid it isn't. We have been hard at work in collaboration with the Feds to trap an individual or individuals who have been feeding information to terrorists," Tom said.

"And how is that going?"

"It's still pretty hush hush. Need to know, you understand."

"I see," he said and then smiled. "How's the leg?"

"Getting better."

"Could you engage in a chase or physical struggle with a suspect?"

"I'll be well enough to do that soon."

"Until then, Detective Chase, you are on medical leave. Get clearance from Dr. Barnes, the department medical supervisor, before you return. Understood?" Tom didn't answer and continued to make eye contact with Riggs.

"As for Detective June, I have selected a new partner for you. You are being transferred to Vice. Report to Lieutenant Fellows this morning, and he will give you a new assignment. Understood?"

"Is that a demotion, Chief? You may remember that I already had a tour of the vice units when I first started," Allyson said.

"Look on it as a learning opportunity, June. Getting away from Chase will be good for you, give you a different outlook."

Tom spoke up after regaining his composure, "I want to thank you for the medical leave, Chief. That will give me a lot of time to meet with the Mayor and the press. I understand that they are hungry to talk to me. Police Celebrity, they have been calling me. Also, it will give me time to work on my politics within the Department, because I intend to campaign for the slot above you when it opens. That, as I am given to understand, will be soon." When he finished, they noticed that Chief Riggs' face was turning blotchy with color. Riggs didn't speak, but his eyes said a lot as the anger was just below the surface.

"Do what you will, Chase. You both have your assignments. Now leave."

"Detective June, will you wait for me in the hall for a moment?" Tom said. After the door closed, Tom leaned across Riggs' desk and glowered at him. "Riggs, your little display of authority just now convinces me that you are the link to the terrorists. You can betray your country and your colleagues just to advance your career? It's appalling, Riggs, appalling, and you won't get by with it. As far as your demotion of my partner...I have contacts also, as you are about to find out. There is always the last resort of the Press. I advise you to retract her transfer right now or be sorry."

"How dare you threaten me, Chase. I am your superior officer and my word on assignments is final. As far as your charges about being in contact with terrorists, I say prove it or get out of the police force."

"Bet you didn't know that the two who were captured are talking since they have seen Gitmo. They are singing a different tune and one that you will find has sour notes."

Tom watched as Riggs lost his confidence for a moment. "If they had implicated me, which is clearly impossible, the FBI would be standing where you are showing me their badges. They're not here, are they?"

"They like to dot the i's and cross their t's. It's in the works, Riggs. Looks like I won't have to campaign very hard to beat someone in prison. Now about June. This is your last chance. If I walk out that door, you are going to find things will turn badly for you sooner than you can say, 'I confess'."

"On that one, it's not worth a fight. As far as I am concerned, she can stay at Homicide. Be warned that she will be in the thick of things, and if she gets hurt, it will be your fault. As for the rest of your bull, give it your best shot and we'll see who is left standing. Things may not turn out as you expect, Chase. Life has a lot of uncertainties, and you have made a lot of enemies."

"No, I haven't a single enemy in the world, Riggs. I didn't even have you as one until you decided to eliminate me instead of competing for this job in an above board manner."

"You'll have to make it that far, Chase. Who knows, you might not live long enough to compete after all." Riggs gave him one of his tight, fake smiles as if he knew something that Tom didn't. Tom hoped that the FBI listeners picked up that last comment.

As they walked down the hall, Tom's cell phone buzzed. "Tom, this is McMurphy. We got it all and it's clear. As far as we are concerned, there is enough of a threat in what Riggs said and how he said it to ask for continued surveillance. I think it will be approved without a hitch."

"At least that's good news. Now that I've stirred the pot, you have a chance to catch him making contact. You can pull him and whomever he contacts in. A feather in your cap for sure," Tom said.

"Where are we headed?" Allyson asked when they resumed walking.

"Homicide. I have a few favors to call in."

"Tom, don't go too far with this. I still have to hold my head up, you know. Besides, I can take care of myself."

"I should know, Bug. I've lost count of the times you saved my life. This is something we need to do to keep you safe until we can bag Riggs. I want to think that he will have no chance to set you up just to get at me. He should know, though, that if it happened, I would suspect him, and walk in there and shoot him in the head. Danger works both directions."

"So what's your plan, Master Detective Chase?"

"I'm going to ask Brannigan to watch out for you. That's one we can trust all the way, and no one is tougher than he is."

After he finished his business with Brannigan, Tom decided to walk toward his apartment to see how far his leg would take him. For the first time in recent memory, he left Allyson back in Homicide to be briefed on active cases without him. He found it very lonely walking without her cheerful presence, but he was happy that he left her in safe hands until his leg recovered. New York is a wonderful place to be on a nice day, and its sidewalks are always full of interesting people and sights. Tom walked slowly with his noticeable limp, enjoying the view and commotion of the city. As he walked he had time to think. This life he walked into from the alley wasn't bad at all. He lost Jeanette but had Allyson. There wasn't as much money to be made by a policeman as an architect, but it was enough to get by. Besides, he had more excitement in this present life than before. If they could only get past this business with Riggs, especially if the Commission appointed him Chief, things would get a lot better. He started to think about himself. What was he? It always seemed like he was an architect pretending to be a detective, but what if reality was the reverse, a dream about being an architect and a real life as a detective? He couldn't seem to think clearly as there was a fuzziness enveloping concepts of his life. Squinting ahead while his mind whirled around, he found himself suddenly stopped while people streamed around him on both sides. A woman about a hundred yards ahead had long red hair that swung from side to side as she walked. There was something ringingly familiar about her that caused him to stop in his tracks. "Jeanette!" he called out to her. She continued walking away from him. He picked up his pace as much as his leg could stand, but she slowly pulled away. The longer he had her in his vision, the more convinced he became that this girl was Jeanette. Her hair, but also the way she moved and the clothing she wore, was exactly like Jeanette. He pushed his leg as hard as he could, but she turned a corner and disappeared. By the time he arrived there, she was gone. Jeanette had not visited him in dreams since she said goodbye forever, and her image had started to fade a little bit. A whiff of her familiar perfume or a girl's green eyes, especially if she had red hair, brought Jeanette's memory flooding back to him along with the same stabbing pain in his stomach. The woman who had eluded him, if only he could have seen her face, he wouldn't have to wonder. As a detective, he knew that most people on a street are seen there repeatedly, especially in some areas of town. There was no shopping or residential dwellings within several blocks and that could mean a high likelihood that she would be on the same street at roughly the same time tomorrow, or if not then, someday. With his leg at its limits, he reluctantly hailed a taxi and went home to his apartment.

The next morning, as soon as he had kissed Allyson goodbye, he headed toward the intersection that he had last seen the red-haired girl. Picking a quiet vantage point, he leaned against the wall and waited. After not finding her among the morning rush of foot traffickers, he went for a cup of coffee at a local grill and rested his leg. He felt slightly like he was betraying Allyson in trying to find Jeanette, but he had to find out if it was her. He hoped that she may be able to help him understand what had happened, especially if the same thing also happened to her. What would he do if it was Jeanette? He didn't know, and he knew it would complicate an already complicated life. The last time he saw Jeanette, she was in California. Seeing her accidentally in New York was nearly impossible, but this whole business has been crazy and inexplicable. Just before noon, he assumed his familiar position and waited in vain. The afternoon went by the same way, and he returned home exhausted both from standing on his still healing leg and from the anticipation of once again seeing his former wife. He sagged into sleep, just after checking his watch and wondering when Allyson would arrive.

"Tom," she murmured. "I'm home. Hope you are hungry." Tom opened his eyes and found Bug's face smiling down at him. "Dream about Jeanette again?" she asked.

"No, actually, I didn't. Haven't seen her since she said goodbye several days ago. She said at the time that we would never see each other again, and she's been true to her word."

"I'm relieved. Something I have to ask you, if you are awake enough to discuss it."

"I'm awake."

"You were seen staking out a corner not far from here. As far as we can tell, you were there all day. Want to tell me why?"

"I thought I saw someone the other day I recognized, and I was hoping that I would see her again. No luck."

"So this is pretty important for you to have stood there all day on your bad leg. A girl you say? Did she have red hair by chance?"

"Yes, long red hair. I never saw her face."

"Oh, Tom. That again. I hoped you would forget about her as she has about you. It was never anything but a dream, you know. You can't find Jeanette as a real person, because you dreamed her up. I'm a little hurt that I haven't been able to get her memory out of your mind. Perhaps, I'm not good enough for you after all."

"Don't feel that way, Bug. I love you without question, and you are the best thing that's ever happened to me. If there is any way to explain those dreams, though, I want to hear it. I thought that if this person is Jeanette, I could talk to her and try to understand why I dreamed about her."

"The other thing, Tom, is that you are making yourself an easy target hanging around on the street in the open. After all, if I heard about it, likely Riggs did too. It's just stupid for several reasons for you to do that. Heavens, if anyone knew the real reason you are there, there would be good reason to commit you for your own safety. Don't go down there any more, do you hear me?" Tom just sat there looking someplace else. She knew that he had heard her but was ignoring her warning. It was because his mind was still remembering Jeanette. She let out a big sigh.

"Tom, tell you what we're going to do. Tomorrow, I will find the patrolmen who work that area and tell them to look for a striking, long-haired redhead. If they see her, they are to attempt to find out where she goes or works. How's that?"

Tom looked up with moist eyes. "That's great. Thanks, Bug. I know you don't particularly want her found, but I have to get this out of my system." She leaned over him and kissed him on the forehead.

"Time to eat," she said.

"Well, it's only been two days, and I have two names for you," Allyson said. She handed Tom a small slip of paper which he eagerly took from her.

Tom read aloud, "They said that both match the description. One is named Catherine and works for a legal group. The other is named...oh, my...Genevieve! Let's see, she works for an advertising firm as a model. I have to see them. Do you mind?"

"I expect to go with you. Do you mind?" she said.

"No, I want you to be there. You might find that I'm not insane after all."

"We'll go tomorrow. I suggest seeing the one named Catherine first, and since she works as the receptionist, it'll be easy."

As she promised, Allyson accompanied Tom the next morning and held the door for him as they entered the law offices of *McGruter, Simmons and Gentry* and walked across the plush carpet toward the reception desk. A flash of red hair was seen above the countertop. Tom craned his neck to look at her, then stopped. "No way, Allyson, it's not her." They ignored the woman's offer to help and headed back to the street.

"Next is the marketing agency. Only two more blocks," Allyson said. They walked slowly and eventually found the office. Once inside, they found a waiting area and sat down. In a few minutes, a young woman came to greet them and inquired about their business. Tom pulled his badge and showed it to her.

"Detectives Chase and June. Do you have a woman working here called Genevieve? Long red hair."

"Has she done something wrong?" the woman asked.

"No, we just have some questions," Allyson said.

"She isn't here at the moment. Anything I can do?"

"Do you have some photographs of her we can see?" Tom asked.

"Be right back," she said and turned around. In a moment, she returned with a thick book of photographs. "You'll find her in here. She's the one with the red hair."

Tom eagerly took the book and took a deep breath. The first picture was enough. "That's Jeanette," he said. The other photos confirmed it for him. There was no doubt that it was her.

"Have you ever known this woman before?" Allyson asked skeptically.

"I was married to her for several years. This is her."

"We'll find out about that," Allyson said and left the room. She came back after a few minutes with a folder. "This is her personnel record. Want to see who she is?" She sat down and they started perusing the records. The woman called Genevieve was born in France and had a stack of recommendations from French photographers. She had only been in New York for six months. She was single and spoke passable English. She owned a Poodle named Sam, and she attended two years of college in France. She lived with two other models near the Park.

"Now I ask you as a detective. Do you see any way that you could have ever known her or been married to her for years?" Allyson patiently asked him.

"No...but it's still her."

"She is a well-known model. You likely saw a photo of her on a magazine cover and your little brain imagined the rest. You have to admit what is obvious, Tom."

"You are right. It doesn't seem possible that I could know her."

"You still want to see her yourself, don't you?"

"Yes, I want to see if she recognizes me. Is that wrong?"

"Not if it will get it out of your system. I want Jeanette gone from your mind forever. You promise that if she doesn't know you, you'll let it go?"

"Yes, I promise."

"In that case, since I trust you, and especially because I have something to do this morning, I'm going to go back to work and leave you here. You'll behave, won't you?" Allyson said. She kissed him on the cheek and left him sitting there alone. He read all the magazines lying around, and in several of them, he found photos of Genevieve looking for the world exactly like Jeanette did in her photos. After two hours of waiting, he had nothing to do except look at the walls. He knew something that Allyson didn't. Jeanette had gone to school in France, spoke French like a native and had worked for photographers while there. There were too many similarities for it to be an accident.

He could detect her perfume before she came into the room. The same brand of French scent that she always wore. They met eyes at the same moment, and he was suddenly reminded of the first time they had ever seen each other. It was at a small party and at the time was a profound moment of intensity, and he still remembered the feeling. The rush of exhilaration just looking at her. The same familiar green eyes in almond-shaped settings looked at him, seeming to bore right into his head then just as she did again now. Tom stood up and turned to face her. She paused and briefly lingered over his face, then continued her stride across the room toward the interior door.

"A moment, *Mademoiselle*," he said. She paused and the green eyes again found his. "Jeanette?" he asked.

"Genevieve," she corrected. "What is it that you wish?" There was that hint of mirth about her. It was just under the surface, but it danced in her eyes and in a tiny, tiny elevation of the corner of her smile. He knew that she was his Jeanette.

"Do you remember me?" he asked.

"Not at all, should I?"

"I remember you very well," he said.

"Impossible."

"Your eyes betray you, Jeanette."

"Genevieve. Must you persist with this?" she said and turned to leave.

"I get it, Jeanette. You are done with me. You told me, didn't you? I just wanted to look at you again and ask how you came to be here in this life."

"It is so easy. I got off an airplane, and here I am!" She lifted her hands with palms up and used a small Gallic shrug. Her eyes smiled at him, letting him know that it was all an act, because, inside, she knew him as well as he knew her.

"All right. I know that you meant it when you said goodbye. I won't bother you again unless you want me to. Here is my card in case there is ever a time you would like to talk. And I would like you to know that I never forgot you, even though you don't inhabit my dreams any longer, and still love you the same as always." She took the card from him with the tips of her fingers and coolly watched as he limped out of the room.

"Goodbye, Tom," she said after he was gone, dropping his card to the floor.

Allyson came home just after dark, and Tom was ready with supper for her. The little oval table had wine and candles, the darkened room hummed with soft jazz playing just at the audible level. She stood at the door and said, "Am I in the right apartment?

Tom, have you become domestic?"

"Enjoy while my leg heals. Won't be long now." He picked her off the floor and buried his face in her neck. "I could just eat you for supper."

She squirmed away and looked stern. "First, tell me what happened with the second redhead."

"Simple. She was not Jeanette. She never saw me before and wasn't even very friendly. She probably thought I was a masher or something."

"So, this thing about Jeanette is over and done?"

"Done. Finished."

"In that case you can start with my neck and work your way down. I'll tell you when to stop." She tousled his hair and gave him a big thankful kiss.

"Hi, Chase, McMurphy here," the phone said into his ear.

"Let me guess. Nothing to report, McMurphy."

"Not entirely true this time, sport. The CIA just informed us that there is chatter about another group of fanatic Islamists coming our way, probably to New York. The info is spotty right now, but we are all tuned in and gearing up. Your boy, Riggs, has been very careful, but we think he is using the old letter drop method of communication, and we saw him drop something in the park last night. There were a lot of people around and we missed the pickup, but at least we know for sure that he's the one. You might have a problem coming your way, so keep your guard extra sharp. I'll let you know if we have anything more specific."

"Say, can't I just push him out of the window?" Tom asked.

"It's a good idea, but it will be hard on your future. Might make no difference if he has already fingered you to the bad guys. You should try to find some other place to live for awhile, but be sure and let me know so that we can keep tabs on you."

"I can't do that and have Allyson go to work. She would just be tailed back home every day. She won't quit the force, you know."

"Yeah, I figured. How's the leg?"

"Couple more weeks. I've been at the health club every day now, and the docs have given me clearance to go back after one more check-up."

"I hate to remind you, because you already know, but this bunch coming at us are the suicide type. They probably won't use guns, and they don't care how many innocents go up in smoke with them. It's a sick world."

"For sure. Thanks for the heads up, McMurphy."

Tom sat down and held his head while he thought. He wasn't ready to die, and he sure couldn't let Bug die with him. For the first time in this life, he was happy and things were going to just keep getting better, if they could just keep the terrorists away. He knew the only real choice was to run. It was the only way to be safe until this batch was hunted down and Riggs was caught. Allyson would have to go with him. Have to. He knew California well from his previous life, and once out there, Allyson was certain to like it, and it might be possible to get her father to move once they got established. If he and Allyson were out of the picture, Riggs would have no reason to pursue them. He opened his computer and started looking at options, and after an extensive search, he thought he had discovered an exciting way to leave. They would board a westbound train and travel in old-fashion style to San Francisco. Once there, with their credentials, they could apply for positions in the SFPD. The more he thought about it, the better it sounded. Allyson was going to refuse, he was certain, but what if he surprised her? He could make it sound like a trip for pleasure and talk her into staying once there. It could work. He opened a page of train departures leaving Grand Central for the Coast. After he found what he was looking for, he grabbed his coat and headed for the street.

Returning was more difficult that he expected, and his leg was throbbing again. One more block, he kept telling his leg. Their apartment building was in the next block, and the top of it loomed over the low buildings beside him. The evening rush was on, and the streets were full of hurried commuters anxious to get home, so that they could get ready for the next workday. As he rounded the corner, the first shock wave hit him, a blast of hot air, followed by noise and light. A second explosion was nearly instantaneous, and the combined force propelled him backward into the concrete. Above the street was an ascending swirling cloud of red and black dust and brick, which started raining noisily to the street amid cries of panic and alarm. Tom lifted his head and looked past his feet to see fire and smoke pouring out of a gaping hole which used to be the front of his apartment building. Swinging his legs around, he propped his back against the nearby building, letting his brain clear. Sirens started in the distance and got louder, and crowds filled the street from nearby buildings. The scene was chaotic, and flames from his building started to grow larger and more ominous.

"You. Are you injured?" a voice commanded from above him. Tom looked up to see a uniformed policeman and then noticed others like him streaming past toward the fire.

Tom held up his badge and said, "I don't think so, but I haven't tried to stand yet."

"Detective Chase," he read. "You were the one at the previous bombing over on Flatbush. Wasn't that you?"

"Yes, I was the lucky one then and now. They were after me. That used to be where I lived," he said as he pointed to the hole. The policeman spoke into the mike on his shoulder and then waved for some help. Two large men picked him up to his feet and helped him over to a nearby patrol car, holding the door for him.

"Please wait here, Detective," one of them said. Tom slumped to the seat in a near faint, and time seemed to stop as he looked at the seat cover in front of his face. In what seemed a brief moment, he felt someone patting his shoulder.

"Tom, Tom. Are you hurt?" Allyson asked. He tried to sit up and get his bearings but could tell that he was still disoriented.

"I think I hit my head when the blast went off. The rest of me feels fine."

"I just can't leave you for a moment, can I?" she said.

"No, you can't. You can see that I can't live without you. It's pretty clear."

"Did you see anything?"

"I rounded the corner at the same time the bombs went off. There was nothing to see."

"Two bombs?"

"Distinctly two bombs. Same as last time. They wanted to make sure." He got to his feet and stood beside the car. Allyson had been crying and her eyes were still red, but she was alive and well and the most wonderful sight in New York. He hugged her and kissed her ear and whispered, "Thank the heavens that you weren't home when it happened."

"Same with you. Where had you gone?"

Tom pulled the train tickets from his jacket and handed them to her.

"San Francisco? Two tickets to San Francisco and the train leaves tonight! Don't you think we could have talked it over first?"

"Sure. We could have been in there talking it over when the bombs went off. There will be a lot of deaths from this, and it's all because of me. Is there any doubt that we have to leave, if no other reason just to save lives?" Allyson looked around at the devastation and the people running in all directions before giving her answer.

"I want to stay and help clear up this mess. It's my job. You are now officially homeless and unemployed. It might be the right thing for you to leave. On the other hand, they might be led to believe that you were killed in the explosion."

"No. Before I came to my senses, I identified myself to a patrolman. That's probably how you knew where to find me. Riggs knows by now." Allyson looked lost in thought and was silent.

"I am in love with you, completely and totally. Wherever you go, I want to be with you, but it's a big commitment for me to leave New York and to think about living on the West Coast," she said at last.

"Let's not plan on a permanent move out there. As soon as the FBI gets Riggs in handcuffs, we will return and claim what's ours, but we have to make it look like we have given up and left. It's the only way. We have to look like we are running, Bug, even though we aren't."

"Your way, Riggs might win. He will end up Chief of Police if he does. Can you live with that?"

"I agree that it won't be easy."

"As you say, it's our only choice," she said after some thought. "Neither one of us has clothes, luggage or anything that we can take."

"We'll start fresh! Buy clothes on the trip and travel light. Will you go?"

"Of course I will, you know that." She checked the tickets and looked at her watch. "I have to call Brannigan. He has to know I'm leaving."

"Don't tell him when or how. Tell him you will know more when you arrive at where you are going. After that, we should go to Grand Central, because the train leaves in just two hours."

Train departures and arrivals are still called on the old public address system, and in the cavernous echo chamber of Grand Central Station, the effect is muddy nonsense, largely unintelligible.

The only thing missing was the escape of steam and the sound of far away whistles to make this a scene from 1940. They found the platform and waited trackside for the conductor to call for boarding. The large crouching locomotives could be seen at the end of the long train of Pullman cars dressed in their silver sheaths of ribbed aluminum. Tom and Bug waited by the door together and instinctively watched strangers slowly assembling in groups.

"Well, Bug, I am happy to be leaving. I hate to admit it, but I think we are heading toward a great future and leaving the past behind. You know, one of those paths you choose which leads away and away. The great thing is that we are doing it together this time."

"You mean like the times that you went through a door and became someone else?"

"I hope I don't mean that. I want to be me and I want you to be you, and most of all, I want us to be us."

"Did you ever see another exit door?"

"Never since I met you."

"You never did explain it to me. What is an exit door?"

"I don't know. It leads to a black nothingness. Completely void of anything. Once I tossed some large stones into one, and there was no indication that they ever hit bottom. A couple of guys in my last life said that if you go in there, you die or at least cease to exist."

"You have the craziest dreams, Tom. At least the dream about Jeanette is finished."

The sound of the big diesel motors starting at the front of the train indicated boarding was to be soon. They both looked over the other passengers in silence as if waiting for an eruption of violence or a suspicious look, but everything appeared as it should.

"Call for boarding. Please have your tickets ready before entering the train," shouted a uniformed conductor as the doors to the train snapped open. Tom and Allyson hung back, waiting for the other passengers to board first as they carefully watched faces. When the platform was empty except for them, Tom took Allyson by the arm and led her toward the door with a smiling conductor patiently waiting.

"This is it, Bug, the start of something new. Aren't you excited?"

"I'm apprehensive. There hasn't been enough time for me to adjust to this." She pushed him ahead of her but held his hand as he entered the door. Just before she took that last step, she paused, looking left toward the rear of the train. Before Tom realized that something was wrong, Allyson let go of his hand and pulled her pistol from under her jacket and pointed it in the direction she was looking. He reached for his own weapon and started back out toward her just as she started firing. Something was holding him back, but the door remained open. He heard return gunfire from the direction she was looking, and then she opened fire again with a burst of three rounds. Tom was struggling to get past the doorway just as the train started to move and his view of Allyson crept slowly away. Tom pounded on the opening and pushed against it, just as it came to him what was wrong. He had entered another doorway and couldn't return. He tried to press his face against whatever it was, but Allyson was no longer in view, and the train started briskly accelerating. He sagged down, his hands above him sliding down the barrier and started screaming, "No! Please, no, not this time. No!" As the train left the station, darkness enveloped the opening, which slowly and inexplicably disappeared, leaving Tom Chase alone and sobbing against the floor.

Chapter 9

Is Knowledge Strength?

r. Chase, is there something wrong? Do you need any help?" a soft voice asked, and he could feel her touch on his shoulder. He pushed his upper body away from the floor and held himself up for a moment with one arm, looking vacantly around. It was a small office, not a train, and he could tell that the gun he always wore was missing.

"Can I help you get up or should I call for help?" she asked. Tom looked up to see a young, soft face expressing concern and sympathy.

"No, I just fell. I'll be all right in a moment," he said as he tried to remember what he was doing here. With some effort, because of his leg weakness, he regained his feet and had a better look around. On the open door he read "Dr. Thomas Chase, PhD, Chairman, Department of Philosophy" in gold letters. His desk was in disarray as was the floor around it. There was one tall window behind the desk, coated thickly with white cracked and peeling paint. Through the glass could be seen the spires of the University around the courtyard and groups of strolling students on crisscrossing paths.

"Can I get you anything, Professor Chase?" she asked sweetly. He shook his head and pulled his leather chair out and sat down. He reached down and rubbed his leg just above the right knee. Where the hell am I, he thought? He started absentmindedly shuffling some papers on the top of his pile while his brain struggled to reassemble his existence. In a habitual motion, he stroked his chin finding a beard.

"About my late paper, Professor. I wondered if I will still get credit?" the girl asked.

Tom suddenly had the urge for a cup of coffee and tried to remember where the image slowly forming in his mind was located. He recalled a dim memory of a faculty lounge close by and decided to try to find it.

"Later, dear. I have to go now. We'll work something out about your paper," he said as he pushed past her into the crowded corridor. He had a walking stick in his right hand, and he felt the familiar carved metal top as he made his way down the hall. Several students nodded to him or waved with friendly smiles. He passed various classroom doors and faculty offices as his head cleared and his memory returned to him. The faculty lounge, he finally remembered, was just ahead toward the end of the hall. He opened the door and just stood for a moment blocking the door as he looked around.

"Well, Thomas, please come all the way in!" a booming voice called from across the room. Tom looked toward the voice and saw Grimes' round, red face grinning at him. Tom went by the coffee pot first and took a cup with him to the table.

"Well, Grimes, your presence here is not unexpected. You are here every time I come in. Do you bother to teach any more, or are you collecting your large salary by drinking the school's coffee?"

"Glad to see you also, you old dog. What's new? Are you porking any coeds yet?"

"That I will leave to you, my good fellow. I am much too old for that sort of thing. Women are an expensive plaything, anyway. Haven't you discovered that yet?"

"Only three wives so far. Stapleton has had five and lots of coeds. He is ahead of me and seems to have a lot of fun. You, my friend, are missing out." The image of little Bug firing at someone beside the train came back to Tom in a rush, and for a moment, he felt that he was going to collapse. Grimes saw his expression and gave him a long look.

"You don't look well, Thomas. Anything wrong?"

"Lots of strong memories are with me today. It causes weakness, but one cannot control his thoughts."

"That's what I tell myself whenever some girl with a tight ass goes by. I can't help wanting some of it." He gave a big and vulgar laugh and slapped the table.

"Grimes, have you ever heard of a person suddenly changing direction or his path and then everything changes for him?"

"Sure, that happens every time I get a new wife or lose one."

"Grimes, be serious for a moment and think about it."

"Thomas, you are always so serious. Loosen up, boy. In answer to your question though, don't you think that we all remember choosing to do something which makes our life different because of the choice we made? We have all speculated what would have happened if we had done something else, another choice. I don't pay it any mind anymore because it is what it is. You can't change anything. Another Thomas once said, 'You can't go home again,' and it's so true."

"This is going to sound weird, but I feel that I have led four lives, all different. I remember all of them, and I have lots of regrets."

"Isn't it also true, Thomas, that you have learned a lot about yourself and life. You probably are closer to understanding the big picture, if you know what I mean. Now you know what is important and what isn't. It's called maturity. Personally, I think immaturity is so much more fun and that is how I want to live."

"Well, then, this is maturity. A lot of aching bones and an empty house. You may be right, Grimes. You do seem to have more fun, that is, until you get sent to prison."

"Frankly, I'm always surprised that a philosopher doesn't have it all figured out. After all, aren't you the ones telling the rest of us what it all means?"

"I teach what others have written. That doesn't mean I agree with them or really understand what they meant. My own views are not so clear."

"That's what I like about computer science. You write code that either compiles or doesn't. The logic is pure thought expressed in symbols and words. There is no interpretation of code. I always thought that computer code was created by God, and we only discovered it. Your subject is always nebulous, vague and changing. To me, we came from dust and will return to dust and nothing really matters. We live, we die. End of story."

"True, Grimes, but brutal. It does matter, because Philosophy gives reasons for life and a code of behavior for us."

"You may know that I have sat in on a few of your lectures, and as I remember, there are vast differences in schools of thought. They can't be all right, if any are."

"And my friend, I have suffered through some of your lectures. Aren't there several programming languages and are they not very different?"

"Yes," he laughed. "I had no idea that you had done that. Interested in learning more?"

"No. I am sorry to say that it was far above my head. All the little ones and zeros. The only thing I understood was the Boolean. George was a great man, wasn't he?"

"There is where we come together after all," Grimes laughed. "I'll make you into a programmer yet!"

"That won't happen," someone said, and they both looked up to see Christopher Penwick. He was small and tightlipped but always dressed to perfection, and today was no exception.

Grimes got to his feet and pulled out a chair. "The illustrious Dr. Penwick. How good of you to join us. How are things in the English Department?"

"Don't start with me, Grimes. To answer your question, though, things in English are always the same. All the undergraduates hate it," Christopher quipped.

"At least, Chris, they speak it. They hate Philosophy and never learn enough to even discuss it afterwards, and later, don't even remember that they took the class," Tom retorted.

Grimes smiled, "They learn enough from me to make a living afterwards. Perhaps the University should just drop your classes and concentrate on the money subjects."

Christopher laughed a nasty haughty laugh, "No, Grimes, your science will change over time, perhaps even disappear, but Philosophy and English are here to stay."

Grimes looked angry and said, "We'll see. Look, fellows, this has been fun, but I have a class." He brusquely got up and left.

"You hit a nerve, Chris. Must have been some truth in what you said," Tom offered.

Christopher straightened his silk bow tie and looked Tom over. "You don't look well, Chase."

"It's because a professor of Philosophy always looks ruffled. We are expected to look harried. It goes with the job."

"Really, Tom. Are you feeling well?

"No. I am troubled by my past and by my future. Also, I have a permanent limp, and I am without a woman to love. There are reasons, Chris."

"To sum it up, you are not happy right now?"

"I have had two beautiful women in my life that I loved and who loved me, and now I have none. Truth is, I don't want a new woman. I want what I had, and either one would do nicely."

"You'll have to live off of your memories then. Is there any other choice?"

"Ever seen an Exit Door that opens into a building instead of out of one?"

"Not that I can remember. I'm not sure I would have noticed though. Why on earth would an exit open into a building?"

"It's an opening into infinity. To go through one is to be finished with life. It's very symbolic, don't you think?"

"Yes," Chris mumbled. "Have you knowledge that there is such a thing?"

"I heard about them a long time ago, and one time I actually saw one. At the moment, I don't know where one is, but I always keep my eyes open. It could prove handy to know someday."

"Like a form of suicide then?"

"Call it an escape from life."

"Thomas, you need a woman or a vacation. Both at the same time would be nice. Perhaps Grimes could suggest a suitable woman for you."

"I don't think I want casual sex like Grimes seems to. A woman who loves only me is my idea of happiness."

"If you don't look, you don't find."

"True, but it would be hard for a woman to measure up to what I've had. It wouldn't be fair to compare someone to either of them. Most of all, I want to go back into the past and resume my happy life."

"Or, perhaps, use a backward exit door?"

"Not yet, Chris, and I have to find one first."

The classroom slowly and truculently filled with chatting students who noisily put their books and bags on the floor or the tables. Tom watched the clock above the entry door, patiently waiting for the second hand to reach twelve.

"Quiet, please," he announced and then waited as the room

settled down. He could see that a few students were still busy getting notebook and pens ready. "The first part this morning is discussion. Do not take notes. I want you to listen and discuss this topic and think about it. At this level of Philosophy, you need to start thinking for yourself and not just memorizing what others have said. Your experience in life is as valid as anyone who ever lived, and what you think is as important. Philosophy is about everything, every human experience requires a philosophy, and there are hundreds, thousands of topics to discuss. Today, I want to discuss dreams and the relationship to reality. This involves the so-called 'Hard Problem of Consciousness' and after the lecture, I will post some links that you can use to clarify this further. It is no accident or through no master plan that I take this subject to you today. It is because I have dreams, just like you do and just like the kings of old did, and we all require explanation at times. First, a question: Have any of you ever had a dream that you knew was a dream at the time?" Tom waited for hands and saw that no one had. "Right. I can never tell while I'm dreaming that it is a dream. The reality of some dreams is at least proximate to what we experience when we are awake. Aren't there times that we gain insights during a dream to daytime problems we face? Sure, history is full of examples we could recall. As all of you know, we have emotions during a dream, some of which are very strong. These include fear, apprehension, love, sexual desire and just about any other you could think of. Often, we awaken and remember every detail just as if it had happened. Philosophers have argued, some of them at least, that perception is reality. In the event that the argument has merit, then dreams are real. See the point?" There was laughter and head bobbing from the class. "I know, you think that is a step too far, don't you? It all relates to consciousness and what it is, doesn't it? Here is another way to look at it. If you trace all the sensory nerves back to the brain, just as you would do with electrical wiring in a house, and you figured out all the places the wires or nerves went, you would still not understand what consciousness is. It's called the explanatory gap. In other words, we still don't know what consciousness is. Presumably and theoretically, you could take a living brain and immerse it in a tank of some kind cutting all sensory input off, and most of us believe that consciousness would still be present in that brain. Would the thoughts in the brain seem real? I feel that it is likely, and I believe that you do also. Recent philosophers argue that our human mind is not yet developed enough to understand our own consciousness. Perception is a word frequently confused with consciousness, and of course, they go hand in hand. It brings to mind another word, 'qualia,' which is defined as an individual instance of a subjective experience. The concept creates a problem for those who explain consciousness as entirely physical or mechanical and, as a result, is controversial. What topic of Philosophy isn't?" There was more laughter, but Tom could tell that he had the attention of the class. All the faces were turned to him and all were intent on the subject.

"Here is a quote from John Searle: 'Where consciousness is concerned, the existence of the appearance is the reality.' Did you get that? Here's another concept: 'An idea or a dream is a copy of the thing it represents, and if all the contents of dreams are ideas, how can we know that anything exists apart from dreams?' "

"Professor?" a short haired blonde female asked with her hand raised.

"Yes, Trudy?"

"Are you saying that dreams are real? I don't understand."

Tom put down his piece of chalk and walked to the center of the room. "Let us consider Sartre for a moment. He contends that human existence is a conundrum whereby each of us exists, for as long as we live, within an overall condition of nothingness. The subsequent dichotomy causes anguish, and therefore, humans may seek to flee their anguish through escapes, visualizations, or dreams. What Sartre teaches is that dreams are a necessary part of our existence. The real question I pose to you is how can we determine when we are dreaming and when we are not? Here we return back to what is real or not real. My point is that we can't tell reality from dreams and that it makes no difference because both are real."

Another hand from the rear of the room shot up, dragging with it a young man, wearing a long pony tail, to his feet. "Dr. Chase. Since I am dreaming, I am going to dream that I got an 'A' in this class. Won't that work?" The rest of the class unsuccessfully suppressed laughter.

"I like that, Andrew. The problem is that I likely won't dream that you got an 'A,' and I am the one who will dream about putting an 'F' on your record. That would be fair, don't you think?" The class sniggered, but there was a general faraway look that Tom knew indicated that most of them were confused.

"Here's a quote from George Berkeley which may help some of you," Tom said and opened his notebook to read.

I do not argue against the existence of any one thing that we can apprehend, either by sense or reflection. That the things I see with mine eyes and touch with my hands do exist, really exist, I make not the least question. The only thing whose existence we deny, is that which philosophers call matter or corporeal substance. And in doing of this, there is no damage done to the rest of mankind, who, I dare say, will never miss it.

"You understand, of course, that Berkeley said the same thing I have being attempting to make clear. Class dismissed." The class got collectively to its feet and filed slowly out, accompanied by the sound of murmuring conversation. All that is except one. She made sure that she was the last by furtively looking around and then came and stood before Tom.

"Professor Chase, could you clear this up for me?" she whined.

Tom looked up to see Rebecca Wartham, the prettiest girl in school, and the most buxom, by far.

"What didn't you get, Rebecca?" he asked quietly.

"Well, I got so little of it that I don't know what to ask. What does it all mean?"

Tom let out a big sigh. "I want you to go read some of the work of Thomas Nagel. You will find that he describes that what is in an individual's mind is beyond the scope of science. What is in my mind is real to me. You cannot objectify what is subjective. Is that any clearer to you?"

"I'm afraid not, Professor. Would it be all right if I called you by your first name? Tom, isn't it? It's so much more friendly that way, and it'll help me relax around you, Tom."

"It's more personal, Rebecca, than I'm accustomed to. After all, we have a student-teacher relationship, not an intimate one."

"An intimate one would suit me very well, thank you, Tom," she said and showed her perfect teeth.

"Rebecca, you are not without attractions, as you likely know, but I'm sorry to have to tell you that I don't get that involved with my students."

"Tom, it's just that without some help, I won't pass this class. I'm willing to let you instruct me in private, and I feel sure that you won't be disappointed with me."

"I wonder if you have had any computer science classes yet?"

"No, but I'm looking forward to taking some," Rebecca said and put her hand on her hip in a way that emphasized her large breasts.

"I have a feeling that you'll do very well in computer science, and if you will permit a suggestion, I feel that you should drop this class and take one taught by Dr. Grimes. Tell him that I suggested it, and I'm sure he will allow it."

"That sounds like a good idea," she said without much thought. "I'll do it, Tom."

"There is an 'A' in your future, Rebecca. Good luck and goodbye."

After she left, Tom felt unusually tired and sat behind his desk organizing his thoughts. It had been a tough day, really tough. Losing Bug was so unfair, because this time, he had done nothing wrong. He had made no mistakes with Bug, and he loved her with every fiber of himself. His last image of her was that moment she was crouching on the platform firing her pistol as someone fired back. What was worse than being unable to come to her aid was that he would never find out what happened. Unable to help himself, he began to cry and put his head on the desk with his hands on top of his head. His head swam with his past lives, even this one. He could remember them all clearly. There were nearly ninety years of lives he had lead, seemingly simultaneously. How could this happen? He considered today's lecture he had given. Is there any explanation in Philosophy which could help? Not from the sources he had used today, he knew. Tom always considered himself to be a realist and thought along similar lines as Daniel Dennett who compared consciousness to magic with its capability to create extraordinary illusions. Was this entire state of mind he had an illusion? It felt real enough. Objects had weight, people had personalities and motives, and his leg hurt a lot. What about the leg? Now he remembered taking a fall on a ski trip several years ago resulting in a fracture. Is it coincidence that the same leg was injured with an explosion only one month ago in his other life? He couldn't answer any of the questions he posed to himself, so he slowly got to his feet and started walking toward his apartment. After he got out into the open air and the warm afternoon light, he started to feel better. It was a nice day for a walk, and it might ease the pain in his leg. Coming toward him on the path were two women walking arm in arm, and as they closed the distance, he recognized them both.

"Well, hello, Professor!" Madelyn said as if she had not seen him in years, instead of just yesterday. "I'm sure you know Elizabeth from Library Services, don't you?"

"Of course, I know Liz. How are both of you today?"

"Well, we were just going for supper. Care to join us today, Professor? I have news of my younger sister whom I was telling you about."

"Well, that's very nice of you ladies to consider me, but I'm feeling rather tired today, and I need to get some paperwork out of the way tonight. Perhaps some other time."

"I just happen to have Carole's picture with me, Professor." Madelyn quickly extracted a large glossy photo from someplace and presented it to him before he could say no. "She's been in France for some time and has gone native. Carole will only be here for a short time, and I am so counting on her meeting you." Just as Tom was about to question why it was important to meet this woman, he unwillingly looked at the photograph. Jeanette was looking back at him from the picture. He could almost smell her perfume. He took it and held it closer to his face.

"Your sister is a very beautiful woman. It seems I know her already."

"You might have seen her in magazines. She has become well-known as a model."

"Why would you want her to meet me? After all, I don't keep the circles she probably does. I suspect that once she sees me, she will not want anything to do with me."

"Oh, that's not true. She wrote me after she saw your photograph in a newspaper when you gave a lecture in Monaco last year. She's most interested in seeing you." Tom could feel his jaw drop open. The thought that Jeanette was alive somewhere and real was almost too much for him, and he felt a little wobbly.

"When do you expect Carole, Madelyn?"

"Anytime soon. She is finishing up a photo session in Chicago and will stop by to see me before returning to Paris. Is it agreed then that you will meet with her?"

"Sincerely, I couldn't refuse. Of course I will."

Tom entered his apartment and noticed that his housekeeper had left her usual note instructing him about the meal she had prepared. He found the plate, poured himself a tall glass of wine, opened the doors of the balcony, and sat down at the little cast iron table. After a leisurely dinner, he came in and settled back in the armchair and picked up his pipe as was usual when he needed to think deeply about a subject. He was still churning about his nearly dual existence, which at times seemed to be both real and also simultaneous. The new wrinkle was that Jeanette could and did exist probably in each of his lives, but she was different as she was also the same. Likely, it was also true for Allyson who may live somewhere yet unknown. It obviously means he will not be able to take back up with either one of them, because they have their own lives which don't include him at the moment. Nevertheless, they both were attracted to him at one time, and one would suppose that is an indication it could happen again. As he puffed flavored balls of smoke toward the ceiling, he thought about the works of the psychologist Carl Jung, who is known for his idea of the collective unconscious. Jung said that "psyche and matter are contained in one and the same world, and moreover are in continuous contact with one another." Jung also felt that "psyche and matter are two different aspects of one and the same thing." It was similar to the ancient idea that there is a universal consciousness of all matter and that what we perceive as objects and things are only expressions of the consciousness of the universe and that would include humans. In that concept, an individual human life and existence is what an intelligent universe decides, and for the first time Tom began to understand why life changed capriciously for him. Tom's pipe slipped from his hand to the floor as he fell asleep.

Chapter 10

Love Returns

The glint in her eye was like a smile or a playful tune. Every time he saw it, he felt good all over, without exactly understanding why. She was so full of energy and life that it spilled out of her like the foam of warm beer making its way across your fingers.

"You are radiant, Bug. I always feel good around you, like I want to jump up on the table and shout joyous things to the world. No matter how long we stayed together, I never got tired of you. It's like a hunger that can't be satisfied."

"I feel the same with you, but it's a little different in that I feel so safe, so loved and secure, that I just want you to wrap me in your arms and squeeze forever." He reached over her shoulder as they walked and held her close to him. The wind was biting cold, the kind that makes your eyeballs ache and your eyes water. Tom pulled up his collar and leaned forward, trying to get just ahead of Bug to break some of the wind from her.

"How much farther, Tom? I don't think I can stand much more of this," Allyson said through her wrap, loud enough to hear.

"Hang on, dear. About two hundred feet," he shouted. Through his tears he saw the opening just ahead. The snow was blowing in small hard crystals which swirled around in the doorways and glittered under the lights, creating a subtle moving rainbow.

The sign blinked, "Tango Argentina," in pink and was swaying back and forth with an urgent squeaking noise. At last, the door handle was within reach of his hand, and when he opened the door, they were treated to a blast of moist air which clung to their faces, instantly turning them white with frost. From somewhere inside, an accordion was already at work singing a mournful and sexually rhythmic tune making Tom's feet feel like keeping time. Through the large opening to the ballroom, dancers clung to each other with eyes that looked someplace else, their feet and legs moving like separate living beings. As Bug looked on, spellbound, a couple executed a deep dip bringing the woman's head low and nearly touching the floor as her split skirt fell away exposing pure white skin nearly to her waist. Tom heard Bug take a deep breath. She looked questioningly back at him as if to say, "You expect that of me?"

"Yes, I do," he said, anticipating her question. Tom helped her off with her coat and pointed to a small set of tables and chairs against the wall. "Let's sit over there and watch for a moment, have a drink and warm up." Bug nodded yes, and on the way to the tables, Tom whispered to a well-dressed woman who smiled back at him. After they were seated and enjoying watching the dancers, the woman arrived with a platter on which sat two gleaming and smoking glasses.

"What type of drink is this?" Bug asked while sniffing the hot liquid.

"*Hesperidina*," he said. "They like to serve it hot here. Sort of tastes like oranges."

"A toast to us, Tom," and she lifted her glass toward him and smiled. She was an open and direct person with no pretense about her. Her feminine charms came naturally without any need for enhancement. Bug had a healthy glow, nearly a well-scrubbed look. At first glance, she could be considered an innocent, but Tom knew that her resume included six deaths by gunfire and several more who had escaped death but with devastating bullet wounds.

He had watched her run down suspects larger than herself and hold them to the ground by force. Tonight, she consented to dress as he wanted and was wearing a silky dress with an open back and long slits along the sides. Tom had picked out black for her, because he knew that it would emphasize her unblemished and flawless skin.

"This is to a most beautiful and desirable woman, and the one I want to spend the rest of my life with," Tom said, then he touched her glass with his. Bug looked excited and nervous as she glanced at the other dancers on the polished floor entwined with pulsating music. "Don't worry, Bug. We are going to have instruction and start really slow. You are by far the most attractive woman who has ever been through the door and that alone will make you look like you know what you are doing."

"Have you taken Jeanette here?"

"I have never taken anyone here before," he responded.

"It seemed to me that they know you."

"Two weeks ago, I came and scoped it out. I met them at that time and discussed taking you here for instruction. Everybody is looking forward to it. If you didn't notice, all the dancers here tonight are professional, and they all are here for you."

"I don't know what to say, Tom. It's so intimidating because I have never done anything like this before."

"I will do anything for you, Bug. I love you."

"I love you also, Tom. There isn't any other person that could get me to do this except you." As she talked, the sequins outlining the neckline of her dress caught the low lights and reflected back gold and red spots. She was wearing one piece of jewelry, a delicate gold necklace with a single diamond which hung nearly to the 'V' formed by her breasts.

"Are you happy in your new life, Tom?" she asked and turned her blue eyes intently on him.

"No, Bug. I don't have you. The only thing in life I want, and it has been denied me."

"Sorry, Tom. Isn't there a way back to me?"

"Something I have realized lately. You are here someplace, but if I found you, you would likely not have anything to do with me. You would have your own life to live. I can tell you something else now that it's all past. The red-haired girl was Jeanette. I could see that she recognized me but she wouldn't admit it."

"Didn't Jeanette tell you goodbye in your dream? You know I'll never do that. If you found me, it might be different this time."

"You'll have a different name and live in a different place. There is no way to find you unless by accident."

"Is there anything I can do, Tom?"

"Just be here in my dreams, Bug. Be here for me forever, because it's the only way I can get through life."

"I'll never leave you, Tom. I'll be here until you stop dreaming."

The accordion started *La Comparsita,* and the well-dressed woman was beckoning for them to come to the dance floor.

Chapter 11

A Jeanette By Any Other Name Smells The Same

The first light of dawn penetrated the bedroom focusing a bright spot on the wall which gave a warm glow of reflected color to everything else. Tom looked at his watch. 6:15. Ms. Hastings would arrive to prepare breakfast sharply at seven. He had to get up, but instead, he rolled over and studied the bland ceiling. Bug was wonderful last night, and he wished that he had taken time to do things like that when she was with him. Thinking about her made him angry that he had been snatched out of that life before...well, before anything. There was so much to do with her. Things that she had never done before, places that she had never seen and gowns that would make her look like a spectacular woman instead of one being hidden under her uniform. He rolled to his feet. Funny, he remembered that in his dream there was no leg pain.

After breakfast, he limped slowly back toward the university spires puncturing the sky. He had walked this particular sidewalk for years, yet this morning he felt like a stranger pretending to be Dr. Chase. When he reached the Liberal Arts building, he headed for the faculty lounge. After he poured a large cup of black coffee, he settled into an armchair with the morning paper. It was quite nice sitting in a flood of morning light, listening to the sounds of students chatter in the distance. He became engrossed in an article and didn't notice Fred Grimes and Kurt Koffman pull up chairs beside him.

"Morning Chase," Grimes said and got his attention. "Feeling better today?"

Tom looked up and acknowledged both of them. "I do feel better, thank you. Did you get the present I sent you yet?"

Grimes furtively glanced at Koffman and wondered if he knew anything about it. "Yes. Lovely present, Chase. I'll take good care of it, I promise." Koffman looked quizzically at each trying to decipher their code. Not being able to discern the subject, he satisfied himself by raising his eyebrows but said nothing.

Koffman cleared his throat to get their attention. "Tom, I have been talking to Chris Penwick this morning, and he mentioned something you said yesterday. Then on the way here, Grimes told me that you feel that you have led four lives. Can you discuss this with me?" Koffman pinched his thick black eyebrows over his thick black horn-rimmed glasses. The unusual lenses in his glasses always made his eyes appear too large, which is why the students invariably, but secretly, called him "Bullfrog". Koffman was professor of Psychology and felt that he was the self-appointed campus confessor.

"You want to analyze me, don't you, Koffman?" Tom asked, feeling amused.

"You don't have to call it analysis. That's for the psychiatrists. I'm only an educated friend, and you don't have to pay me a cent."

"You will want to know a lot of personal detail and then you will give an opinion about what's actually wrong with me. Isn't that how it usually works?"

"No, Tom. I just am interested in how you have lived three, or was it four, lives. And then there is this thing about an exit door. The subject matter is very appealing for me, and I am dying to discuss it with you."

"Koffman, you should have attended my lecture yesterday. It was on the subject of dreams, and I quoted some of the leading authorities on dreams and discussed what they mean. Let me ask you first about your dreams. Have you had dreams which seemed real at the time you were dreaming?"

Koffman sputtered. "You are trying to distract me. Of course, I have had realistic dreams. Doesn't everyone?"

"Yes, that is the point, Koffman. I dream and remember my dreams, and it seems that I have a life in my dreams. Now, does that seem so unusual?"

"Not when you put it that way. Now that you've opened up to me, I want to know if the same persons show up in your dreams most of the time."

"To be truthful, there are, or were, two women whom I have dreamed about. I seem to know them very well in my dreams."

"Were? Then there is only one lately?"

"Last night was the first for one of them. I don't dream about them at the same time."

"Brother, never have two women at the same time. Trouble. And you can believe me," Grimes interrupted and laughed loud enough to attract attention from several of the other faculty.

"All right, Koffman, I have another question for you. Ever dream about having a dream? And I mean a dream within a dream, but one you can remember?"

Koffman looked blank for a while with his large eyes rolling back and forth. "I don't recollect such a dream. You have this type of dream?"

"Here is the truth, Koffman. I feel that I am living a life in one of those dreams, and when I sleep in my dream, I dream. It is the only explanation for what I remember. I dream about another life, but I can remember during my dreams all the other lives.

Complicated?"

"Fascinating, Chase. Enough so that I want to consult with a friend about the implications, if that is all right with you."

"I have no problem with you doing that. Tell me what your friend has to say about it."

"Yes, Chase. I'm sure he will be interested. Now tell me about the exit door."

"Not much to tell you. I saw one in one of my dream lives. It seemed to be a black hole into nothing. That's about all I know."

"Tell me Chase. At the time you saw the exit, were you happy or despondent?"

"I'm not unenlightened about what you are getting at. I understand without you telling me that you feel the Exit Door represents a symbol for suicide, an escape, a permanent escape. Isn't that what you are thinking?"

"Of course, but you didn't answer my question fully. Let me put it this way. In a happy dream, do you ever see the exit door?"

"No."

"One last question, Chase. What do you think will happen if you enter your exit door in your dream?"

"Cease to exist, Koffman. Gone."

"Does that mean that you'll wake up?"

"I'm not sure. The object is very fearful. It would take more nerve that I have to enter one. A point you should know, Koffman, is that during one of my dreams, everything seems to be completely real. It would be a deliberate act of suicide to enter an Exit Door." Just as he finished, the bell rang indicating classes were to begin in exactly ten minutes. There was a sound of chairs being pushed back around the room as members of the faculty arose to prepare for class.

After the last student was seated, Tom began, "Today we are going to discuss dreams. We are going to start with what is known from recent brain research and then discuss the historical significance which has been attached to dream interception. You recall that yesterday we discussed the suggestion that dreams and reality may be hard to differentiate, and we mentioned the theory that what you perceive is real, regardless if in a dream or while awake."

"The main tool of recent research is the EEG which, as you know, is a recording of brain waves. More recently, PET scanners are giving us an understanding of brain activity and what it means. Yet, no matter what we find in the brain activity, we still don't really know the significance of dreams or how to interpret them. A study has been made of things which influence dreams, and we all know from personal experience that our daytime lives have an important effect. Until recently, we didn't know, until research proved it, that odors, such as the smell of familiar flowers or perfume, will, in part, determine what the dream is about."

"The duration of dreams is an interesting topic. Usually, dreams occur in brief periods of several minutes or up to fifteen minutes. You are more likely to remember the first dreams of the night than the latter dreams, which tend to be more chaotic. That dreams occur only in REM or rapid eye movement sleep is now known not to be completely true. We may dream during non-REM sleep, and the origin of the electrical impulses comes from a different part of the brain. In short, REM sleep arises from the emotional centers in the limbic system. NREM sleep arises from other parts of the brain and is considered to be where analytical dreams arise. It is worth mentioning that the mental disorder, Schizophrenia, seems to be similar to dreams in that the subject cannot tell what is truly reality. For us, as philosophers, where dreams arise in the human brain is not as significant as the dream itself. We view dreams to be a connection to the unconscious mind. Dreams are usually not in our control but can give us inspiration or become a creative force in our awake state."

"You should all be aware that Sigmund Freud had a rather narrow interpretation of dreams and usually tried to relate dreams to a childhood experience, usually a negative one. Dream interpretation goes back to the earliest civilizations, and for all we know, beyond. Greek and Romans felt that dreams were messages from gods and had a predictive value for the future. The Greek god of dreams was Morpheus who acted on those who slept in temples. Every ancient culture had similar views on the importance of dreams, and dreams remain interesting to people and to scientists."

Just as Tom finished his sentence, the door opened and two women entered, attempting to be quiet, but the entire class, including Tom, came to full attention. One was Madelyn, who nodded secretly at him on their way to the back of the room. The other one was stunningly beautiful, and every male in the class followed her with their eyes in rapt attention. From that moment on, her long red hair and her figure was imprinted on their brains forever. When she sat down and faced Tom, the sight of those green eyes took his breath for a moment. The woman was clearly and undeniably Jeanette. Tom knew every part of her, every inflection of her voice, and every tilt of her head by heart.

"Welcome to our visitors. I want all the heads turned toward me, including the fellows, please. To continue where I left off, I was about to mention Carl Jung. He differed with Freud's views in that he felt that dreams are messages and present the person dreaming with answers which help resolve emotional issues. A survey of people around the globe has established that most people feel that their dreams reveal meaningful hidden truths. Once again, I mention that some early philosophers frequently discussed the idea called Skeptical Hypothesis. They concluded that the so called real world is, or could be, an illusion or a dream."

"Dreams are important in art, literature and history, and recently several movies have created fanciful tales of dreams intertwined with reality. I want to leave this topic with a quote from Shakespeare's, *The Tempest."*

> *We are such stuff*
> *As dreams are made on and our little life*
> *is rounded with a sleep...*

"Assignments are on the board. Class dismissed." Tom waited until all the students left and, during that time, couldn't take his eyes from Jeanette's face. She smiled at him and seemed to be entirely different than the last time they had met. He walked back toward them and leaned on a desk with his arms crossed. "Hi. Your name is Carole, isn't it?" he asked.

"Yes, that is my name. And your name is Tom Chase," she said with a hint of humor and reached out to shake his hand. He took her hand in his, and the memory of touching her became an electric charge within him, recalling all the memories of having her envelop him with her love.

She turned to Madelyn and smiled. "Do you mind very much giving us a moment?" Madelyn nodded approval, gathered her things and left with a last look from the door.

"I feel that I know you, Tom. Your photo was in a paper I picked up by accident, and your face was so familiar to me. I have been thinking and dreaming about it since...about you, I mean. I had to see you for myself, and now I am certain that we have a connection in some way."

"May I ask, Carole, have you ever been married?"

"Twice. Both times unhappily. I wish that I could find the right man for me. Looking at you, something tells me that I have been looking in the wrong places."

"I realize that you have been told many times, and don't need to hear it from me, but I am compelled to say that you are beautiful beyond words. Just looking into your face is thrilling and mesmerizing."

"Thank you, Tom. I have never heard it put that way before. For me, looking at you gives me peace and comfort in some way that I don't understand. It's like I know you very well, perhaps have known you for years. Do you have an explanation?"

"Not one that you might believe. Does the name Jeanette or Genevieve have any connection to you?"

"No. I have always been called Carole. Is there a reason that you asked?"

"One thing more. When I appeared in your dreams, what did I say or do?"

She held her hands in front of her mouth in mock surprise. "Really, I couldn't tell you that, Tom."

"So, in your dreams, I was your lover?"

"Yes, perhaps more."

"In answer to your obvious question, I feel that I know you also and have for a long, long time. You even wear the perfume that I expected when I saw you."

"Tom, it seems ordained that we should have a relationship, don't you think?" After she spoke, Tom looked away and stroked his beard for a moment, gathering his thoughts. There was this little problem of Bug. He loved Bug in every way possible. This time things were reversed with Bug as a dream and Jeanette real, but now he understood himself better.

"The way you look would attract any man including myself. It would be a privilege just to keep you company or be seen with you. But...I don't think I'm a match for you because I am just ordinary, a lowly college professor with a bad leg. You are a world-class beauty. I couldn't make you happy. You would eventually leave me for someone more exciting, and I don't want that again."

"Again?"

"You really don't remember? Please tell me the truth."

Tom could see the old Jeanette under the new name. It was her. The laughing eyes and the slight smile said it all. She knew him from before, in her other life. Of course she remembered and dreamed about their encounters as did he. She didn't want to admit that she remembered the other life, because it would cause him to recall that she left him. After all, she was the one who said goodbye.

"Well, in my dreams, you seem to have known me for a long time. We were happy," she admitted.

"You left me, and you should recall that I never left you."

"Yes, I wanted a life. Now that I've had what I thought I wanted, I realize what I lost. Can you forgive me?"

"I forgive you, Jeanette. I understood that you did what you had to do at the time."

"Now that the truth is out, can we start over, perhaps?"

"You walked out on me, even as I begged you not to, Jeanette. My heart was torn out and thrown away. Another truth is that I was always terrified of losing you because you are so attractive. You always could have had any man you desired. I counted my blessings every day that I had you in my arms, but I suspected that there was a day that you would find someone new. It happened, didn't it?"

"Yes, I made the rounds and made my share of mistakes. I found that your love was more true all along. I regret losing you. Don't you want me any longer?"

"It would destroy me to have to say goodbye again, Jeanette. I don't want to have that feeling arise within me again. I'm just not good enough for you, and we both know that. All I have are my dreams, but that is all I need."

"Then the answer is no?"

"Regrettably. The answer is no."

"You recall the lovemaking we had?"

"I don't dream about you any longer, mostly, I have learned not to think about you at all. For a long time, memories of you gave me a lot of pain, but I have adjusted to this life. We aren't exactly the same people any longer, Jeanette. You are the same girl whom I sought and won, but it was a long time ago. You should keep looking for that perfect mate you want and need, and let the past be the past." She started to weep, softly at first and then uncontrollably. Tom took her in his arms, and she rested her head on him as he stroked her back. It was a familiar feeling to Tom, and she felt warm and good there, like nothing had changed.

"I love you, Tom. Isn't that enough?" she said and looked up with her reddened eyes and puffy lips.

"The old Tom loves you still. This one can't let himself. He has too much to lose."

After she left, Tom felt hollow and near collapse. It was what he wanted, to have Jeanette back in real life, and he just let her walk out. Then he remembered Bug. He loved Bug in a different way than he had loved Jeanette and, for the first time, realized how important Jeanette's looks had been to him and how unimportant Bug's looks were. He loved Bug for herself, and he would never give her up, even if she were only a dream.

Chapter 12

Only In My Dreams

Sunlight glinted off the moving water of the lake, creating flickering waves of light on the trees and on Bug's face. It was charming to see the sparkle of her eyes mix with the sunlight and to see brief shadows play along the contours of her face. She was happy and energetic and looked around with wondering eyes, taking in a graceful summer afternoon. Off to the left, a ball game was being staged on a grassy slope amid the shouts of encouragement from scattered, interested spectators. A vendor just ahead was shouting incentives to buy his bratwurst, alternately singing a Neapolitan tune in Italian. Across the lake, they could see the irregular city skyline and the high rent apartments of Park Avenue.

"You look happy today, Bug. It makes me feel good to look at you," Tom said.

"Yes, I'm very happy. Yesterday was the last day of my old life, and today is the start of my new one."

"So the divorce wasn't contested, even a little?"

"No, he wished me the best happiness and even gave me a gift to remember him by. I told you that Peter always treated me good. He even loved me in his way."

"Does that make you mine forever?" Tom asked. She pulled him close, smiling at him with love in her eyes.

"Yes, I am yours for as long as we live, or as long as you want me." They continued slowly walking down the path accompanied by the swish of her dress and the soft footfall of their shoes against the pavement.

"I know that you had another chance with Jeanette. Thank you for choosing me."

"Wouldn't it be better if we could be together other than in my dreams?"

"Yes, Tom. Like we almost were."

"I was thinking about you. Finding you, that is. I have seen Jeanette in two different lives. I know that you are around someplace. Where could I look for you?"

"As you told me, Jeanette has a similar life wherever she is. Perhaps I am the same. You could look in New York and check all thc policewomen there."

"How could I do that? They would never share photos of police officers with anyone without cause. There could be thousands of women working for the NYPD. You might not even be a cop. Even If I find you, you might not know me or you could even be involved with someone."

"I've got it! You could commit a crime and then your wanted photos would be broadcast. I might see you and remember."

"Thanks, Bug. Get real."

"I don't know how, Tom. In any case, we are together now, aren't we?"

They stopped by the food cart where Tom ordered two coney dogs and drinks, and they found a close park bench to sit down. Bug was like a little girl unwrapping her Christmas gift as she peeled back the paper around the bun. She loved life and was full of both. Tom looked at her soft blonde hair which wrapped around her ear and spilled onto her collar.

"Your hair is getting longer. Looks good."

"I got jealous of the tango dancer's long hair and decided to try it out. Don't you prefer long hair?"

"Your hair is always right as far as I'm concerned. Don't grow it just for me." He paused to wipe some mustard from her upper lip, and she did the same for him as they laughed at each other.

"This tastes great. Can I be dreaming if I can taste the food?" Tom asked.

"Humm. Try my lips and see if you can taste the mustard," she said, then puckered and closed her eyes. He kissed her as she asked while he lightly held the back of her neck.

"Yup. I taste the mustard, and I taste you. This is real enough for me," he said.

The alarm clock vibrated and chimed, and Tom opened his eyes to squint at it. He resolved not to take it out on the poor clock, but the dream was just getting good. Rolling slowly to his feet, he felt the pain in his right leg come back. He briefly wondered why he never felt the pain in his dreams. Another day of class, another day without Bug in his life, and another day of loneliness. He sighed and pushed himself to his feet.

On the way past his letter box outside the faculty lounge, he retrieved a pink tinted slip of paper asking him to report to the President sometime today. He folded it into his pocket and opened the door to the lounge. A round face looked up and Grimes called and waved to him.

"Morning, Grimes. On your second cup yet?"

"Listen, Tom, something's come up, and it might involve you."

"I'm all ears, Grimes."

"Remember Rebecca Wartham, the coed you sent my way?"

"Big chest, very forward. That one?"

"Yes, I had her in my office for some 'counseling' and things...well, we got frisky, if you know what I mean."

"You show such marvelous restraint, Grimes. Nothing new

there, though."

"Her daddy is a local bigwig, an attorney. He already found out about it, and there's going to be trouble."

"I fail to see how that involves me," Tom said.

"You sent her to me."

"I didn't send her for sex. That was between you two. I wasn't there, as I recall."

"Doesn't matter. They'll say you knew that was what was going to happen."

"I did know. But, that is what she wanted, and as I recall, she is of age of consent."

"There will be a big stink about this," Grimes said, and Tom could see the sweat beads on his brow making their way along the horizontal creases of his forehead.

"You are right," Tom said and pulled out the pink slip. He studied it for a moment and stroked his beard. "I don't see how I have done anything wrong, Grimes. You, on the other hand, went too far too fast. It's happened before, but this time you got caught. What did you expect, for them to give you an award?" They both turned to see an approaching figure. Chris Penwick was rapidly approaching with a cup of coffee in each hand.

"Two cups, Chris. Isn't that being greedy?" Tom asked.

"No, my critical friend. One is for you, if you want it. I noticed that you didn't have one."

"Touché, Penwick. I had that coming. You look especially pert this morning."

"Well, in my class yesterday, we were working on Robert Frost, and I ran across a couple of lines that I had forgotten, but it hit me, while I was reading aloud, how it applies to your problem."

"What do you see as my problem, Chris?"

"Paths. Your story is of choosing a path and not being able to return. Isn't that about it?"

"One difference, Chris. In my case, I never chose a path. It seems to choose me."

"You willingly go into a room or through a door. That's choosing. We usually don't know in life that we are making an unrecoverable choice until it's too late."

"Point conceded. Go on with the Frost quotes then, and we'll see."

> *Two roads diverged in a wood and*
> *I took the one less traveled by,*
> *And that has made all the difference*

"Right on target, wouldn't you say?" Chris said expectantly.

"Not exactly the same. I don't know if it was less traveled. Wasn't the poem set in the woods?"

"Yes, but here are another couple of lines which may be closer."

> *Yet knowing how way leads on to way,*
> *I doubted if I should ever come back.*

Tom squinted, "That one hurt. Never come back. Goodness, I hope that is wrong. There is someone back there that I have to see again. The part about way leading to way describes my experience, though."

Grimes struggled to his feet. "It's been nice and all that. I have an appointment about my path and my choices. Hope to see you again tomorrow, but I have my doubts." He ambled away, and Tom and Chris followed his back as he left.

When he was gone, Chris asked, "Something I need to know?"

"The call of female flesh has its costs," Tom summarized.

Tom knocked on the door just under the brass, "President Henry Lawrence," sign. A voice from within said, "Enter," and Tom pushed the heavy door open. President Lawrence sat up and pushed his papers aside, then leaned back into his armchair. He had an unusually stern look and was dressed in a somber dark suit which made him seem more formidable. The paneled walls were decorated with plaques of various honors or degrees along with some personal photos. The President's desk was an heirloom of extravagantly carved walnut passed for generations into this office and was an exact copy of George Washington's.

"Well, Professor Chase, we have a problem."

"We, sir?"

"A student here has accused one of the faculty of sexual harassment. It's a serious charge, and one that can do this institution no good."

"How am I involved?" Tom inquired.

"You are named as procuring the young lady into the hands of her harasser."

"I did no such thing. My record is unblemished regarding my treatment of female students. I respect women in general and go out of my way to be considerate."

"Never mind your record, because that won't help you in court."

"Can you share any details of this accusation?"

"The young woman is a second-year student with a poor academic record, and I am informed that she is most attractive. That alone puts her in a vulnerable position. As the record stands, she was your student and then transferred to Computer Science on your advice. There is where she met Professor Grimes and the trouble commenced."

"As I recall, she was completely lost in Philosophy, and I asked if she were interested in CS and she said yes. You made the rule that all transfers must be approved by the head of the department, and so I sent her to see Professor Grimes. There was no mention of sex or anything similar to either one of them. I see no fault in my actions, do you?"

"No, not the way you tell it. Was there any hint of misbehavior on her part when she was in your class?"

"She insisted on calling me by my first name and hinted that we should get together privately. I didn't like it, but there was no mention of sex."

"So you had some inkling that she was available, wouldn't you say that was true?"

"I told her that I didn't form out-of-class relationships. I wanted to remove her from my presence."

"You have, of course, heard the rumors about Grimes and women?"

"As have you, I'm sure."

"So you will admit you sent a vulnerable young girl, who already expressed tendencies toward misbehavior, into the grasp of a professor who liked that sort of thing?"

"As I see it, Grimes' behavior is not my responsibility. It's yours."

"You are attempting to pass the buck to me. I resent it."

"If this gets to court, they will simply prove that you knew about Professor Grimes' antics for a long time and took no action. Like I said, I did nothing wrong, because I don't hire and fire teachers, you do."

"I don't like your tone. There is no choice for me here other than to suspend both you and Grimes until this is cleared up."

"Since you have no direct accusation to fling at me, then my suspension will be with pay or you will hear from my attorney. You should also know that cases like this one will drag on for years. It's a long vacation for me. Good luck with finding my replacement, sir." Tom turned and left the room before President Lawrence could rethink his position. Free at last and with pay! It was a burden lifted off of him, and his leg even felt better. He strolled out of the building, ignoring that he had two more classes scheduled and several conferences later in the day. He straightened his back and with a smile looked ahead toward a distant door to the outside.

"Professor Chase!" a voice beckoned from behind him. He turned to see Madelyn hurrying to catch up. "I have to ask you what happened with Carole yesterday. She wouldn't discuss it with me. Did you two have an argument?"

"Not at all. I enjoyed meeting her. Such a gorgeous woman. It was simply a delight. She had some feeling of *deja vu* when she saw my photograph. Turns out that we have never met and have little in common. I think she was disappointed, that's all."

"She hasn't left yet and has been crying most of the time since she met you. I was concerned."

"That's unfortunate. I rarely have much effect on women, so I'm not sure that I shouldn't have some elation about her feeling that way."

"I'm sure that she wants to know you better. Is there any chance?"

"No, I'm afraid that I am headed to New York to find someone that I lost. Wish her the best from me, if you will. I mean it, I would like to see her happy."

"I will, Professor. Good hunting in New York."

Chapter 13

Bug Hunt

*T*om pulled a map from his jacket and held it up against a brick wall studying the route to the next police station. Two more blocks. This was the third station out of dozens he still had to visit. As he predicted, no one was willing to help him even a little. He didn't know the name of the female police officer and was unable to provide a reason for finding her. Usually, they just laughed at him or threatened him. At least New York's Finest were willing to protect their own. As he walked, he decided on a new tack this time. After the last corner, he finally could see the sign ahead. There were several patrol cars in front and two uniformed officers taking an outside smoke.

"Greetings, Officers," Tom began. "I am a college professor visiting from Connecticut, and I am trying to find a female police officer, but I don't know where she works or her name."

One of them stood, in a slightly confrontational manner, and said "Why do you want to find her?"

"She helped me when I fell off the subway platform. Saved my life. I want to thank her in person."

The other one also stood. Close up, they were both larger than Tom. "When did this happen?" he said.

"Several months ago," Tom said.

"Why are you seeking her just now?" one of them said. Good question, but Tom was ready.

"I had a head injury and just recently recovered."

"If you had a head injury, how can you remember what she looked like?"

"I remember that she was young, with short blonde hair and very friendly and attractive."

"Where did this happen. I mean exactly where?" the first one asked.

"The platform at Grand Central Station. That's 42nd Street, I think."

"Do you have a date? We could look it up, because she would have filed a report."

"I'm not sure of the date, officer. My head, you know."

They looked at each other, then studied Tom carefully. "Let me see your ID, fellow," the second one said. Tom complied and handed him his university identification. The officer studied it and handed it to the other officer.

"Professor Chase. Tom. Is this correct?" he asked.

"Yes, that is my photo, is it not?"

"Seems to be, Professor. Tell you what, we'll check this out, and if there are any police officers who fit the bill, we will tell her that you came calling, and she can get in touch with you, if she wants to. All right?"

"Do you know any woman that works here who looks like I've described?"

"We just can't give out that kind of information, sir. It's the best we can do. You are free to go inside and just sit there and watch for her, if you want." They handed him back his card and smiled a particularly unfriendly smile at him. He realized that if he went inside, they might make it hard on him in some way.

"No thanks, Officers. I'll just move along," he said and limped slowly down the street and out of their view.

The door was marked with "J. Philip Jessup, Investigator" from the reverse side in flaking gold leaf. There was an ascending crack in the glass, which would eventually reach the signage. Tom tried the knob, but the door was locked, and the room appeared dark inside. He checked his watch, 9:30 a.m., precisely. He was on time for his appointment, but where was Jessup? While he stood there pondering what he should do, he heard the latch on the door and saw the lights come on. He tried the knob again, and this time was admitted to a seedy front office adorned by two hardwood chairs in poor repair and a metal desk complete with a busty young secretary.

"Good morning, sir. You must be Professor Chase. He is on time and waiting for you." She fussed with her hair while talking and without looking at him. Tom didn't feel the need to acknowledge her and proceeded to the private door. Behind his cluttered desk was a large man with an even larger neck which hung over his collar. He smiled at Tom, showing a couple of missing upper teeth and others darkly stained. He seemed to be of indeterminate age.

"Well, hello, Professor!" he said in a booming voice. "What brings you to Jessup Investigations?" He offered a thick, hairy hand to Tom, and he reluctantly accepted.

"Mr. Jessup," Tom began "on the phone we discussed my need to find someone who might be working for the NYPD. Was I correctly informed that you were at one time a police officer yourself?"

"You can call me Phil, son. Yes, I was a detective at one time. Pickings are better on the outside, you know. Now, exactly who is this person you seek, and why do you seek him?"

"It's a her. I don't know her name or exact age, but I put her at between 28 and 38. She is attractive and has short blonde hair. I'm not sure she is even in the police force. I need to find her for a personal reason."

"Well, son, that's not much help. Not much at all. You need to be more frank with me. Level with me, son. I need to know how you came to know this woman."

"If I do, you won't take the case. Before I tell you any more, tell me how you would go about finding such a person."

Jessup leaned back and the chair squeaked threateningly against his weight. He lit a cigarette and blew a column into the air. "Here's a suggestion. The Police Academy at Gramercy Park is a two-year program and turns out about seventy per year. There is no album, like a community college would have, but they usually take group photos at the graduation ceremony. Unfortunately for you, there is no legend of names to accompany the faces, but it could be a clue to finding out if she is even on the force. The other thing is that only about half of the force is from the Academy. Now, who is this woman to you."

Tom sighed audibly. "It's complicated. A short version is that I saw her in my dream. She was on the NYPD in the dream, and I have to find her."

"A DREAM! You gotta be kidding me. I should kick your nutty ass out of here for wasting my time." The chair returned to the horizontal, and Jessup leaned across the desk.

"Look at it this way, my friend. You charge for your assistance, I assume. Can you afford to turn down an easy and straightforward request for help?" Tom said.

"No. I can't. Well, I'm free this morning, and we can go over and peruse the wall of photos in the lobby. Two bills per, understood?"

"Agreed."

The lobby was a busy place, and Tom and his obese companion stood before the wall of group photos. It was behind a glass door, and the glare wasn't helpful to see the small faces, especially those on the back row. A quick glance showed only three or four blondes per year so perhaps this wouldn't take long. Tom started with the one taken ten years ago and had to tiptoe to see it well. As he was looking a young man in a suit approached with a concerned face.

"Can I help you gentlemen?" he asked.

"Hi. We are looking for my niece. I think she'll be in one of these photos. Is there a problem?

"If you can give me her name, perhaps I can look her up for you. What year did she finish?"

"Her name is Allyson June but she might be using a different last name. Broken home, divorce, you know how it goes. I'm not sure which year she finished," Tom said. The man nodded and wrote something down and left.

"You are the accomplished liar, Professor. I even believed you for a moment," Jessup said. They continued to look at the photos knowing that their time was limited once the man returned.

Suddenly, Tom tapped on the glass in front of him. "There she is. I'm sure."

Jessup put on his glasses and squinted at the photo. "If you say so. It's nutty though." They heard footsteps behind them and turned to see the man returning with a paper in his hand.

"Did you find your niece?" he asked.

"Yes, that one." And Tom tapped on the glass over the photo. The man looked at the photo and the date above it.

"It fits. Same year. I couldn't find a June but the name Allyson was the only one in the database. Says here that she used the last name of Simpson. Sound familiar?"

"Yes, that was her real father's name. It's her all right. Does it say where she works now?"

"Well, this says that she went to Midtown South. Choice slot. She must have had connections. That's on 357 West 35th Street, if that helps."

"Ever so much. Thanks a million," Tom said beaming. He stood back for the first time and looked at the postings as his head cleared. There at the top he saw a familiar face smiling beneficently down at him. Riggs. He was Chief of Police.

As they walked out, Jessup tapped Tom on his shoulder, and he stopped and turned toward him. "How is it possible from a dream that you could know a real person? You even got her first name correct. Tell me the whole story, or I'll feel compelled to tell the cops what I know."

"It gets weirder and weirder, Jessup. If I told you the whole story you would want to take me to Bellevue. It's pretty much as I said. It's a dream but a really complicated one. There is no malice here. I deeply love this girl, and I want to connect with her. Want to help some more?"

"For a buck, I'll do almost anything. Any more surprises?"

"Just a word to the wise, that's all. Chief of Police Riggs is corrupt."

"How do you know this, Chase. That's a tall accusation."

"Dreams. I dreamed it up, but it's true." They started walking again, and Tom searched the streets for a yellow cab.

"Wait, Chase," Jessup said and put his hand on Tom's shoulder. "I just remembered something about that cop. That Simpson of yours is a detective, and she was in the papers recently. Something to do with terrorists. We need to look this up before we try to find her. Did you know anything about that?"

"Again, it's complicated. Let's look at the newspaper and I'll know more.

In the Public Library they read the newspaper column at the same time with Jessup looking over Tom's shoulder. Detective Allyson Simpson had shot and killed two suspects and wounded a third on the train platform at Grand Central Station. There was a photo of her receiving an award from none other than Riggs himself. The story detailed a series of attacks by terrorists, one on a New York hospital. There was no mention of a Detective Tom Chase. The photo, without question, was of Bug. She was assigned to Midtown South Precinct, exactly where they both had served. Tom had chills along his spine. Things were similar but not exactly the same. Bug had a different last name, and a Tom wasn't with her now. Would she remember him at all? He was determined to find out.

"Still think that she's the one?" Jessup asked.

"She is positively the one. In my dream, I saw her shooting at them. I was on the train."

"Couldn't you have seen this story someplace and dreamed the rest?" Jessup asked.

"That is the way it looks, but my memory of the event is much more complete than this story. I need to talk to Allyson. Want to help me find her?"

"No. All this talk of terrorists and you want to walk in there with a wacky dream story. Not a chance I want any part of that. You pay me for my time today, and I'll let you handle the rest." Tom opened his wallet and gave Jessup his money.

Chapter 14

Pillow Talk

om rolled over, still half asleep, and covered his head with his pillow, trying to shut out the morning light. The day came creeping in past the pillow and through his closed eyelids, and his awareness came to him in small jolts. He noticed that his left side was warmer. He sleepily reached over to pull the cover back when he felt a soft solid shape beside him. He turned his head to see blonde hair above the edge of the cover. He gently pulled the edge of the blanket back and Bug's blue eyes opened, slowly at first, then fully, letting her intelligence pour out and envelop him.

"Good morning, sweetheart," Tom whispered.

"Good morning, lover," she answered with a brilliant smile. Tom reached around to pull closer and felt bare skin covering her lovely curves. As they embraced, he realized that he was also nude. Full body contact is such a wonderful sensation, he thought. They kissed a long, slow, and lingering but tender kiss, parting with reluctance.

"I love the taste of your lips and your breath on my cheek, Bug. I love the sound of your special little voice and your blue eyes. There isn't anything about you that isn't perfect. For me, this moment is as good as it gets."

"Not what you said before you fell asleep!" she teased.

"Every moment with you is dear to me," Tom said and kissed her nose. She snuggled even closer, wrapped in his arms.

"I've been thinking about when you find me," she said against his chest.

"Will you know me? That's the big question."

"You are part of my image of myself. You can't be separated from me without leaving a void. Even if I had never seen you, I would know that you belong to me. I did from the first time I saw you, and I will again. It has to be that way."

"That's fine and I believe you, but what if you are involved with someone else? The way you are put together, you would never give a hint of interest in me, even if you felt it. I've been through that before with you, and I know how you react."

"Yes, I have a loyal streak, but I assure you that I still feel inside what I can't show outside. Have patience with me, if that happens, because I still won't let you down."

"You know that Riggs made Chief?" he asked.

"Sad, isn't it? Think you can still get him?"

"We have to know if this Riggs is working with terrorists before we accuse him. He is in a very powerful position and I'll need proof, lots of it."

"That's where I can help, Tom. I am incorruptible. It comes from the soul, and mine is pure. Convince me of the facts, and I will help you."

"You have saved my life so many times that I've actually gotten used to it. It's just something I have come to expect from you. I have finally found what I want in life and it's you, Bug. If you reject me, there isn't anything left for me to live for."

"Don't doubt me then, silly. Have I ever let you down?"

"No, Bug, and I'll never let you down either." They embraced tightly and kissed passionately once more and then Bug flung off the covers.

"I'm going to take a shower. Care to get up and make me a cup of coffee?" she said and sat up, dangling her feet off the bed, her bare back glowing in the soft light. After watching Tom nod yes, she stood and walked toward the bathroom, twisting slightly to look back at him. Yes, he was watching. Her beautiful curves were implanted deeply in his brain and, seeing her, activated nearly every emotion within him. Such a lovely and perfect creature. How lucky he was to be a man and have the gift of her shape before him. When the shower turned on, he could hear Bug softly singing to herself, and he slowly drifted off to sleep again.

Chapter 15

Face To Face

Tom recognized the building and its entrance. He had been through these doors thousands of time in his eight years on the force. He resisted the temptation to walk in as if he still worked here. By habit, he caught himself reaching in his jacket for his badge, which, of course, wasn't there. Looking around, he realized that he knew nearly everyone he saw by their first name. He felt more at home here than back at the University. Somewhere upstairs, Bug was sitting at her desk, bent over her pen, working on a case. What had happened to his desk, he wondered? Or his locker? He stood in the middle of the floor with people walking around him while gathering his thoughts.

Pete Summerly tapped him on the shoulder. "Help you, Buddy?"

Tom nearly called Pete by his first name but caught himself. "Thanks, Sergeant Summerly, for asking. I was hoping to talk with Detective Allyson Simpson."

Pete looked at his chest to see if an ID was visible. It wasn't. "How do you know my name? I don't remember seeing you previously."

"You just seem familiar for some reason, and your name popped into my head. Our paths must have crossed at some point." Pete looked Tom over carefully gauging him for misbehavior or risk before deciding that he was harmless.

"Get a visitor's badge from the desk and then go up to Level Three. They will direct you from there."

"Thanks, Sergeant," Tom said and gave a small salute. Pete watched him walk away with some lingering interest.

Brannigan met eyes with Tom when he got off the elevator. There was some hint of recognition in those eyes, Tom thought, but not enough that brought comment. Brannigan watched as Tom made his way among the desks toward Bug, who was busy at her desk and didn't see him coming. Just before he got there, he felt a big hand grasp his arm and turn him around.

"What's your business here, Mister?" Brannigan asked. Tom saw that his brow was wrinkled, and he carried a sort of forward body position. His usual mark of aggressiveness.

"I came to talk to Detective Allyson Simpson, not you, Detective Brannigan." Tom answered with as much assertiveness.

"How in hell did you know my name, Mister?" Brannigan said as he squared off.

"Maybe I'm clairvoyant. You figure it out," Tom said as he sharply pulled away and resumed walking toward Bug, who now was looking at him.

"Leave this one to me, Brannigan," she said and sat up and looked at Tom carefully. Tom could feel Brannigan's presence just behind him, like a circling pit bull.

"May I sit down?" Tom asked.

"Certainly," she said and motioned toward the chair beside her desk. Brannigan sat at Tom's old desk just beside her, watching Tom carefully. Tom removed a card from his wallet, identifying him as a university professor from Connecticut, and gave it to her. Bug turned the card over carefully and then handed it to Brannigan.

"So, Dr. Chase. What brings you to see me?"

"I was on the train when you shot those terrorists, and I have some information which may interest you," he said, looking at her with familiarity. He could feel Brannigan watching his eyes. Bug was Bug. Everything was the same. He remembered her embrace and kiss just this morning and the natural, wonderful smell of her hair against his nose.

"Well, I'm waiting to hear. Spill."

"Is there any way to talk privately? I don't feel that this is the place for that, and I don't enjoy the hostility from your big pal." Tom looked at Brannigan to see if he got the message and caught his glare. Bug tapped her pursed lips with her pencil, trying to think of a place they could talk.

"Might I suggest the rear conference room? As I remember, it's glassed in and Brannigan could keep an eye on me," Tom said. Her eyebrow raised a little, and she looked at Brannigan.

"How could you know about that room?" she said and looked at him again. Tom discerned that there was interest but no hostility from her. Perhaps she was right this morning when she said that her soul would recognize him even if she didn't show it.

"I know a lot, and I have a long story to tell you."

"This should be interesting. Come on then and you can tell your story to me." She stuck out her hand and said, "Allyson Simpson." Tom took her hand and felt the electric moment happen. The first touch, the passage of unexplained energy, went both ways, and suddenly, he could see something happen in her eyes. She softened just a little, but only he knew her well enough to detect it. They pulled up opposite chairs across a well-worn wooden table. Tom remembered all the interrogations they conducted together in this room. He stood for a moment and flipped a hidden switch, turning off the microphones. Bug looked at him with increasing interest.

"Who *are* you?" she asked.

"Someone who knows everything about you and everything about this place and the people in here. I can't explain it to you until I get your confidence and trust. Will you give me a chance?"

"I'll listen without making promises. Talk."

"I'll give you a sample but don't feel threatened, please. I'm on your side more than you could ever know, and I have important information you must have, but you have to trust me first. About Brannigan, his first name is Mike, but everybody, including you, calls him Spike. He was married to Linda but got angry and hit her in the face one day, and she and the kids left for good. He has a sister, Eloise, who works down the street, and they often meet for lunch at Club Sandwich. You know Dick Murphy, Tom Sneed, and Ralph Emory, who are all your friends and who ogle you every time they get the chance. Tom is married to Gloria. She is as fat as he is, and they argue constantly. Dick has two daughters who are bankrupting him with their private schooling. Ralph has a brother in prison and a daughter hooking over in the Broadway area. You love jazz and body lotion. There is a small mole on your left lower abdomen which you keep meaning to have taken off but never get around to it. You take your coffee with cream but never sugar. There was a dog named Cecil that you loved and cried for three days when he died. Your father has a cabin in the lake counties west of here that you all went to every summer, but you haven't been there in eight years. You don't think of yourself as attractive but everybody, especially men, think differently. You love taking showers twice a day, and you never learned to like sushi. Should I go on?"

"No, I feel threatened and invaded. How is it remotely possible that you know all this information? You better have a good answer, or I'll let my big friend throw you out of the window."

"Look, Allyson, I know things about you that only someone could know if they lived with you and loved you. Anyone ever call you Bug?" He watched as her mouth dropped open.

"My father's nickname for me when I was young, an infant. No one has mentioned Bug for many years. How did you know that?"

"I'll tell you something that will shake you up. There is a thing which might be called parallel lives. Someplace in another life, you and I were both detectives. We were partners for three years. You saved my life and I saved yours, and we became best friends, then lovers. I still dream about you. I worked out of this office and among these same people, and I know them as I know you, like the back of my hand. Another item I didn't ask you before, but were you married for awhile to a man named June?"

"Yeah, we divorced recently. You could have read about that."

"No, you told me. It was the final step before we married. That's how I started calling you Bug. You know, 'June Bug.' " That's what I call you in my dreams. Last night you told me that something in you would click when we first met. That I will fill a need within you, just as you do for me. Is there anything happening?"

"I find you interesting but frightening. This is too unreal to believe. Why did you come to see me today?"

"Because I am in love with you, but I understand that it will take some time with us together for you to really see and understand me. There is one other very important thing you have to know. In my other life, Chief Riggs is dirty. He is in contact with the terrorists for some reason, and he marked me for death, because I also wanted to be Chief, and I had a good chance. You and I fled to your father's cabin, and you had to kill one of them there. Another batch of terrorists blew up my apartment over on Twelfth, and you and I decided to get out of town. That's what I was doing on the train. We were leaving together when they showed up on the platform, and you had to kill two of them."

Allyson got up, opened the door and signaled Brannigan. "You still have this guy's card? Go check him out. I want photo ID and everything you can find."

"You will find that I am a Professor of Philosophy and a resident of the state of Connecticut. You won't find that I ever lived here or worked as a detective. It won't explain how I know about eating lunch at Rita's with you almost every day for three years or the times we went out for beers after a hard day. I know that your former husband is gay and that he traveled with his lovers frequently, and you still stayed with him out of duty, not love. Your mother cheated on your father with his best friend which broke his heart and that neither of you attended her funeral when she died. You have never traveled abroad but would like to go to Paris someday. I know that you have never had dance instructions but have dreamed about learning the tango. You almost never use perfume but usually use an expensive French soap, one of your rare extravagances. Your best friend in high school is named Ashley and works as a nurse only a few blocks from here, but you haven't gotten around to seeing her because you are still offended by her 'tomboy' joke that she took too far."

Allyson sat back down and just stared at him. "There was a building on Twelfth hit by two suicide bombers. We never understood why. Did you ever see my father's lodge, by the way?"

"Not inside. We stayed across the lake because we were rightly afraid that they would find us. My leg had been fractured by a terrorist bomb, and I was an invalid at the time. They burned your place while we watched, then came for us. Your friend, Charlie Chuck, arranged our hideaway. He ended up shooting three of them himself."

"That's amazing. No one knows those details except me. Most of that happened, but you weren't there. To be frank, my recollection of the whole event is fuzzy. The more I look at you the more goes on in my head. I don't recognize you, but I find you familiar in some way that I can't put my finger on. It seems that I have a memory of you in some dim way. Is there a Jeanette associated with you?"

"My first wife. She left me after you came into my life. You do remember."

"It's like the memory is just out of grasp, but the more I sit here and look at you, the more I recall. You shot two in the head and a bomb, no two bombs, went off. Did that happen?"

"Yes, over in Flatbush. Afterwards, they attacked the hospital I was in."

"You saved my life that day," she remembered.

"True and you repaid me many times. That was the day we admitted, for the first time, that we loved each other."

The door opened and Brannigan came in with some papers. He gave Tom a dirty look. "The Professor is real. Here's his stuff but obviously something is missing which would explain how he knows so much."

"Come in, Spike, and sit down. Don't speak, just listen," Allyson said. "Go on and tell your story about Riggs, Tom. We will listen." She patted Brannigan's hand to reassure him that it was all right.

"First, I want to know if a Special Agent McMurphy has been in touch with you?" Tom asked.

"That's top secret. How did you find out?" Brannigan said angrily.

"Remember, Spike, I asked you to be quiet," Allyson repeated. "Yes, he has been in touch with us. Just us."

"Agent McMurphy told me that one of his agents saw Riggs do a drop in Central Park, but they couldn't get there in time. I figured that if he is still using the same system, he could choose to do the drop in Gramercy Park which is only two blocks from the Academy. If we catch him with a drop, we have him for sure," Tom said.

"That fits with what we were told. Good thinking about Gramercy. They are still looking at Central. You might be on to something," Allyson said.

"Wait, I'm not buying this guy. Something is fishy, Allyson,"

Brannigan blurted.

"Tom, give this boy the works like you did me," she said.

"Brannigan. You can bench press 223 pounds. I helped spot the first time you did it. Your youngest daughter is twelve, and you affectionately call her 'Cootie'. You had a bulldog that your wife named Little Spike after you because you looked so much alike. You were having frequent oral sex with Veronica, the file clerk, and your wife got wind of it. That's when you stupidly hit her, and she left you. Your attorney's fee was over three thousand, and you lost custody nevertheless. I told you so. You went to high school in Queens and played football until you hurt your right knee. You rose to the rank of corporal in the Army and achieved Expert on your rifle skills. Should I continue or are you stunned yet?"

"Whatthehell! I ought to punch you out," Spike said and clenched his fist.

"Was he right about Veronica? Even I didn't know about that," Allyson asked with a smile and a punch to his shoulder.

"Yeah. Yeah, he's right about all of it."

"Then sit right there and look at him as I did, and he will come back to you. I remember him better and better. You will too."

"Spike, I am the one who asked you to look after Allyson when I was injured and Riggs suspended me. I see that you took it seriously, and I am delighted to see that I was right to trust you. Sorry about the Veronica story, but I was the only one here that knew so I had to use it," Tom said and extended his hand for a shake.

"Did you tell Linda about Veronica?" he said leaving Tom's hand extended in space.

"No, Veronica called Linda herself trying to break up your marriage. I kept my mouth shut."

"How did you know?"

"I guess you don't remember that I walked in on you two and

saw for myself. You and I discussed it later, and I swore to secrecy. I kept my word until now," Tom said. Brannigan slowly reached out and shook his hand.

"I think I do remember something about you now. Tom, is it? You are an expert with a handgun. Is that right?"

"You are getting there, Brannigan. Yes, I am, or was, the best on the force."

Bug was listening with glistening eyes. She suddenly threw her arms around Tom and kissed him hard on the lips. "Oh, Tom. I remember everything. I thought I lost you forever when that door closed and you slowly dimmed out." She kissed him again and again while Spike looked on perplexed. "Where did the door take you?"

"I woke up on the floor in my office in Connecticut with a student standing over me. You should hear my lectures in Philosophy. I'm pretty good!"

"You are never, never getting away from me again. If I had gone first through the door, perhaps we could have gotten away together," Bug said and then kissed his face all over. "The little doctor beard has got to go, you know."

"You have been with me every night in my dreams. Last night you advised me how to act if and when I met you again. You were right about you."

"I finally remember!" Spike said. "You old sonofagun! God, it's great to see you again." He slapped Tom on the back so hard he started coughing.

"Geeze, Spike. Save the hits for the bad guys," Tom sputtered. They did a three way group hug and danced around the room.

"I gotta tell you the truth, Tom. Good thing you came back when you did because this lady was starting to give me the hots. I was always jealous of you and her together."

Tom put his hands on their shoulders and looked serious. "We have to work together in secret to get Riggs. It's our duty as cops and as Americans. You two are the only ones who know that I'm back, and I think that I'll leave the beard on just now, because it might help disguise me. Bug, can you check with the Academy and see if they own a complimentary key to Gramercy Park? If they do, I'll check in at the Gramercy Park Hotel, and we'll start to stake the place out."

"Does that mean that you will still go home with me tonight?" Bug asked with a hopeful pout.

"I was hoping to, Bug."

Chapter 16

Gramercy Park

om was escorted to the park by the hotel representative and watched as the gate was unlocked and locked behind him. He was dressed appropriately for a distinguished professor and wore a grey three-piece suit with red silk tie. His walking cane added to his appearance. He chose a quiet bench and sat down to study the little park. It was fenced with intricate but massive cast iron and had limited access. His prior research discovered that there were only 383 keys to the park in circulation. Assuming that he was correct about Riggs using this little two acre park as a drop, it narrowed the recipient suspects a lot. He reasoned that the pick up party would likely not know when Riggs would drop a message and would have to frequently check the site. This party would therefore have to be a regular and have access. For the moment, Gramercy park had no other visitors, and Tom settled down and thought about his confusing recent past. The evening air was warm and there was good shelter from the sun from the many trees. After a while, he walked to the center of the park to inspect an interesting bronze statue. He was looking at the figure when someone spoke to him from behind.

"Know who that is?" the man asked. Tom turned to see a dapper older man approaching from the rear. He was short, plump and had thick grey hair topping a very wrinkled face but carried himself much like you would expect of a dignitary of some importance.

"I was just getting ready to read the plaque. You know, apparently?"

"Edwin Booth, and the bronze was dedicated on November 13, 1918. He was the brother of John Wilkes Booth, of assassination fame, but was really known for being a great Shakespearean actor." Tom detected a hint of accent from this stranger, but his English was faultless.

"Thank you very much for the enlightenment, sir. Let me introduce myself. I am Professor Tom Chase from Connecticut where I teach Philosophy. And you?"

"Agar Sulliman. I am part of the Lebanese Delegation to the United Nations. I am also a dedicated history buff, and this part of New York is very historical. The list of the famous and rich and important who lived around this little park is long, and if you listen carefully, you can hear the echoes of history."

"A question, Mr. Sulliman," Tom inquired. "Do you live around here?"

"Yes, I own a little piece of number eighteen south. It entitles me to a key, and I find myself, weather permitting, here frequently. I use the quiet time to contemplate the future of the Mideast and how I can help make it better."

"Admirable, sir. And how is that going?

"A struggle which will require many lifetimes. As you probably remember, Lebanon was admired for centuries for its beauty, but now...well, it could be better. Many factions are struggling for their share of a little country, and there are abundant outside forces at play. Once again, Lebanon is but a pawn in a big game and its people suffer."

"As we hear. You seem well-informed, Mr. Sulliman, may I ask if you hold any degrees?" Tom asked.

"My, yes, my new friend. You may call me Agar, sir, if you would give me your first name."

"Tom."

"Thank you, Tom. I have a PhD from Oxford in Political Science, and it has been useful many times in my life. You, Tom, are a philosopher, is that what you said?"

"No, I teach Philosophy. There is a large difference. I attended Yale, by the way."

"Excellent. In your studies, did you become involved in political philosophy at any time?"

"Of course, we studied that, but political thought is a very separate branch of Philosophy and has been sullied over time since Plato."

"True enough. I wonder if you recall the great philosophers of Islam such as al-Kindi or Ibn Sina or even Ibn Khaldun."

"The names seem distantly familiar but, in truth, my education about religious doctrine is scant. I seem to recall that the core of Islamic Philosophy revolved around two concepts: that of the *ijtihad*, or search for the truth, and the Asharite view that reason and truth are subordinate to the Quran. As I understand it, the latter prevailed."

"I am taken back, Tom. Your depth of understanding is greater than most Western scholars. Our problem in Islam, at the moment, is more political than theoretical."

"If I may, Agar, didn't Khaldun, whom you mentioned, state that government should be restrained to a minimum as a necessary evil, and doesn't that differ from the Islamic governments of the present?"

"True, Tom. You impress me more by the moment. But, I will respond by asking you if the founders of the American Constitution would accept your present government?"

"Agar, I would admit they would not. It seems that our world is not presently in its golden period," Tom said.

"It may be wise not to cover our new relationship with the mud of politics, my friend. May I ask why you are in New York and more to the point, why you are in this park at this moment?" Agar asked.

"Unfortunately, I am being treated at Memorial Sloan–Kettering Cancer Center for an unusual tumor. Chemotherapy. I decided to treat myself to a decadent life style while I have time."

"Is the future bleak for you, Tom," Agar asked with feeling.

"There is always hope, Agar. I am hoping to change things while I am here, and the future will be brighter."

"Then, I look forward to our evening discussions, Tom, while you are here. We must have dinner together someday. I want to test your knowledge and perhaps add to it." Agar Sulliman gave a short bow and touched his hat and left the way he came. Tom studied him carefully as he left to see if he looked at any particular place too long but couldn't see anything unusual. After he had disappeared down the outside sidewalk, Tom picked up his phone.

"Bug, I just had an interesting meeting with a fellow who calls himself Agar Sulliman and says that he is attached to the Lebanese Delegation. Ask Agent McMurphy to very discreetly check him out. We sparred a bit, and I'm sure his people will check me out. I told him that I was a patient at Sloan–Kettering so you need to get someone to hack into their system and insert my name in case they inquire."

"I'll get right on it, Tom. Are you staying there for the night or coming here to be with me?" she asked.

"My plan is to sit here until just before dusk and then catch a cab to your place. Acceptable?"

"I'll be waiting anxiously. Good luck over there."

Just as he rang off, there was a click from the other iron gate and a squeak when it opened. He turned to see a small figure carefully closing the heavy gate. Evening was approaching, and the light was fading fast. He watched as the small figure came slowly toward him, and he started to see the outlines of an older woman carefully watching her footsteps. She came directly toward him and smiled as she got close.

"Well, hello there. You are new here, aren't you?" she asked.

"Yes, I'm staying at the hotel and came here to enjoy the park. You know everyone who comes?"

"Not everyone, but I've been around a long time and I come frequently, at all times of day, so I've gotten to know most of them."

"My name is Tom Chase," he said and offered his hand.

"Glad to meet you, Mr. Chase. I am Gladys Furnachi. I live over by the corner," she said and pointed to the north end of the park. "My family has owned that place for over one hundred years, so I'm one of the old timers."

"Have you seen any of the New York Police Force in the park?" Tom asked.

"Odd you should ask that, Mr. Chase. Usually, the only time we see police here is when someone in the area calls them. Lately, we have had Chief Riggs himself visit the park fairly frequently. He doesn't live around here, but the Academy is about two blocks away. We assume that the police have a key so perhaps he uses that one or there might be another reason."

"What would be another reason?" Tom asked.

"The key could have been illegally duplicated. That has happened before, so they change the locks every year and issue new keys. But, since he is the Chief, I haven't seen the harm, so I don't ask any questions."

"How often would you say that he comes here?" Tom asked.

"I don't know, but I have seen him at least five times myself.

Always the same time of day for him, so I probably missed him on days that I came early."

"Can I ask what time of day it was the last time you saw him?"

"About now. Just before dusk when they close the park." She looked around as if expecting him. "Now, about you," she said looking at Tom. "What are you doing here?" She held his eyes, and Tom understood that Gladys Furnachi was the unofficial and self-appointed guardian of Gramercy Park.

"You don't have to worry, Ms. Furnachi. I will be returning to my teaching in Connecticut as soon as my medical treatments are complete. Two more weeks, I'd say."

"No, dear, you can't get away from me that easily. Come on over here, and we'll talk about us and our history until they close the park." She took his sleeve and led him to a nearby park bench, and they sat down together.

"Now tell me where you went to college, dear," she said and patted the back of his hand.

"Yale. Undergrad and grad. Got my doctorate there."

"Nice school. My oldest went there. He was killed in Vietnam, and I never got over it." She paused for a moment, then continued, "So you teach?"

"Philosophy...eight years. I'm head of the department."

"My, my. I went to Dartmouth and studied law. I did not excel at Philosophy. Too far above my head."

"By the way, the Police Academy doesn't have a key for the park," Tom said.

"So, that was why you asked about Chief Riggs, wasn't it. There is more to your being here than by accident."

"Clever as you are, you were bound to figure it out. I actually am what I said, though," Tom said.

Gladys thought for a moment and then said, "I saw Agar Sulliman coming out as I left the house. Meet him?"

"Yes, we talked."

"What did you think?"

"Educated, sophisticated and Arab."

"Too smooth? That's what I thought also. He is here frequently at that time of day. I asked him once if he had met Chief Riggs yet, because they come nearly at the same time. He said no, but the way he said it was funny. Too quick to answer and then seemingly not interested. Strange."

"Ever see either one do something odd?"

"See that trash can over there?" she said and pointed to one just inside of the gate.

"Yes."

"There is something interesting about that can. If I didn't know better, I would think that they both are recycling aluminum cans like a street person."

"Have you ever talked to Chief Riggs?"

"Tried to a couple of times. I thought that he didn't have time for old ladies, but now I'm not sure. He just brushed me off with his artificial smile, like a politician would. I wish I had kicked him out of the park. If he shows up today, I plan to ask him how he got his key."

"Listen, Ms. Furnachi, don't do that just yet, and don't ever say anything about me to him. Will you do that?"

She looked at Tom for a time and said, "Something about you, dear, makes me want to trust you. Can you let me in on what's going on?"

"Someday. Right now, it's better that you just act normally and trust me. You will, won't you?" Tom asked. She patted his hand and nodded to the far gate. Riggs was just coming in.

"Now we'll just talk like we're old friends, and he will ignore us. When he leaves he will go by that trash can and look in, I guarantee it," she whispered.

"I watched Sulliman leave, and he didn't leave by that gate. He wasn't anywhere near that trash can." Tom whispered as Chief Riggs approached.

"You might have scared him off," she said lowly. As Riggs strolled past, they both looked up and smiled to him. Riggs looked back hard at both of them, nodded briefly and strolled past. He continued once around the statue and then left slowly by the other gate and past the notorious trash can. Once there, he stopped briefly to adjust his tie and quickly looked in and then continued to walk to the gate. They could hear the jangle of keys against the gate and then he was gone.

"Told you. That's what always happens. Sometimes he pretends to put something in that trash can, but the way he does it makes it look like he is taking something out."

"There is a chance that he does both or either," Tom said.

"I never thought about that. Do you think they are sending messages to each other?" she asked.

"Looks like it, doesn't it?"

"I thought that gays were out in the open these days. Why don't they just hold hands like all the others do and dispense with all this mystery?" she asked rather loudly.

"I really don't know. Perhaps they are both married." Tom said very seriously.

"Are you really getting medical care, Tom?"

"No, that's just a cover story. I'm actually a college professor, though."

"Then why is a college professor from Connecticut chasing gays in New York?"

"Gladys, you said that you trusted me. Don't ask that just now. They likely aren't gay anyway."

"This is pretty exciting, Tom. You'll be here tomorrow then?" she asked.

"Same time, Gladys. We'll talk some more. Meanwhile, don't tell anybody anything. Okay?"

"Okay, partner!"

Tom tapped lightly at the door and listened for footsteps. Suddenly, the door was opened, and Bug flung herself into his arms, wrapping herself around him and burying his face in hers. He walked in holding her around the waist and kicked the door shut behind him. She slid to the floor laughing and gave him one last squeeze around the waist before pushing away to look at him again.

"I just can't get over it, Tom. You are here with me, but I remember a life without you and with you. I thought about it all day, and I don't understand at all. It's like losing my mind. I thought for a while that I imagined you, and you weren't coming tonight. That's why I am so elated to see you just now."

"For once, someone understands what my life has been like. I was a cop, then I was never a cop, and now am I both? I don't get it either. I remember more than just those two. There are two more lives that I recall in full, and there are lifelike dreams almost every night. That means I'm not crazy if you aren't, and you don't look crazy, just appealing." He bent over and kissed her on the forehead and worked down to her mouth. "It doesn't matter to me if I'm crazy. I have you again, and that's all I want in life."

"I remember working with you for years, but then I remember being without you and not even knowing who you are. Let me ask you this, Tom. Are you a cop?"

"The answer is technically, no. I don't have a badge and am not in the system. Everything about me appears to confirm that I am actually a college professor. Tell you what, give me your gun and let me find out if I know anything about guns." She reached behind her and handed him her sidearm, a 9mm Beretta. Tom took it and hefted it, turning it over and over. He pulled back the slide ejecting the round then released the magazine. He flipped the safety on and off and then released the slide, disassembling the gun. He put the parts back together quickly and handed it back.

"Well, it seems I know about this one. Now if I knew that I could hit a target, I would feel better," he said.

"Try this," Bug said and pointed across the room. Without understanding what she meant, he pointed also. "Now close one eye at a time and find out if you have a trained eye or not." He did and discovered that one eye was accurately aligned with his finger. The target eye. He had forgotten about that trick. Indeed, he remembered how to shoot after all.

"Riggs was there, and he looked in a trash can for a drop which wasn't there. They are communicating in both directions. His contact is that Sulliman I told you about. Any news about him?" Tom asked.

"Agent McMurphy didn't know about him, but he was taking it to the CIA tonight. We'll know tomorrow. No more Riggs talk, Tom. I have plans for how I want to spend the evening and night. Rested up?"

Tom woke up and reached behind him. She was there, all right, just as she was when he drifted off. She stirred as his hand touched her thigh, and she snuggled closer.

"Get any rest?" she asked. He couldn't see her face, but he could feel her warm smile in her voice. He turned over toward her and they embraced.

"Isn't it nice to have me back?" she asked.

"Wonderful. Better than a dream," he said sleepily.

"I resent that," she mocked and smiled. He could barely see her face in the scant light, but he could see the smile lines on the side that was up.

"I don't understand, Bug."

"I was very good to you in your dreams, didn't you think? I made you happy, you told me," she said.

"Yes, the real thing is just better, that's all."

"One thing you should know, Tom. I'll be expecting you to tell me what you are going to do next. Are you staying here or going back to Connecticut? And what do you expect me to do?" Tom noticed that she used I'll be rather than I am. It was an odd way to phrase the question. It made him wonder for a moment, but then he took his hand and swept her contours and felt the temperature change from spot to spot, and when he pressed against her back, he felt her exhale slightly. She was as real as he was. He kissed her gently on the cheek and caressed her hair.

"I haven't thought that far forward, Bug. I guess I have to ask what you want to do and what you want me to do."

"Yes, you will." Her question opened his eyes wider. He put his nose in her hair and inhaled. It was Bug, no question.

"I am waiting to hear your views, Bug. I will do anything I have to do to stay with you."

"Me? I want to stay right here in your arms. That's all I ever want. I am happy all the way through. You'll still have to ask me in the morning."

"Am I dreaming, Bug. This whole thing is a big dream. I really don't have you back?" He could feel his pulse climbing, and he started to feel hot.

"I'm back. Don't I feel real to you? It's just that you have to ask me when you awaken." Tom started to get up and think this out. He was starting to be confused. Was anything real? He felt that he wanted to splash some cold water in his face, see if he could feel it.

Something was shaking him, and he slowly opened his eyes. Bug was right beside him in bed and smiling at him. "Were you having a bad dream, Tom? You were talking in your sleep. It's time to get up, we are going to have a big day." Bug leaned over and kissed him on the mouth, and he felt her warmth radiate through him. His eyes were open, and the world slowly came back.

"You are real after all!" he said. "I actually have you back!" He threw his arms around her and pulled tight.

"Yes, Tom, I'm real and that makes it hard to breath. If you don't want to be punched, relax a little."

"Did I ask you what you want to do now that I'm back?" he asked.

"We haven't gotten past the tearing off clothes part, but I would like you to ask that question."

"Didn't I just ask you that?"

"Not yet. Are you asking me now?" Bug said.

"Yes, Bug, what do you want to do now that I'm back?"

"The way I understand it, you were a cop but aren't a cop, or something like that. You are a college professor who was a cop, or something like that. All I know is that I'm a cop and I'm in love with whatever you are. Where you go, I go."

"Simple enough, Bug. Let's get Riggs, then see what happens. I feel the same. I want to be with you, and that's all I want."

"Is Brannigan coming over here this morning, Bug?"

"Anytime. I expect he'll have some news for us. By the way, who did you dream about last night?"

"You and only you. I couldn't tell if I was asleep or awake. For the first time you were in both places and always in my arms." There was a loud knock at the door and Bug got up and unlocked it, admitting Brannigan who was smiling broadly.

"Morning, guys. Did either of you get any sleep?" he said with a laugh and looked back and forth at each of them to see their response.

"News for us, Spike?"

"No sense of humor. That means that you didn't get any sleep. Yeah, good thing that we hacked the hospital database, because last night someone did the same thing looking for you, Tom. They found the dummy file so they should think your a legit patient. The CIA reported to our FBI man that Sulliman was always suspected of being connected to Hezbollah. He is linked to arms shipments, and his family is worth as much as anyone in the Mideast. He's likely our man. One more thing. The CIA took a look at Riggs and checked his background. Looks like some of his documents are fake, and it goes way back to his childhood. More on that later."

"Well, my trip to the park wasn't wasted. The characters Sulliman and Riggs are doing drops there on a regular basis, and I think it's a two-way. Now that they have checked me out, they might continue to use the park for a while. It's our chance to catch Riggs and maybe Sulliman also," Tom said.

"If you plan to single-handedly bring them down, Tom, you aren't thinking straight. You aren't even a cop, and you don't have a gun. Riggs has both," Bug observed.

Brannigan scratched his head and took off his cap. "It depends on what they are passing. A laundry list wouldn't put them in prison. It would have to be something that would tie them to terrorists. You have to get a look at what they are dropping before we can act."

"Photo surveillance would be helpful also. Spike, can you get the Feds to help plant a camera?" Tom asked. Brannigan nodded and picked up his telephone.

While Brannigan was busy, Bug pulled at Tom's sleeve and whispered, "I have an extra pistol and holster. You need to wear it next time you enter the park. Riggs wouldn't hesitate to shoot you if he finds out what you are doing."

"And I would love an excuse to shoot him. I have an advantage this time. He doesn't even know that I'm alive."

"It worked out perfectly, didn't it. Almost as if you had dreamed all this up," Bug said.

"Yes," Tom answered, then looked far away as he stroked his beard. Was this a dream? No, he thought, last night was a dream and then he woke up. This is real and he could really get killed if he wasn't careful. Better take it seriously and be alert.

Brannigan put down the phone. "Yes, they are going to do it this morning. No problem. They want proof before any arrest, because they never got any real evidence on Riggs. All they have is suspicion, so far.

Chapter 17

Spycraft

om sat down on the park bench and waited. He squinted at the statue but couldn't make out the camera which reportedly had been installed on the top of the bronze head. There were no other current visitors and the sounds of traffic came mixed with calls of songbirds. Before Tom sat down, he carefully inspected the contents of the trash can by the gate. He tried to memorize what was there so he could spot anything new. Sulliman was right about this being a nice and historic park. Tom brought the guidebook from his hotel and studied the history of the area while he waited. Gramercy Park was founded in the 1830s and was an early attempt at city planning. The area has remained exclusive since its inception. Because it was originally a swamp, the height of buildings has always been restricted, which adds to the flavor of the scenery. Tom's hotel dated from 1925 but had been remodeled and maintained carefully. He looked at the long list of former residents around the park, and many of the names were famous like Edwin Booth, Tom Edison, Booth Tarkington, Jimmy Cagney, John Barrymore and Daniel French, the Lincoln sculptor. He looked around, lost in history, until he heard a distant click and squeak of a heavy iron gate. Agar Sulliman was making his way toward Tom in his slow deliberate fashion. He was dressed, as yesterday, in an expensive, tailored suit made from fine bold grey wool interspersed with white threads. He gave Tom a polite little wave of acknowledgment.

"I hope your treatments are going well, my new friend," he said and extended his hand. Tom stood, shook with him, and they sat down together. Sulliman noticed Tom's guidebook and said, "You are catching up, aren't you? I hoped that I had stimulated your interest in this place."

"I fully credit you, Agar. Thanks for giving me incentive. It's never a good feeling to be ignorant of the world around you. And how are things at the U.N.?"

"Politics, Tom, politics. Factions who hate each other and pretend to cooperate. The whole structure is a house of cards or as Faulkner would say, 'Full of sound and fury, signifying nothing.' "

"Do you, as a politician, have goals that you aspire to, Agar?"

"Peace. That's all I want. People should be able to live and make money and children and worship *Allah*.

"That sounds slightly different from the American version, 'Life, liberty and the pursuit of happiness.' "

"You Westerners, especially Americans, have put religion out of politics. We Muslims cannot separate our faith and our politics. It guides us in everything in life."

"That means that your Imam is the channel through which *Allah* speaks and directs your life?"

"That is comparable to your Pope, is it not?" Agar asked.

"The modern Pope speaks to the way people live and conduct themselves but has little voice in politics. This is very different, Agar, and fundamental."

"Is this your faith, Tom?"

"No, Agar. I am a man of the world. I claim no faith, and I object to none."

"In the Muslim world, you are still an infidel, you know," Agar said and patted him on the shoulder as if to console him.

"No doubt I am viewed as that in both camps, but I have conducted my life with malice to none, and now that I am nearly at the end of it, I can say that I never persecuted anyone in the name of religion."

"At least that is somewhat redeeming in the eyes of *Allah* when Judgment Day arrives," Agar said.

"Can you say that, Agar?"

"I'm afraid that I am directed by my faith which teaches that Muhammad is the only prophet." There was a click of a distant gate, and they both looked up to see the crouched familiar slow figure moving toward them. Agar sighed deeply and struggled to his feet. "I must go, my friend. This is a person who has stronger opinions than even I do, and I have learned to avoid her. It is nearly time for evening prayers and so I will bid you farewell. Will you be here tomorrow?"

"I would like to be, and I will try, especially if we can continue our conversations, Agar. Until then I bid you *as-salamu `alaykum*," Tom said and stood and offered his hand.

"Most gracious of you, Tom. See you then, *Insha'Allah*." He turned his back to Gladys Furnachi and strolled toward the gate, pausing to toss something into the nearby trash can.

"Chase him off, didn't I?" Gladys chuckled. "Good riddance. Did you see him throw something into the trash, just like I said?"

"Yes, he did," Tom said.

"Don't you think you should go see what it is?"

Tom was silent for a time, then said, "No, Gladys. He might want me to pick it up. It might be a test to see if I am what I claim to be. We'll let that one go."

"Are you going to shoot him someday, Chase?"

"Now, dear, you know that I'm not a policeman, only a college professor, and my kind of people don't shoot other people." He patted her withered hand and smiled down at her. He could see a pout forming, just like she probably did when she was three.

"Then, what are you here for?" she demanded.

"I am enjoying the park with my new friend, Gladys Furnachi. Isn't that enough?"

"Tell me about yourself, Chase. Any women in your life?"

"I've had a couple, and yes, there is one now who is important to me."

"Then why aren't you married or is your relationship with her strictly sex?"

"Gladys, you are forward, aren't you. I'm beginning to see why Sulliman fled when he saw you. To answer your question, though, I am planning to marry her as soon as I can. I just found her again after a long separation."

"How long a separation?" she asked and looked steadily at him with her faded blue eyes. Just as Tom was struggling with formulating an answer that she might understand, there was another click from a distant gate.

"Right on time. That'll be Chief Riggs. You watch him, sonny. He's going to go to that trash can before he leaves," Gladys said and thumped her cane into the gravel for emphasis.

"Listen, Gladys, try not to look at him. Pay no attention. We will look at each other and talk and ignore him. I don't want him to think that we have a care in the world about what he does."

"Then you can talk to me about your women. That'll keep my interest. Why did you lose the first one?" As they turned to face each other, they could hear the footsteps of Riggs in the loose gravel of the path. He walked past them and around the circle of the statue and slowly made his way toward the gate and trash can.

"I can see him, Chase. Want to know what he's doing right now?"

"What, Gladys?"

"He's leaning over the trash can and looking at us under his shoulder. I can see his eyes."

"Stop looking, Gladys. You don't want him to see you interested. Look at my face," Tom commanded. Gladys looked closely at him as he requested.

"We could have had a grand time in bed if I were younger, Chase," she said dryly. Tom could hear the key in the gate as Riggs left. Tom sat up slowly and methodically, looked at the perimeter fence, trying to act casual. In the distance, and on the outside sidewalk, there was someone looking into the park. Riggs. He was observing them for interest in the trash can. Tom realized that his instinct was correct. This time they were being tested.

"Thanks for the compliment, Gladys. I guess we will never find out if that would have worked, will we?

"Aren't you going to look in the trash can, Chase?" Gladys asked impatiently.

"Not tonight. They were checking us out. There would be nothing of interest in there. Don't you go look either. Those two are very dangerous. I want you to behave yourself."

"At my age, there isn't anything else I can do but behave, Chase. But if we would have met when I was your age. Fireworks."

After saying goodnight to Gladys and walking her to the street, Tom thought it wise to return to his expensive hotel suite at the Gramercy. He stopped by at one of the hotel's bars and had a cocktail. No one seemed interested, so he quietly took in his lavish surroundings. There was an abstract painting of some size at the end of the bar, and while he gazed at it, lost in thought, he felt a tap on his shoulder.

"I seem to know you from somewhere," Riggs said. He was standing at Tom's shoulder and had a puzzled but offensive look about him. Tom swiveled on his stool and turned to face him.

"Not that I can recall. Just who are you?" Tom asked.

"You have been in the park for two days. What were you doing there?" Riggs asked.

"Not that I can see that it's your business, but I also saw you there for two days. What were you doing there?" Tom asked in retort.

"I happen to be Chief Riggs of the NYPD. I get to ask all the questions."

"You were in the park, I assume, on official police business. How did you get access, I wonder? I had to pay for mine." Riggs started coloring and stepped back in anger.

"I asked you a question, and if you don't answer me, I'll have you hauled in for questioning."

"I am Professor Chase of Connecticut. Here is my card. If you are in need of philosophy counseling, I am your man. Otherwise, go away."

"Your face looks familiar, have you been in New York previously?"

"Never. I've only been here for four days. Perhaps we've met in Connecticut? Now, it's your turn, Riggs. How do you have access to a restricted park?"

Riggs sputtered in anger, threw Tom's card on the floor, and stalked out. Tom called to him just before he left the room, "See you tomorrow, Riggs." He regretted making a scene, and it might make the task of nailing Riggs more difficult, but he couldn't step away from his hate. After all, Riggs had tried on several occasions to have him and Bug killed.

Tom dialed Bug, and she picked up right away. "Hi, sweetheart. I'm headed that way in a moment, but I just had a confrontation with Riggs in a bar. He's suspicious and thinks he knows me. He just can't remember, but I predict as he churns it over, some of his memory will return.

"Wow, Tom, that's not a good way to be secretive! I have some company here, and we all are waiting on you. Some interesting findings," Bug said.

Chapter 18

Preparing for The Drop

om, I have some interesting news!" Spike said excitedly into Tom's ear as soon as the door opened.

"A moment, please," Tom said and scooped up Bug in his arms, kissing her with passion. "Have I told you in the last minute or so how much I love you?"

"No, dearest, I am waiting," she whispered in his ear.

"I love you, my little Bug, and I am so happy I found you."

"Now can we get to brass tacks?" Spike asked impatiently. "You two have all night."

Tom looked past Spike's large shoulders and saw an unfamiliar face seated on the couch with his laptop opened. He let Bug slide gently to the floor and walked into the room.

"Tom, this is Andrew. He's CIA, and you remember Agent McMurphy over there, don't you?"

McMurphy got up looking puzzled. "I'm supposed to remember you but I don't," he said and shook Tom's hand.

"Give it a moment, Agent McMurphy, you will," Bug said.

Tom gave them both a little wave and said, "What's this all about?"

"We were watching you and Riggs in the park live. Andrew has some comments you'll want to hear," McMurphy said.

Andrew cleared his throat to get attention and twisted the laptop around so that they all could see. "They asked me to look at this, because I have a lot of experience with this sort of drop. First, the two you are interested in are more experienced than you knew. This is a case of 'Duel Drop,' meaning it's more complex than you thought. On observation, and at first glance, it appears that they are using a two-way method involving a singular trash can. It didn't happen that way. They are just good enough to make it look like the trash can was the drop site. Look at this clip." The camera zoomed on Sulliman as he came through a gate. His hand came up to the lock in a casual manner just before the gate swung closed. The maneuver looked natural, as if he had steadied himself when the heavy gate began swinging. Tom looked at Spike and at Agent McMurphy.

"I didn't see anything. Did I miss something?" he said.

"Now watch this," Andrew said and started another video. This time it was Riggs in the close up. He left by the same gate as Sulliman and did the exact same thing with his hand.

"I must be dumb, fellows," Tom admitted. "I don't see anything."

"It's all right, Tom. I had to watch it a dozen times before it clicked," Spike said.

"There is another angle from a different camera. The thing to know is what they are leaving is a small memory chip, like the kind that fits in a modern camera. The object is only two centimeters across and black. Watch closely now," Andrew said and started another video. This one was from a camera entirely different, and the magnification showed only the hands and metal gate in the visual field. This time, Tom saw a glimpse of a very small object being placed on the underside of the lock. It adhered with a brief touch and came off into Riggs' hand just as quickly.

"Well, I just learned that I am an amateur at the spy game. That's amazing. Say, you people were lavish with the cameras, but it sure paid off," Tom said.

"Andrew is the expert. We may not have spotted the drop except for his skills. As for the cameras, it's better to have overkill than miss something," Agent McMurphy said.

"You all have to know that Riggs followed me back to my hotel and had a confrontation with me. We had some back and to, and he left angry. It's only a question of time until he recognizes that he has seen me previously. I predict another swarm of terrorists intent on blowing me up when he remembers."

"He's going to check you out first. When he finds that you have a history in another state, he might not connect you in time to prevent being caught," Agent McMurphy said.

"Tom, don't you think someone else should go to the park? I'm worried now that he has seen you up close," Bug said.

"No. I have to do it. Someone new would definitely be suspicious. Both of them have checked me out, and they think that they know all about me. Besides, I have to get Riggs myself, it's important to me."

Agent McMurphy stood and looked around the room. "Here is what I think should be the next step. Tom, you are going to be in the park tomorrow, just as always. We will be nearby in a van monitoring the cameras. If they do a drop, we will buzz your phone once, just once, and that is the signal for you to go retrieve the chip. I have a device that you will use to download data on the chip in under three-seconds and then you just have to stick it back under the lock and sit down like nothing happened. Simple, yes?"

"Does the chip reader send the data to you in the van?" Tom asked.

"Even better, it sends it to FBI headquarters, and the computer team there will decode it and send the results right to me. Might only take a few minutes. If we find incriminating evidence, we will buzz your phone twice."

"Then it's all settled. What if the results confirm that both are involved in a conspiracy with terrorists?" Tom asked.

"We'll round them up on the spot and take them both in for intensive interrogation. If we can't get what we want out of them, we give them to the CIA who guarantees results," McMurphy said. They all shook hands, agreed to meet later in the afternoon tomorrow and were shown to the door by Bug.

"Alone at last!" Bug said and smiled impishly. She took Tom by the sleeve and led him to the couch. "Sit and talk. We have lots to discuss."

"First, a kiss or two, perhaps more. Then we talk," Tom suggested.

"Talk first. Then we have the entire night without interruptions." She raised her eyebrow and seemed resolute. "All right, I'll start. Whatever happens tomorrow, we have to make plans for the future. If Riggs is jailed, can you still be Chief of Police and live in New York?"

"Before I got on the train, that would have happened, but this seems, in part, to be a different reality. I am a tenured college professor, not a cop and not even a New Yorker. I don't see how I can even be considered. Everything has changed."

"That's my next question. What do we do now?" Bug asked. Her face reflected some apprehension, and she looked somewhat lost. Tom settled back and thought about her question. He wanted to be with her more than have all the money and power in the world. Nothing else mattered to him, and her happiness was something he had to preserve to keep her.

"I have few options, really," Tom said. "One is that we both go back to Connecticut. I have a good paying job and local respect. We can buy a house, have a family and live our lives. The other option is that I'm willing to do anything it takes to make you mine, and all you have to do is ask me."

"That sounds like what we should do, Tom. I'm willing to give up New York to be with you, and I'm willing to be the mother of your children."

"Then there is only one remaining question, Bug. Will you marry me?"

She pulled him down toward her as she slid backwards on the couch and held his face in her hands. "Of course, I will marry you. I love you as much as you love me."

Tom picked her up and carried her to the bed and carefully laid her down and stood for a moment just taking her in. She was so lovely and girl-like the way she looked back at him with her hand listlessly draped above her brow.

"Tom, can you explain what happened to you and us? It's confusing that I seem to know life with you and without you. How can that be possible?"

"My whole existence is a mystery to me. I come and go helplessly through a life which seems to be a dream, and dreams which seem to be real. It's as if everything has been written on a hidden tablet by some unseen force. Call it destiny, perhaps. I believe my life has been hammered and shaped to form a sharp-pointed spear leading up to this moment with you. Being with you seems to be the end point, a final destination, and nothing else matters or has ever mattered." Bug beckoned to him with arms extended and tears in her eyes.

Jeanette tossed her long red hair over her shoulder with a slight jerk of her head and half-turned toward him. She was wearing a long red sequined gown, low cut in front and back and complimented by a dazzling diamond in her hair. The pose she struck with her hand on her hip was good enough for a magazine cover. Her alluring pout was enhanced by her glossy red lips, and when she turned the spotlight of her green eyes on him, something deep in his brain wakened like a sleeping monster and stirred. She walked toward him with a slight sway so familiar and yet so provoking, her preceding perfume enveloping him, penetrating some primal area that men try in vain to civilize.

"All I have to do is touch you, and you will be set on fire," she said in a murmured voice and then moved close enough that he could feel the warmth of her body, nearly but not quite touching him with her breasts. Tom felt the hair on the back of his neck quiver, and he felt his face flush.

"Yes, Jeanette. You could always do that. I have been forever helpless to resist you when you wanted me to notice. Why would you do this after you have forsaken me?" In some distant room a band was playing and the sound of the instruments and singer drifted in like little echoing waves of surf, advancing and receding but always there.

Only you…you are for me
It's you…waiting for me
No matter how far I go
You wait for me
It makes my life complete just to think of you

"I felt lost without you. You wouldn't come back to me, and I had to try to make my life over, discovering that there was never anyone that would love me like you did, Tom. I need you to complete my life, because without you it seems to be a hollow dream." She moved closer, and for a moment, he thought she was going to kiss him. He leaned forward to accept her face against his, but at the last moment, she pulled away, leaving the fragrance of her lipstick coursing through his nose. He urged his body to resist until his thoughts returned clearly, but the memory of her moving against him only separated by a thin film of sweat welled up and seized him in a steel vise of passion. She moved away and turned slowly in a small circle. Her animal curves reached out and forced his eyes to penetrate her clothing, seeing her once again in her marvelous perfection. A symphony of skin blended with subtle shades of color, shadow and motion dimmed as her green eyes came around and held him captive in their depths.

> *Endless days and nights*
> *I think of you…starving for you*
> *And when this torture is through*
> *I'll make love to you*
> *Be by your side, endlessly*

"You like seeing me again, Tom?"

"You know that I do. Once again, I am stunned by you."

"How do I compare to her, Tom?"

"You realize that I'm in love with Bug. Love is a form of passion, and she makes me feel like my life has meaning as well."

"Do you want me, Tom? All you have to do is to want me."

"Those moments when we joined and held each other so tenderly that we felt that we became one being instead of two are still in my mind. I could never experience such intensity as that again. You are the physical perfection that can only be created by God. I have not forgotten you, Jeanette."

"Wouldn't you rather be with me than anyone else, Tom?"

"If I could return to what we had, the answer would have to be yes. I loved you beyond my capacity to tell you or to demonstrate it to you. After all, I am only an imperfect being full of changing emotions. But, life has taken us down different paths. Some we chose and some we fell into or walked through without understanding, but we can't ever go back into the room we left behind. You know this, Jeanette."

Just as the last waves of music left the room in silence, she moved toward him and reached out and touched across his lips with her index finger. "Can you be so sure you have left me, Tom? One fine day you might wake up to find me back beside you, and that is the moment that I live for. I won't leave you ever again once you come back, and you will come back."

Something was pulling him upward from a depth, some cavern of the earth, and the light grew as he ascended, breathless. Her lips were on his and her bodily flavors poured over him, covering his soul and his willingness to resist her.

Bug's kiss was wet and full, and Tom opened his eyes to see her's floating like indistinct blue orbs on some distant horizon. "Good morning, Tom! I love you," she said and buried her head against his neck, covering his lips and nose with her fragrant blonde hair. He put his hand on the small of her back and found it warm, contrasting the coolness of her buttocks. As she turned, he felt her muscles tighten and relax, covered by her perfect, seamless skin. How could he dream of a woman more desirable than this? Wrapping her in his arms in utter happiness, all thoughts, other than her, faded into nothingness. He wished he could lie there with Bug forever, but the thoughts of the present crept in, followed by a relentless flood of fear and doubt, crashing into his mind like a rogue wave.

Tom patted her bare buttocks and said, "Time to get up and start planning. This is the day that it will all come together or fall apart. Something about this day is important, inevitable and ordained. I dread it like the imagined monster hiding in an odious dark cave. It's not the fear of death, it's the fear that we will be separated like last time. My fear that we will not have another night like last night churns my insides."

"I'm afraid for you, afraid for both of us, Tom. But, we aren't going to let Riggs take away something beautiful from us. We aren't going to let evil win over goodness. He had his chance to kill us, now it's our turn."

"I'm not going into the park today without a weapon. If Riggs' memory comes back, he won't hesitate to shoot me, and he would probably get by with it. This time, he's not getting out of the park to unleash his dogs on us again."

"Remember, Tom, that you have to have a reason to shoot, or you will have the law against you. We don't want to be running from the law, so I want you to be levelheaded when the time comes."

The time drew close and then became the moment to leave. Tom checked his watch one last time, then removed the Beretta from his shoulder holster, pulled the slide back to release a cartridge into the chamber, and snapped the safety on. He adjusted his silk tie and dusted off his jacket. A quick pat over his pocket found that the card reader hadn't moved. He was ready. Tom dialed Bug's number. "Hi, leaving now," he said, then opened the door of his hotel suite.

As he approached Gramercy Park, he couldn't detect any visitors. He made a point to enter the same gate which was being used by Riggs and Sulliman, and as he passed through, he quickly felt for the area which would contain the chip. It was bare, for the moment, and he continued down the path toward the center of the park dominated by the bronze casting of Booth. Since no one was present, he seated himself on his now familiar bench and pulled out a small book of the history of New York, pretending to read, while being alert to his surroundings. In the distance, he could just see a glint from the windshield of the van containing video monitors and Bug. He tried to imagine what the inside of the van looked like, but it was no use because all he could think of was Bug and the way she looked when they parted. She had held him by his hips and looked into his eyes without speaking. There was really nothing more to say to each other which hadn't been either said out loud or by exchanged glances. Her face was imprinted in his mind for all time and could never rust away or deteriorate. This moment was his to keep eternally, and he would keep her just as she was at that instant, full of love and selflessness. *Oh, Bug. To be separated for an instant is torture, forever is death.*

While an erratic and puffy wind played in the trees masking its sounds, the city hovered outside like a sleeping mountain leaving the nest of the park encapsulated in its fist. The distant click of a gate came to him as an electric jolt. The adventure was about to begin.

Chapter 19

A Drop Into The Abyss

Ah, my friend, Tom. I have looked forward to this moment most of the day," Sulliman said. Tom rose, and they shook hands, using both hands in a sincere clasp while smiling at each other like lost relatives.

"As did I, Agar. We can resume fixing the world and its problems, can we not?" Tom responded.

"We must be honest with each other, Tom, and I want to confess something to you." Tom expectantly waited not knowing what was coming next. His mind raced with possibilities.

"It was necessary for me to turn your name over to my security personnel. This age we live in, you know. They checked and found out that you are exactly what you told me," Agar said, unsmiling and serious.

"Well, I'm also glad that I am what I thought I was. It's a relief to be reassured by experts," Tom said with a laugh.

"One problem remains, however," Agar said. "Your records only include your educational history. Your family history and life prior to college was not found. They seem to think that this is a problem. So, my first question for tonight is...who are you, Tom Chase?"

"Who do you think I am, Agar?" Tom asked.

"I'm not sure, Tom. There is more to you than meets my eye. I come from a troubled part of the globe, and we have had to learn not to trust too far. You recall the *Doveryai no Proveryai*, Trust but Verify, proverb of the Russians. A good motto."

"You understand that it works both ways. I have not had any background checks run on you. Little matter that I don't have the ability to do it. I had no reason to for I accept you as a civilized, well-read and intelligent companion as long as our friendship lasts. Fear not, Agar, because I have nothing to hide. I am not from an intelligence agency or from the police. As you know, I am a simple college professor who has a terminal illness. The few times I have been abroad were for speeches I gave regarding Philosophy. More importantly, if I could have my wishes granted, I would wish that your part of the world would learn to live in peace."

"You still, my friend Tom, have not addressed the question that I asked so politely."

"Agar, I had to change my last name to avoid ill will generated by my father's sex crimes. You need to know no more than that. It's a subject which is off limits."

"Well, I am most satisfied by your answer, and I will put the question out of my mind. My sympathy is with you and your family. Now we can get back to our far-reaching topics." Agar smiled and gave a slight tip of his hat.

"Now, perhaps I can impose a difficult question on you," Tom said. "In your conflicted country, how do you avoid being drawn into pursuing the interests of one faction over another? I guess my question would be better asked as how do you represent the people in your country against the wishes of belligerent neighbors?"

"A difficult question. The simple answer is that you cannot avoid the pressures of ends justifying means. To exist, you have to choose sides."

"And which side are you on, Agar?"

"That's easy, Tom. I am on my side."

"I understand. Here is an observation from a philosopher, if you will. This America that we admire so much has a very short temper and, once angered, responds with overwhelming violence. Just examine our history. So many times, we have been misjudged, because we are tolerant and peaceful by nature, and our enemies always forget that we have killed millions and will kill again if provoked."

"Your point, Tom?"

"Be careful not to awaken the sleeping beast, Agar."

"No, no, Tom. I intend to leave a very small footprint while I am here. I want to make no waves, no loud noise, and hopefully escape being seen at all."

"Others that you trust could make loud noises on your behalf, and the spotlight will turn toward you."

"I only act as a go between. I have never personally been responsible for any harm to anyone. My hands are clean."

"In a rifle, the trigger fires the shot, but the spring makes it possible. They are part of the same unit and cannot be separated as to their actions." When Tom paused, he saw that Agar became beaded with sweat and looked uncomfortable. He appeared agitated and looked around as if expecting someone or something to start chasing him. The clank of the far gate echoed in the moving air like the piercing call of a dragon master, and Agar jumped to his feet.

"It is time for me to leave, Tom. This meeting has been most enlightening for me and has clarified the air I breathe. I don't believe that we will meet again, but I can say to you that you would be a most worthy opponent in any game of intellect. There are events which may require me to soon return to my home country in haste. We depart friends and soul mates, and I earnestly can say that you are entitled to my respect. May we meet again."

Tom slowly rose to his feet and extended his hand, "My regards,

Agar Sulliman. We shall meet again, I'm sure." He remained standing as Agar made his way to the drop site at the north gate. Agar gave one last look over his shoulder toward Tom and closed the gate behind him with a clank. Tom's phone buzzed once.

"Salutations, Chase. Did I run that Sulliman off again? Good riddance, I say," Gladys said with a chuckle as she slowly neared their bench.

"Greetings to you, Gladys. Why don't you sit here and wait just a moment for me," he said as he patted the seat beside him. After Gladys sat down, Tom found his card reader and hurried to the gate. The memory card was just where he expected and the slightest touch caused it to come away into his hand. As instructed, he inserted the card and watched the red LED appear and quickly go out. He unplugged the card and positioned it back under the lock. It wouldn't adhere and fell off. He tried again with the same result and then looked more carefully at the card. There was a thin film of adhesive which had been dislodged by the card reader. He attempted to move it back into position as he heard another click in the distance. Riggs was early. He had no choice but to pocket the card and regain his seat before Riggs could see him by the gate.

"Gladys, make no eye contact with him. Just watch me, dear."

"I like watching you, Chase. I wish you would watch me just as intently," she said. They could hear footsteps on the gravel path getting closer. Tom quickly adjusted his jacket so that his weapon could be quickly drawn.

"What do you want to discuss, Chase? I suggest sex, a most interesting subject," Gladys suggested enthusiastically.

Tom's hair started tingling as Riggs approached, and he tried not to look that direction. "Sure, Gladys. What about sex?" he asked.

"Here in spite of my warnings?" Riggs said as he approached.

Tom looked up, and they made eye contact. Riggs was searching Tom's face, seemingly trying to recall any memory of him. There was something about Tom that riveted his attention. Even though neither moved, there was a sensation of two wolves with yellow, narrowed eyes circling each other, waiting for an opening.

"Chief Riggs," Gladys croaked, "How do you get access to this private park? I see no police business for you here, so unless you have an apartment nearby or are staying at the hotel, you need to leave right now, or I'll have you ejected by force." She stood up, all five feet of her, and glowered as threateningly as it was possible for a short, older woman to glower. Riggs ignored her and moved closer to Tom.

"I should search you, Chase. There is something about you I don't like."

"Go ahead, Riggs. I would like you to try to search me so that I can break your arm."

Riggs opened his coat so that Tom could see his weapon hanging under his shoulder. Tom didn't move or blink and remained seated. Riggs obviously could see an implied threat in Tom's eyes. He could tell that Tom would react suddenly and with violence, and he decided that it wasn't worth the risk. He walked slowly away keeping his eyes on Tom for as long as possible. As usual, Riggs walked around the statue and headed toward the north gate. Tom held his breath when Riggs' hand went to the lock area. Riggs froze for a moment with his hand under the lock and looked back at Tom. He knew. At the same moment, Tom's phone buzzed twice, the signal that the data had been decoded and was sufficient for an arrest.

"Chase!" he called from the gate. "You have something of mine, and I want it back!" Riggs pulled his handgun from under his jacket and started toward Tom and Gladys. In the distance, they could hear faint sirens drawing closer, and Riggs stopped and looked around.

"You are finished, Riggs. Give up now. Put down the gun,"

Tom commanded. Instead, Riggs threw open the gate and took off at a run, crossing the street without looking back. Tom got up to follow and tried to sprint toward the gate, not remembering his bad right leg. He pulled up in pain for a moment, but then clenched his teeth and forced himself to run after the figure growing smaller in the distance. Riggs rounded the next corner heading toward Park Avenue. Tom remembered a subway stop only two blocks away. Riggs had to be headed toward that station, he thought. Tom turned the corner just in time to see Riggs disappear into the maw of the subway staircase. He drew his pistol and started down the stairs, wary that Riggs could abruptly start shooting at him from any number of hiding places. He found the platform deserted with no guards in sight and no sign of Riggs. Upstairs, the sirens grew louder, then suddenly stopped with the screech of tires. Tom walked to the edge, looking cautiously down at the electrified tracks. Looking both ways, he saw no sign of Riggs. From deep in the tunnel, a train approached with an ominous rattle and the screaming sound of metal against metal, its headlight reflected from tiles lining the tunnel creating a mosaic of white lights. The train grew louder as Tom could make out footsteps from policemen descending the staircase.

"Looking for me, Chase? Or should I say, Detective Chase?" a voice said from behind him. Before Tom could spin around, he felt a violent push on his shoulder toward the abyss of the tracks. He lost balance and felt himself falling sideways, but managed to twist in time to see Riggs' malevolent grin. Tom raised his pistol and fired into that menacing face just as the headlight from the oncoming train seemed to light up the world. He felt himself fall off the platform and continued to fall, spinning in a void as if there was no bottom. Light became dark, and Tom fell into a black world, crashing hard into something, his face grinding into the dirt, just before he lost consciousness.

Chapter 20

Where Old Friends Meet

Tom sat up and felt around. There was a brick wall behind him while under him appeared to be concrete with a large amount of overlying dirt mixed with garbage. A foul odor came from someplace close, and nearby was the rustle and squeak of rats. Tom rubbed his shoulder where he had impacted the ground and looked up, trying to make out the subway platform, but all he could see was blackness. "I'm down here!" he called, but the only response was the scurry of rats from several locations near his feet. He stood slowly and brushed himself off. He realized that he no longer was wearing a tie, and his jacket had a front zipper. Looking around, trying to find any recognizable landmarks, he began to see another wall opposite to where he was standing. This place is some sort of alley, he thought. At one end was impossible blackness, but the other had a reddish, slightly detectable ambient light which was intermittent, almost like a flicker. He started walking toward the light, keeping to the middle of the alley. His leg and shoulder ached, and he could smell the odor of alcohol on his clothes. As he approached the lighted end, he could see shadows of people moving back and forth in front of the alley. When he finally made it to the opening, he looked up at the source of flickering light. A neon sign said "Bar" in red letters, and as he watched, it endlessly blinked on and off. He seemed to remember something about that sign, but the thought wouldn't come clearly back. Fatigued, he propped himself up against the corner of the alley to rest.

"Tom? Back for some more? Got any money left?" a woman said and laughed a husky condescending laugh. Tom looked across the alley and saw a plump blonde with heavy sagging breasts leaning against the other wall. She was smoking and blowing the smoke high into the air.

Her female companion quipped, "I don't think he can handle any more, Betty. Mister, you best go home and sleep it off." They both laughed again. Betty's name and the neon sign made Tom remember with regret where he was. He was back in his second life, and this was the alley with the Exit Door. At the same moment, he realized that he was intoxicated and smelled of booze and sweat. In the dim light, he saw that his clothes were tattered, then he remembered the rest. He had been fired from his job with Talic and, last week, lost his apartment. Seven days of living on the street, and all the money he had in the world was in his pocket. He decided to get away from this place and started to walk in a direction chosen by chance. People he passed looked at him with disgust, avoiding eye contact.

Frequently, he could hear their comments after they safely passed him. "They should pick that bum up. Did you smell him?" The streets and the lights went on and on, seemingly without end, and Tom passed places that he would have liked to take shelter in but didn't have either the money or the nerve to enter. Down the street, he thought he recognized a familiar sign. As he drew closer, he remembered. *Thursday's* was the name of the bar he first entered from his real, his first, life. That was where he first became aware of openings that you could enter but not go back through. He peered in through the large window, zipping up his thin jacket against the cold. It looked the same as he remembered. The squat bald bartender was still tending bar and two men with their backs to him...what were their names? He tried to recall. They were the ones who told him about the Exit Door. Frank and Vance? Wasn't that their names? He drew himself upright and pushed the glass door open. The bartender eyed Tom with malice on his face as he approached.

"Whoa, Bubba. You ain't coming in here. We don't allow no beggars. Hit the road, or I'll have to show you my club," the bartender said and leaned over the bar with his large tattooed arms. The two men on stools swiveled around to see the newcomer.

"Hey, Vance. It's our old friend. Tom, isn't it?" Frank remarked.

"Yeah, Tom. Come over here, Tom," Vance said. "We won't let him throw you out yet. Not until you join us for a couple of drinks. We've wondered what happened to you. Nothing good, it appears."

"Hi fellows. I was hoping to find you here. You are right about nothing good. My life is a shambles and getting worse. It's good to have someone to talk to," Tom said with relief.

"Well, sit yourself right here between us," Frank said and moved over one stool. After Tom sat, the bartender glared over the bar top at him. "Got any money?" he asked.

"Not much, I'm afraid," Tom admitted.

"No matter, Tom, we're buying tonight," Frank said. "Barkeep, bring him a whiskey sour. That's a man's drink for our old friend Tom."

"Say, what happened after you left that night, Tom?" Vance asked. Tom paused thinking how to tell a complicated story of three lifetimes in a couple of sentences. While he thought, he looked at the area of the wall that once was the arch he came through from the ballroom. Now, there was only plaster and brick and no opening, just the same as the last time he saw it. He remembered that, for a short time, he could still see Jeanette sitting at their little table, and the thought brought tears streaming down his face.

"Well, if it's that bad, you don't have to tell us," Frank said. A short glass was slammed down in front of him, and he looked up to see the large bald head of the angry bartender looking at him.

"I did find an Exit Door. You were right about that. It is like a hole into nothing. No sound, no light and no bottom. It's a couple of miles from here, in an alley frequented by hookers."

"Did you see anyone go in?" Frank asked.

"No, it frightened me, and I left as quickly as I could. After that, I went through another door and into a different life. I've had two different lives since I met you that first night," Tom said between sips of his drink.

Vance leaned over and said, "How did you get back here, Tom?"

"I was pushed off a subway platform in New York by someone who wanted to kill me. When I fell, I ended up in the alley near the Exit Door." They both started to laugh and slap their hands on the bar. Even the bartender smiled.

Vance tried to suppress his sniggles long enough to ask a question but was unable to complete a sentence without breaking out in a big horse laugh. Finally he managed to say, "I recall that you said that you were an architect before you came through the wall. What, may I ask, were you in your other two lives?"

"I was a police detective in New York and was fleeing terrorists when I went into a train and became a college professor of Philosophy in Connecticut. Then I went back to New York seeking a woman named Bug whom I met when I was a police officer. Sounds strange when I say it, but it all actually happened." The laughter was loud and prolonged. Vance actually fell off the stool, clutching his abdomen, and all three of Tom's audience were red in the face from laughter.

The bartender said, "Let me see if I got this. This bum walked through a solid wall one night claiming to come from another life and now says that the same thing happened twice more. Each time he became another person. Now he ends back here begging for a drink. Is that about it?"

Frank put his forehead to the bar and slapped the surface with both hands, roaring with laughter. "Please, I can't stand it. I give. This has to be funnier than the night he came in thinking he just walked through a solid wall."

Vance was wiping tears from his face with his sleeve. "Yes, this bum entertained us that night with his crazy story, and we even got him to buy us three drinks." He started whooping again and held his face in his hands. "We made up a story about an exit door. You know, some spooky story about going through and vanishing, and he bought it. Now he even thinks he saw one. It's the most hilarious thing I've ever heard. Can you beat this?"

"You mean I didn't come through an opening that closed that night?" Tom asked.

"You silly drunk. You stumbled in here through the same door you came in tonight. You were so lit that you believed anything we said. No, it was the alcohol that made you think what we said was true. You are just a homeless bum, sleeping in alleys. You never were anything but that, but you are good for some laughs," Vance said and then slapped Tom on the back. "Tell you what, Tom. I'll buy another round because you made us laugh so hard tonight. What'll you have?"

Tom slid off the stool and hung onto the bar. "You mean that none of this ever actually happened? I dreamed about the whole thing, and there never was a Jeanette or a Bug?" The laugher started again in earnest, and all three were holding on to each other for support. Even a few people farther away were laughing and looking at Tom.

"You poor alcoholic. Your brain is hollow. I'm surprised that you can still think, much less dream. Now get out of my bar, because you are stinking up the place. No more free drinks for you. Get the hell out, and don't come back," the bartender said while he wiped his hands on his apron. Tom could tell that he was on the verge of being harmed and decided to leave without a fight. As he walked out, they were still laughing.

"Hey, Tom! Who the hell would call his girlfriend Bug?" someone called out.

"Likely, a man who sleeps with bugs!" another answered to the sounds of guffaws.

The sidewalk was a welcome relief from the bar and its humiliations. He pulled up his collar and wondered where he could go for the night. He walked slowly and zombie-like, letting his past lives run through his mind like a stream passing among trees creating little waves of memories. The barflies were wrong. He remembered the actual events of his life so well that he couldn't have dreamed them. Some of the dreams were real enough that he remembered them as well, just as if they also had actually happened. In the most important ways, they did actually happen. A cool gust of wind hit him and smelled of rain coming shortly. He was sore, tired and hungry and had about fifteen dollars in his pocket. He remembered his resolve to change and become a better person. Guess it didn't happen that way, he realized. Ahead was the relative darkness of a park that he frequently slept in until police chase him out, and he instinctively headed toward it. Along the paths were other homeless men sleeping on scattered benches covered by newspaper for warmth. He stumbled along, looking for an out-of-the-way place to lie down. Most of these men would gladly stab him if they knew he had any cash in his pocket. As he stood there calculating his next move, he heard a scraping sound behind him, and he turned to see an older man pulling a large cardboard crate behind him.

"Hi, want to help an old-timer?" the man asked, smiling a gap-toothed smile. He wore dark, dusty clothes and had a respectably long beard in grizzled grey.

"Sure," Tom said and grabbed a corner of the box. "Where are you headed with this thing?"

"I always find a dark corner over there where the police don't go. You're welcome to share my box tonight, if you like."

"I would. What's your name, old-timer?"

"I'm known by several rather disgusting names, but I prefer Dugan. My mother gave me that one, and it fits me rather well. What's your handle?"

"Tom Chase, Dugan."

"Had anything to eat, Tom?"

"Afraid not, Dugan. Any ideas?"

"Don't worry. I raided the trash behind my favorite restaurant on my way here, and there is enough for two hidden in a corner of our temporary home. We'll eat before retiring."

"That sounds wonderful. You seem more resourceful than most around here, Dugan." They reached the selected site nestled between giant trees and shrubs which would make their temporary shelter undetectable until daylight. The box unfolded quickly, and Dugan supplied some twine to secure it to the adjacent trees. It was big enough for both to lie side by side and close the flap.

"It won't do if it rains a lot so keep your fingers crossed, Tom." Dugan took out his sack of discarded food and passed it to Tom. "Eat all you want. We can go back for seconds if we need to. Free of charge, of course."

After eating, they slid into position and settled in for the night as the night creatures stirred in the park. The crickets were first out and gradually became a rhythmic serenade lulling them into relaxation.

"Well, I'm ready to hear your story, Tom. Why are you in this fix, sleeping in a cardboard box and going hungry? Want to share with me?" Dugan asked.

"You first, Dugan. You are smart and streetwise. It doesn't seem right. You don't even reek of alcohol."

"I am, or was, a clinical psychologist. The whole thing began when I started spending a lot of time with street people whom I thought were in need of some counseling. At first, I began to identify with them, then later realized that I enjoyed their lifestyle. I became one of them, and I don't regret it because I've been out here for twenty years, and I'm more healthy than I was when I had a home and all the food I wanted to buy. No cares. That's the main thing. You live from moment to moment and don't worry about things you can't change. I never drank alcohol or used drugs so that makes me different and better off than the others. There is no time I devote to feeling sorry for myself, and I don't feel inferior to others. Being free is all I want, and I have it. Now you."

"It's complicated and admittedly unbelievable. You'll just think that I have some delusional dementia. Perhaps I have. I don't any longer know what I am or what I have been," Tom said.

"Try me. I expect that I've heard most of it before."

"Okay, here goes. I have led four separate and complete lives. Loved two women and lived in widely separate parts of the country, and I remember every day of it. I have drifted from one life to the other without wanting to and can never fully return. That is except for today. This is my second life and the worst of the bunch, and I am back against my will."

"Are these dreams, Tom?"

"No, my dreams are different. I always awaken from them and know that I was dreaming. That doesn't happen in my real lives."

"Except for this current life, are you a successful person surrounded by a single, or perhaps several, beautiful women in your other lives?"

"Exactly. Successful and admired. I have two women who are there but never together at the same moment. They always are with me in my dreams."

"Of course, Tom, you must know that what you have described is clearly impossible. A more likely explanation is that they are all dreams of wishful thinking. A necessary escape from reality. Your reality right now would not seem to be a desirable life. You live for your dreams or in your dreams, if you will."

"Dugan, you've obviously been around. Ever hear of an Exit Door?"

"We are surrounded by exit doors, Tom. Some are real and some of them lead to a better life. That kind are allegorical, are they not? Unless you mean an exit from life, then you are describing a suicide. A final release. Which one are you referring to?"

"I don't know, Dugan. There is one on the west side of town in an alley. I opened it once, and it seems to lead to nowhere. There is a nothingness on the other side, and it frightened me. Ever hear of such a door?"

"I have not seen it, Tom. It would be consistent with your history of seeming to live different lives. You have created this exit door with a desire to have an escape route. Did your other lives have such an exit?"

"No, it's the only one I have seen."

"It makes sense for it to be here in your present life. If you were to venture in, I would expect something very bad to happen to you. End of you, Tom."

"Metaphorically speaking or for real?" Tom asked.

"It all ends the same, doesn't it?

"I don't want to die, Dugan. I want to regain a respectable life and share love with a good woman. Unlike you, I don't want to live like this. I want more from life than scraps."

"First you have to give up wanting things, Tom. Freedom and happiness doesn't come from having things to take care of. They are all a burden. You can become happy devoting your life to a person or even a nation. Something bigger than a physical thing and something that can't be taken from you like a possession can. You have to expand your horizons to understand why we are all here. Was it just to pillage the forests and the earth of its treasure or was it to try to help inspire people like you to see the real treasure of being alive?"

"I never thought of life in that way. But I know that if I had the right partner, I would devote my everything to making her happy. Right now, I am willing to make any effort required to make me happy."

"First things first. You have to stop indulging yourself with booze and cheap women. Ask yourself if that's making you happy or just making you forget for a moment that you're unhappy. Then get a job, any job, and work hard at it. Try to do it the best that you can, no matter how trivial it is. Third, find someone who needs help and give them all the help you can. Suddenly, you will become more happy. Being totally happy is almost never achieved. We, after all, are human, and complete happiness is not possible. You must start tomorrow. Delay is death, Tom."

"I want to, Dugan. You sound like you have discovered the truth and have shared it with me, and I appreciate it. I'm afraid that I might not be a strong enough person to do what I should. This day started when I got up in the Gramercy Park Hotel, and it quickly transformed into a rat infested alley across town, and now I'm sleeping in a cardboard box. It's hard to tell what is real any longer."

"Be thankful for small things, Tom. Your stomach is full, and you are warm and dry. Isn't that good in itself? Do you really need more?"

"Yes, Dugan. I want one of my lives back. Any one but this one."

"And, perhaps, Tom, this is your life. You can't live a dream, because you always wake up. Make do with this one, because it's the only one you'll ever have."

Tom closed his eyes knowing that he would be able to see Bug again. He had so much to tell her, and he wanted to feel her next to him and feel her lips against his. He tried to make himself comfortable against the cold ground. Even if separated by a thin piece of cardboard, the ground was still hard and unyielding. The crickets did their job, and he eventually fell off to sleep.

Tom rubbed his eyes and saw that he was still wrapped in cardboard. He never dreamed last night! The only thing he could count on and even that was taken away. He sat up and noticed that Dugan was gone. Tom pushed one flap open so that he had more light. There was a message written on the flap in pencil.

"Dear Tom. Enjoyed meeting you last night and enjoyed our conversation. I hope that I have been some help to you in getting started in your new life. I had to leave early this morning, and I am giving you the cardboard house, if it makes it through the day, that is. One other thing. I took your money because you needed to start at the very bottom so that you can only go up from here. Hope we meet again when you have begun your path back to a whole being.

Dugan."

Tom beat his fist into the cardboard house punching a hole through it. This was the bottom all right. No money, no job, no Bug, and he had a wrenching headache. He stepped out of the box into the morning sunshine and stretched.

"Hey, you! Yes, I mean you!" someone shouted. Tom looked around and saw a uniformed policeman headed his way carrying a long billy club in one hand. Tom looked around for a quick exit, but there was a high fence behind the box on both sides. He was trapped.

"Don't run, stupid, or I'll chase you down. See the sign?" The policeman pointed to a "No camping, No sleeping" sign posted on the closest tree.

Tom said, "We came in after dark. You couldn't see the sign then. I'm sorry, officer."

"I can arrest you, but the city would have to feed you at the people's expense. We have a better way. First, you clean up your mess and put it in the trash bin, and then I'll put you to work cleaning up the rest of the park. Work all day and I'll let you go. Understand?" he said and pointed his big club at Tom's face.

"Do I get any food for working?" Tom asked.

"Hell no, you stupid bum. You can drink all the water you want out of the fountain, but you don't get any reward for disobeying the law. Get to work or taste my club."

Tom had little choice, and remembering what Dugan had said, he started working, determined to do the best job he could. After a couple of hours of hard work, he became lightheaded with hunger, and food was the only thing he could think of. He watched as visitors bought and discarded parts of doughnuts or ends of hot dogs in waste cans. After a while, he made his way to one and found edible portions. It was disgusting to him that he had to stoop to eating trash, but he had little choice. To work, he had to eat. The hot sun took its toll of him, and by evening, he was dragging, unable to move quickly. One policeman changed into another, but they all had the same instructions. Keep the bum working until dark.

"Okay, bum. You can go now. Don't ever come back in here or next time we'll get rough. Now get out of here," the latest one said. Tom stumbled toward the park entrance and sat down on the sidewalk. Too exhausted to think, he just stared ahead, listlessly. He had no idea where he was going to sleep, but he knew that he wasn't going back to the park. As he turned to see the source of a close-by noise, he felt something hit his back, and he fell into the street, face down.

"Got any money, fella?" the young tough snarled. "Gimme what you got, or you'll get a beating."

"I don't have a cent. It was all stolen last night," Tom said. They began kicking him. He couldn't tell how many were involved, and the only thing he could do was curl up, trying to avoid kicks to the face. It went on until a passing car slowed, and somebody yelled at them. They left Tom crumpled in the street, blood running from his broken nose and split lips. He felt someone pulling his legs and then felt his body scraping over the curb. The person rolled him onto his back, and Tom looked up to see another uniformed policeman standing over him. He squinted to see the brass name badge on his chest reflecting specular light from the nearby street light. Riggs.

"We can't let you sleep in the street. Get up and move along, or you'll regret it," Riggs said.

"I've just been beaten by several thugs. Surely you saw them," Tom said weakly.

"They help us clear the streets of you people. You are the one lying in a public street. Now get up and move along, or I'll start with your feet and move up to your empty head."

Tom got up painfully to his feet and stood to face Riggs. It was him, all right, but this time he was only a sergeant.

"I remember you. Seems like I've rousted you before. I recall that you are a worthless piece of trash. Why don't you go crawl into a hole and die?" Riggs hissed and pushed him in the chest with his black club for emphasis. Tom understood that protest would only be rewarded with more physical pain. He turned and shuffled away as fast as his battered body could move. Pain caused him to place his hand over his chest, discovering the sharp edge of a broken rib and noticing that the front of his jacket was torn and covered by blood. He decided to return to the alley, hoping that once there he could somehow walk out and return to his life with Bug, like he did last time. It was his only hope, and it was two painful miles away.

He frequently was forced to rest, leaning against any nearby object. People who passed were careful to give him a wide berth or crossed the street before they crossed paths with him. Not a single person spoke to him or offered any help.

After what seemed to be an endless walk of pain, he could make out the flickering neon sign ahead. He was weak enough that forward progress was only possible while holding on to the buildings he passed. Breathing consisted of short painful breaths, and he seemed to be losing focus, objects appearing more and more blurry. Two female forms near the alley entrance were watching him come toward them.

"Look at this piece of trash, Betty. Didn't you make it with him a few times?" Rose said loud enough for Tom to hear.

"Yeah, I did, and I never got enough dough for doing it. Looking at him tonight, he would be finished off for good if he had a piece of me." They both laughed a nasty, coughing laugh. Tom was forced to walk around them into the alley, and he did so without looking or returning their taunts. He just wanted to lie down for a moment and get some strength back. Stumbling into the darkness, he occasionally kicked up some piece of scattered trash while feeling the despising looks of the two hookers striking his back. The alley grew darker and darker, and he had to feel along the wall to know he was still moving in the right direction. Here and there was the rustle of rats and the squeak of mice. He could just make out the flicker of a dim sign on the other wall a few yards from him. Fear welled up into his throat, and he could feel his pulse increase. It was the Exit Door. It was waiting for him.

Tom turned to look back at the alley entrance. It looked the same, and he could see the two women each time the bar sign flickered. The previous time the Exit Door was visible, he had walked into a different life when he left the alley. He limped and dragged himself back toward the entrance while the two women indifferently watched his progress, smoking their cigarettes. Just before the corner, he took a deep breath and closed his eyes in hope and pulled himself past.

"What in hell are you doing now?" Betty asked. Tom opened his eyes to see that nothing was changed. There was no entrance into another life here. He couldn't leave this miserable existence after all, and he slid slowly down the brick and sat on the sidewalk, tears streaming down his dirty and blood-crusted face.

"If I were you, I'd crawl back in that alley before my pimp sees you. You are bad for business sitting there, and he won't like it," Betty snarled.

Tom feared another beating and rolled to his hands and knees and started very slowly disappearing back into the blackness of the alley. His hands and arms started quivering from effort while grit and chips ground into his knees, but he made steady progress, and ahead could start to see the outline of the Exit Door. As he got closer, his fear seemed to lessen, and when he was directly below the dim, flickering sign he felt relief. There was no longer any reason to keep living. This Exit Door was finally welcoming Tom as a long lost friend, and he knew that his struggles would soon end. He felt a peace wash over him, and his pain diminished as he struggled back to his feet, clutching his broken rib. Today, he would leave behind all the things he couldn't fix, all the things he would never do again, and the women whom he loved and who loved him in return. Before he touched the handle, the door swung inward with a rusty, creaking sound, causing the nearby rodents to flee in other directions. It was a hole as black as black could be. The opening was as if deep space was on the other side of the jam, with no light and no sound possible from that dark rectangle of nothingness. With a small smile and his head up, Tom stepped into the opening and disappeared.

Chapter 21

From The Depths Into The Light

om had the sensation of being deep below the surface of the sea and being able to look around. There was a dim light from far above him which grew brighter as he slowly ascended. Bubbles streamed from his nostrils, but he felt no need to breath. Up and up he rose in silence, save for the tiny bubbles brushing past his ears making little tinkling noises. There seemed to be nothing on the smooth surface above him except for the motion of little waves. He felt weightless and all his physical pain was gone, and he felt happy and free for the first time since his birth. If this was death, it was very pleasant indeed. Tom thought about the past and remembered it, but none of it seemed to matter any longer. It was the water and Tom and nothing else. A few feet from the surface, the light grew impossibly bright, and at first Tom feared breaking the surface. He squinted to shut out the light and readied himself for whatever was there, allowing his body to rise face first into the light.

A crack of his eyelids allowed an explosion of light into his brain, and as suddenly, his ears were aware of voices and noise. His name was being called by a familiar voice that he couldn't place, and a warm towel was being used to wipe his face and around his eyes.

"Tom. Tom. Tom, can you hear me? Tom. You can open your eyes, Tom. Come on and try, Tom. Can you hear me, Tom? Try again to open your eyes, Tom." The voice was sweet and feminine. He struggled to know who was calling him and where he was. He tried again to open his eyes, and the light poured through the small slits like the bright opening of a furnace door. There were shadows moving in the light, back and forth. "Tom, you almost have it. Try again to open your eyes, Tom," the sweet voice said. He tried again and saw the unfocused head of someone leaning over him. "You have it, Tom. Welcome back!" she said. He opened his eyes more fully and started to make out a woman's face and short blonde hair. She was almost in focus now, and she was gently patting his bare shoulder. "Hi, Tom. We've been waiting for this day for a long time. Can you talk, Tom. Try to talk, Tom. Can you understand me, Tom?

"Yes," he heard himself croak. "I hear you."

"Wonderful, Tom! Now look right at me and tell me what you see," she said. He tried to see her. Something was keeping her blurry, but she seemed so familiar, like he should know her from somewhere. He felt the warm cloth on his eyes again as she wiped them clean. "Try again, Tom. Look right at me," she ordered. He did and this time her image was clear. She was beautiful, and the light from the ceiling lit up her hair as a blonde halo. He could see her perfect teeth and smiling lips. "Hi, Tom. I'm Allyson, and I'm your nurse." Of course, I know her, he thought. My Allyson, my Bug. I'm back again. Inside a feeling of warmth radiated, making his limbs come alive, and he felt able to move again.

"Hi, Allyson. Remember me?" he asked.

"I should. I have spent every working day for the past two months taking care of you. If ever two people were closer, then I don't know about it," she laughed her familiar and sensual laugh that he loved so much. The room around him came into focus, and he looked around. It was a brightly lit room with a large window at the end. The walls were darker lavender, and there were a couple of chairs and a bedside stand for trays. Tom realized that this was a hospital room of some sort. Allyson was right beside him and started taking his blood pressure, and the cuff on his arm tightened for a moment.

"Where am I?" Tom asked.

"You are in Parkside Rehab. Been here for two months or so. Remember anything?" she said.

"I seem to remember you very well. It's like I know you."

"I always talk to my patients a lot. Sometimes about myself. We wonder if they remember, and it seems that you did. I'm glad to finally talk to you, Mr. Chase, and have you talk back. Do you remember your accident?"

"I remember being at a ball. We were dressed up. We had an argument. I recall a balcony overlooking the sea and music. That's about all. Jeanette. I remember Jeanette. We were married?"

"Yes, you were married," Allyson said.

"Is Jeanette all right? Was she hurt?"

"No, she's fine. You suffered a fall off the balcony."

"Balcony?"

"They told us that you were standing on it and fell backward."

"I don't remember. Did I get hurt?"

"You broke your right leg and your head. The surgeons fixed them right away, and they are all healed."

"I've been unconscious that whole time?"

"For three months."

"Oh."

"Now, I want you to close your eyes and rest again. It's going to get easier from now on, I promise. Your physician will be in this evening, and I want you to show off for him, because I was the only one who knew in my heart that you would awaken some day, and I want him to tell me that I was right."

Tom closed his eyes and seemed to be floating on the surface of the ocean through which he had just risen. He heard gulls overhead, and as the sun warmed his bare skin, he stretched out on the water, just bobbing along in small waves feeling enormously happy. Someone was calling to him from nearby, and he turned to see a woman in a swimsuit beckoning him. He floated toward the pier, and she extended a hand and helped him up on the platform.

"Tom! I'm so happy that you are back," Bug said. She threw her arms around him and kissed him all over his face, and he picked her off the ground with his embrace. "I thought I lost you, but here you are!" she said and beamed at him.

"Bug, I love you so much it hurts. I thought you were never going to visit me again. How is it that you are here?"

"I have to guide you, like I did before. Your nurse likes you, but doesn't know that you are in love with her. You have to take it a step at a time, and she'll come around. Step at a time. Got it?"

"What happened to Jeanette?" Tom asked.

"Allyson will tell you all you want to know. After you recover a bit more, you can ask."

"Are you back with me to stay, Bug?"

"I hope so but that depends on you. You'll wake up and start your real life now, and you'll find that you've changed. Time will tell."

"No. You are the one I love. I must have you back with me. All the adventures we shared and the times you saved my life. Nothing can change that."

"Something you have to know, Tom. You have been in a coma and weren't expected to return to normal life for a long time, if ever. Allyson believed in you, and yes, she saved your life more than once during that time. I and all the others were a fantasy inside your coma. It was all a dream, the entire thing. You put bits and pieces together from the things you heard and made an entire story about them. Several stories, in fact. You are going to wake up to the real reality now, and you will learn that your life is what you will make of it."

"One more kiss, Bug. The last or the first of many more. Let's hope for the latter." He picked her up and kissed her tenderly trying to inhale her scents, trying to absorb her through his skin.

"Tom, your doctor is here. Time to wake up and prove me right," Allyson said and gently shook his shoulder. Tom opened his eyes more easily than before, and after a moment, he could see a somber, older man dressed in a pale blue lab coat standing next to the bed. He had bushy eyebrows that went up and down with an individual intelligence behind thick glasses.

He patted Tom's shoulder. "Welcome back to the world, Mr. Chase. I had my doubts, but Nurse June never did. She always said that you would come out of it, kept insisting on it, and this moment is hers. Good work, Allyson."

"I'll second that," Tom said and smiled at Allyson. He remembered her telling him to "go slow" a few moments ago. "What happens now, Doc? Do I just get up and leave?"

He leaned over Tom and his name badge twisted so that Tom could read "Dr. Greystone, Rehabilitation Medicine." "No," he laughed. "Wish it were that simple. You have been lying down so long that your muscles are pretty much worthless. You have lost weight and strength, and we don't even know about your brain function yet. I predict that you'll be here at least another six weeks if everything goes well. We are going to make you function close to normal before you can get away from us."

"Do you know anything about my wife, Dr. Greystone. Has she been here?" Tom asked.

Dr. Greystone stood up and glanced at Allyson, then pursed his lips. "She was here. Often at first. I haven't seen her recently, Tom, to be truthful. First we need you to get on your feet and gain weight and all that other stuff will sort itself out. I will stop by at least daily, more often if you need me, but you are in good hands with Nurse June. All the physicians here wish we had more of her to spread around the hospital. You are as healthy as you could be right now, and it is all due to her diligence. She just wouldn't give up. Well, Tom, seeing you awake has made my day. I'll see you again soon. All you have to do now is whatever Nurse June tells you."

After Dr. Greystone left, Allyson was still there smiling at him. "We, you and I, are going to sit you up and see what happens, Mr. Chase." He could hear a motor running, and the bed started to elevate at the head. He tried to sit up more fully and realized that he couldn't.

"Not so fast, Mr. Chase. Be patient and it'll come back."

"Can we dispense with the Mister? Call me Tom, please."

"All right, Tom. You can call me Allyson if you like."

"I planned to, Allyson. I've had you in my dreams for...two months?...I developed strong feelings about you during that time."

"That makes two of us. Something about you made me want to know you as a person. It's thrilling to talk to you in real life after all this time," she said.

"Do you mean that I was in your dreams also?"

"Yes, Tom. I guess my mind created something that I wanted and couldn't have."

"Can I ask, Allyson, are you married?"

"No, Tom."

"Were you ever married?"

"No. Not yet."

"Can you tell me about Jeanette? I could tell that there was more to the story from your looks."

"We should wait, Tom, but we'll discuss it when the right time comes. You'll have to trust me."

"I do trust you, Allyson. More than you know."

Every day was spent with gradual physical rehabilitation. After breakfast, the first trip to PT, then lunch and back to PT. Evenings were saved for counseling. Allyson's shift was over at 3 p.m., but she usually waited to leave until Tom returned to his room after the second physical therapy session. He grew in strength rapidly and was walking with assistance after ten days. His evening counselor was a middle-aged but kindly woman who insisted that she be called by her nickname, Kentucky. They worked on Tom's comprehension and verbal skills, and she seemed to try and avoid any serious social issues, especially conversations about Jeanette. One evening, Kentucky said, "I think you have a visitor waiting for you, Mr. Chase, and if it's satisfactory, I'll show him in when I leave."

"Of course, Kentucky. I'll see you tomorrow then?"

"You are approaching normal, as far as I can tell. There isn't any real reason for us to meet again," she said.

"Aren't you the one who should be discussing my return to my job and to my wife? We never talk about Jeanette. I'm tired of being kept away from her, and it's time I know what is going on."

"I'm not that kind of counselor, Mr. Chase. My job is to make sure you have no learning disability or mental handicap which will prevent your discharge. Perhaps you should mention your concerns to Nurse June in the morning."

"Getting out of it again, huh? Very well, I'll do that. Thanks for your help, Kentucky, and I hope I haven't been a problem patient."

"No, Mr. Chase. You have a lot of admirers in this facility, me among them. It's been a pleasure."

After she left, Tom sat expectantly in one of the bedside chairs waiting on his guest. There was a gentle rapping at the door which soon opened and admitted Eric who came in smiling from ear to ear holding a bouquet of mixed flowers.

"Tom! Goodness, it's good to see you looking so alert! It's been too long. They just told me yesterday that you had come out of it. We were about ready to give up on you. And here you are! How do you feel?"

"How do I look, Eric?"

"Thinner. Looks good on you. I should try it," he laughed. "You must have gotten good care here."

"I had a good team but one outstanding nurse."

"Yeah, the blonde one. Good looking dame. I hit on her a couple of times, and she quickly put out that fire. She seemed to like you, though."

"How's business?" Tom asked.

"Busy with you gone. That plan that we completed just before...well, the Mall is nearly complete. There's been good publicity about the design and I...I mean we...are getting loads of calls wanting projects. Some big. You woke up at the right time."

"Good. Soon, I hope. Hear from Jeanette lately?"

"Not for a while. Nope, not a word." Eric looked at his feet and avoided eye contact. Even he didn't want to talk about Jeanette.

"Eric. You and Jeanette. Anything there?"

"Not me. Not even if you were dead. Anyhow, she wouldn't give a slob like me the time of day. Not a chance. I never even thought that way, buddy."

"I'm relieved. What's going on with her? Why isn't she here?"

"Have they told you anything?"

"No one will talk about it. I want to know what you know right now."

"You got to know, Tom, that they were telling her that you weren't ever going to be the same and likely would die without coming out of it. At first she came all the time, and I even came with her a couple of times. She cried and cried about you, how unfair and how stupid it all was. That sort of thing, you know. I heard that she left for Europe, Paris I think, about two months ago. She probably gave up. That's about all I know. I haven't talked to her, but I still send her the money every month. She made sure about that."

"She leave with anyone?" Tom asked.

"That I don't know anything about. If she did, I don't know who. You need to talk to these people here about her. They'll know more than I do."

"That news hurts a lot, Eric."

"Sorry to be the one, Tom. Anyway, if you need anything, get hold of me. I'll look forward to you returning to work."

That evening, Tom saw Dr. Greystone when he came by making his rounds.

"Evening, Mr. Chase. Your progress is excellent. Speech, cognitive ability and memory retention are normal. You are making strides walking and in strength. Not much longer now. Anything you need?"

"Yes, Doc. I want to know everything you know about my wife, Jeanette."

"I'm not sure that I know more than I have seen with my own eyes. Rumor isn't fact and that's most of what I know. Your wife was here a good deal at first and then her visits grew sporadic. She pinned me down on a prognosis for you, and frankly, it wasn't very good at that time and I told her so. After that, she only dropped by occasionally, and those visits became more infrequent. At this time, I don't know anything about her or even where she is. Sorry."

"Who knows, Doc. Who can I ask?"

"Your nurse will know more than I do. Your attorney has been here. He likely knows the rest."

"I don't remember having an attorney, Doc."

"Ask Nurse June. She might know."

They were sitting on a park bench which overlooked a lake, and the weather was warm and sunny. Bug wore her hair up and had dark sunglasses. Never before had he seen her wear makeup, but this time was different. She had a gloss to her lips which he couldn't stop looking at. Just watching her form words was arousing, and when she moved, the small diamond necklace caught the light just so. She was different. More worldly, more mysterious and Tom liked what he saw.

"You are unusually beautiful, Bug. Very exciting. Is this a new look for you?" Tom asked.

"I thought I would try it out on you. Like?"

"Anything you do is all right. I have seen you in just about every possible situation, and you are always perfect. You don't need to change for me, Bug."

"We all grow, change and morph, Tom. Even you will change. We throw off the old and put on the new. It keeps us young inside. We just have to be careful to change together."

"I see your point. This change in you is good, but I don't want to give you the idea that I want you to change. You might change and not want me around any longer."

"I'm not Jeanette. Any change I make will be for you and you alone."

"What do you mean? Was there someone else with Jeanette while I was away?"

"Not to criticize her, Tom, but she seemed to be mostly engrossed in herself. That kind of woman wants to be the center of attention and doesn't want to waste any of her precious youth on waiting. It's what you buy when you get a woman like that."

"And you are not Jeanette, are you?"

"Remember me shooting at some perp or kicking down a door? You never saw me flip your unconscious body over and wash it, but I did. I just wanted you to know that there is another side of me as well. I can be as attractive and desirable to you as any woman."

"It's working, Bug. Good thing I'm sort of civilized or you would find out right now."

"That's what I wanted. You'll never miss Jeanette with me around, Tom."

"Can you tell me what happened to her? Nobody else dares say it."

"Ask me this morning, and you'll find out. It's time you do."

The noise of the food cart outside the door woke Tom, and he looked around the room, confused at first. The door opened and the aid sat the tray down and gave him a little wave. Before he could start to eat, Allyson came in and moved the tray into a better position.

"Awake now I see. Feeling good this morning, Tom?"

"Seeing your face always makes me feel good. How are you this morning?"

"Good. Didn't sleep well, though." Tom watched her face and understood that her concern was over him.

"Allyson. Time to tell me everything. Come on, I'm ready." She sighed and pulled up a chair and sat down. Opening the nearby side table drawer, she took out an envelope and handed it to him without comment. Tom took it and saw that it was addressed to him with the return address of a law firm. He opened it and started to read, then put it down.

"This is a divorce decree. I'm not married to Jeanette any longer. Is this legal? Can they do this to someone just that easily?"

"She was here one long, painful day. She was crying every time I was in. I think that she told you goodbye that day, because she only came back one other time, just before she left for Paris. I think that she wanted to be sure you were still unconscious. That might have eased her conscience to see that you were unchanged."

"You won't believe this, but I think I remember her telling me goodbye. I thought I dreamed it, but even in a dream, it broke my heart."

"I know you heard her, because I saw your tears for myself. It was a moment that I wanted to scream at her that she should wait. That you were going to come back, if only you had more time. There was another part of me that wanted her to go, to prove that she wasn't worthy of you, so I didn't say anything."

"I have to ask, Allyson. Was there another man?"

"She had one with her the at the last visit. He was the pampered, haughty sort who feels awkward in a hospital, and he just hung around, smiling a slick smile. They won't last long, because they both are just alike."

"Is that when she left this envelope?" Tom asked, holding up the divorce paper.

"No, that came later. A suit delivered it and introduced himself as Attorney At Law Forrest Riggs. A nastier man you could not imagine. He seemed to delight in flinging it on your chest and left the room laughing. I wanted to trip him down the stairs."

"I dreamed about a Riggs. He was a very bad, very corrupt policeman. In my dream, I shot him in the face as he pushed me into the path of a subway train. I remember him very well."

"I didn't want to tell you this stuff about your ex-wife. You are strong enough to take it now, so it was time."

"Anyone ever call you Bug?" he asked.

"Only about a million times. Goes with June, right?

"May I please, please call you Bug?"

"I always sort of liked it. You may, but only if we are alone."

Chapter 22

Some Things Should Not Be Seen

You look better with a bit more weight, Tom. They are talking discharge soon. Are you ready," Allyson asked.

"No. I'm not leaving."

"Don't you want to get back to work and your home?"

"Jeanette sold our house and furniture and piano and every single thing I ever had, including my clothes. I have to start over, but that's not why I want to stay here."

"I'm listening."

"You, Bug. Not seeing you every day...I can't hold this back any longer...I'm in love with you. You are there in my dream every night, and you were with me in my dreams while I was in a coma. I feel that I've been with you for years, and I've made love to you a thousand times. Your voice, your perfume and those eyes are part of me now."

"Patients often fall in love with their heath care provider. It's happened to me before. You'll lose interest in me once you are out of the hospital."

"Absolutely I won't. Listen to me. I asked you to marry me in my dreams, and you said yes. Twice you said yes. This isn't a thankful patient talking. I love you. Do you want me to start shouting it while running around in my gown?" Allyson started to laugh at the idea.

After she regained control, she looked serious and took his hand in hers. "I felt like I brought you back to life. It didn't happen that way, I know, but I wanted you to live so much, I willed it to happen, then it did. You opened your eyes. At that moment, I felt that I owned you or created you. Yes, I love you also, and it's against every rule and recommendation out there, but I do and I can't help it. Now I can admit to you that I told you that I loved you while you were unconscious. I thought my love would give you strength."

"Bug, if I had only known, I would have flung myself through the Exit Door a long time ago."

"Exit door? What are you talking about, Tom?"

"The Exit Door is a gateway to some other place. I thought it led to death, but it led straight to you. I've only seen one, and it's backward. The exit goes into the building, not out, and the door opens inward. There is a sign above that says 'Exit'. The one I saw gave me the creeps, until I had no other choice except to go through."

"There are four exit doors in this wing alone. How do you know by looking at them?" Allyson asked.

"I'll bet you will know if you ever see one, but I hope you never do."

"Back to us, Tom. We have established that we love each other. Now what?"

"We marry, we live together, we reproduce and we rejoice in having each other to hold until death."

"Are you asking me?"

Tom instantly fell to his knees in front of her and looked up adoringly. "My beautiful, wonderful Allyson, otherwise known as Bug, please marry me. Please."

"Aren't you supposed to have a ring? This is my first time, and I want to do it right you know."

Tom looked anxiously around to see if anything could be used as a substitute and found a pen. He carefully took her left hand and isolated her ring finger. She started to laugh and move but he persisted, carefully drawing an "IOU" on the back of her finger, then kissed her hand with a big smacking sound.

"More? I have a lot of ink left," he said with a straight face.

"That's enough. Yes, I will marry you, Tom Chase."

Tom stood and brought her up also. "This will be my first real kiss with you, but I already know how if feels, and it's going to feel so good."

"Eric? Tom here. Yes, I feel fine, and I'm coming back at the end of the week. I have to have a place to live, but I need some money. What's there of mine that I can use?"

"Your wife had a lawyer, Riggs I think, serve some papers on us requiring us to pay her whatever your salary would be every month. You still have your retirement because they couldn't get that until you were declared dead. To answer your question, nothing. She took, and is taking, every penny she can get. You might be able to borrow some funds from your retirement but you'll need some legal advice to do it. As far as I'm concerned, you get all the checks from now on, and if you send her anything, it will be up to you. That help?"

"Clears up a lot but doesn't help much. Looks like I have some work to do, but I'll still see you Friday."

Tom lay back on the bed that had captured him for so long. He had gained forty pounds in less than six weeks, and he felt strong and alert. It was time to move on and start his life over. Tomorrow would bring tomorrow, and whatever was there he could face. His dreams had prepared him for adversity, with their highs and lows and dangers, and, above all things, he had Bug with him forever. The first thing to do tomorrow would be to hunt for an apartment and buy a car and, of course, a big diamond ring. The bedside phone rang and he picked it up with a smile expecting Bug's voice.

"Hello," Tom said.

"Hello to you," Jeanette said back. "Know who this is?"

The End

www.ingramcontent.com/pod-product-compliance
Lightning Source LLC
Chambersburg PA
CBHW051300210726
48287CB00002B/595